2019

TROUBLE PURSE
SUED

TROUBLE PURSE SUED

MARIANNA HEUSLER

W🌐RLDWIDE®

TORONTO • NEW YORK • LONDON
AMSTERDAM • PARIS • SYDNEY • HAMBURG
STOCKHOLM • ATHENS • TOKYO • MILAN
MADRID • WARSAW • BUDAPEST • AUCKLAND

Recycling programs
for this product may
not exist in your area.

Trouble Purse Sued

A Worldwide Mystery/September 2019

First published in 2017 by Hilliard & Harris.
This edition published in 2019.

ISBN-13: 978-1-335-45558-1

Copyright © 2017 by Marianna Heusler

Printed in U.S.A.

Dedicated to my dear sister-in-law, Jamie Ramondetta, and her four beautiful children, who have read everything I've ever written. Love you, guys.

ONE

Twelve Years Ago

SHE HAD NEVER thought of herself as a blackmailer, and it was something she would never resort to in ordinary times.

But these weren't ordinary times. She desperately needed money. No one was buying her photographs, and, after all, a girl had to live. Too bad people didn't appreciate real art. While other photographers focused their attention on nature, on forests and mountains and streams, she photographed back alleys, desperate people, the seedy, the sad, the lonely, the forgotten.

Fate was with her that day, because not only did she capture a picture of stark realism, but a photo of the most primitive act of all. Murder.

The murder of Victor Holtz.

And it was certainly true what they said.

A picture was worth a thousand words.

Only in this case, it was worth ten thousand dollars.

Of course, it was ridiculous—blackmailing a murderer. Anyone who watched those crime shows on television knew that. Ridiculous and dangerous! If someone killed once, why not kill twice? They said each time it got easier. So she would have to be very careful. She would lie, say she had left a note with a relative, which would be mailed if she should meet an unexpected

end. She had to make the killer understand that all she
wanted was the money. Then she would disappear, no
threat to anyone at all.

She left the house on that cold, chilly morning,
locked the front door and checked one more time that
she had the proof, both the picture and the negative
tucked away in a place no one would think of looking.

Safe and sound.

She reached into her purse for her gold compact with
her name etched in sequins—Dagny. A little powder
would hide the sheen of sweat which had pooled unto
her chin.

She was staring at the cold sore on her mouth, now
sullied with red lipstick, when she missed her footing
on the icy steps. She tumbled head forward, her shoes
flying into the snow, her brand new handbag, opening,
scattering the contents on the frozen snow and her head
hitting the concrete with one final thud.

Her last thought was a regret—that no one had cap-
tured her death in a photo.

TWO

The Present

"Julia?"

Mrs. Hopwood's eyes snapped wide open as she reached for her watch in a panic Was it a school day? 7:30. Had she overslept? Why hadn't the alarm worked?

It was Saturday. Who had the nerve to call this early on a weekend?

"Julia, are you there?"

Her sister, Roseanne, the eternal early bird.

"It's seven in the morning," Mrs. Hopwood grumbled, "one of the few days I get to sleep in."

"Aunt Eunice is dead."

"Who?"

"Aunt Eunice. She was married to our great uncle, Vito."

"She had to be ancient."

"Ninety-eight. Don't you remember? I told you I've been taking care of her for the past three months."

"I'm very sorry for your loss," Mrs. Hopwood said half-heartedly, She was in a hurry to hang up before she got roped into attending a funeral for someone whom she barely knew, and wasn't even a blood relative.

"You're in her will."

Mrs. Hopwood bolted upright.

"We all are."

Mrs. Hopwood, one of five siblings, wondered just how much she would actually receive when it was divided among so many people.

"That was very kind of her." She decided to be blunt. "How much money are we talking about?"

"I'm not sure, although I'm the executor. I'm thinking at least a couple of thousand. The funeral Mass is on Tuesday and I'm going to need you to do a reading."

"I work and I've taken so much time off already because of Alex. You know I had to leave the country and drag him back from Taiwan…"

"Isn't the principal, Mrs. Jones, your best friend?"

"It's Mrs. Johnson and friendship extends only so far."

"Another thing," Roseanne rambled on, "you have to help clear out Aunt Eunice's house."

"I work," Mrs. Hopwood repeated.

"Well, you can do it next weekend. Gina is going to tackle the cellar. You've been assigned to the attic. You can have whatever you find. Otherwise make arrangements with Goodwill or just trash it. She has a lot of stuff because remember, she owned that second-hand dress shop down on High Street." Mrs. Hopwood remembered no such thing. "I have to go. The nursing home is calling me. Cousin Rachel isn't doing well and I'm her health care proxy."

Left with a dial tone, Mrs. Hopwood placed her cell phone on the corner table. She hoped she would be receiving enough money to redecorate her bedroom with a white upholstered headboard, a mirrored make-up table, crystal lamps and ivory wall to wall carpeting.

She also wondered if there was any way she could possibly hide the inheritance from her husband, Mont-

gomery, who thankfully had gone for an early morning jog. No doubt he would want to use the money for
something useful, like repairing the roof.

But Mrs. Hopwood held firmly to the adage made
famous by Coco Chanel, *Take care of the luxuries. The
necessities will take care of themselves.*

Mrs. Hopwood shut her eyes and dreamed of more
luxuries.

THREE

NANCY SUGARMAN PUT the seventh grade morning work on the Smartboard. Today it consisted of completing math problems which—if the truth be told—she would be hard pressed to solve herself so it should take the students a good twenty minutes to complete. After a bit of mutinous muttering, they got to work.

She'd have twenty minutes of peace and quiet while she finished her lesson plans, lesson plans that had been due on Friday. But Mrs. Johnson had left early—something to do with a tennis match and her twins—and today Mrs. Johnson had a meeting with the superintendent, so she would be late arriving at St. Polycarp.

Mrs. Johnson had confessed to Mrs. Sugarman that she didn't want to be principal in September and had every intention of returning to her seventh grade classroom. That news elated Mrs. Sugarman, who had been yanked out of the library to replace Mrs. Johnson after the unfortunate incidence in the fall.

The plain truth was that Mrs. Sugarman did not like children at all, which was precisely why she had none of her own. What she loved was a calm environment with civilized people, who spoke in hush voices. While growing up, when other children dreamed of becoming actresses, teachers, lawyers, nurses and funeral directors, Mrs. Sugarman wanted nothing more than to be a librarian.

Not a school librarian.

Libraries, however, were not what they used to be. Book shelves had given away to computer stations, hardcover novels were replaced by Kindles, and local libraries were being shut down by young politicians.

When the library on Maple Street closed its' doors and Mrs. Sugarman's husband, Chester, died suddenly without leaving one penny of life insurance money, the only job Mrs. Sugarman was able to find was at St. Polycarp. And the only reason she was able to get that job was because Chester was a regular parishioner.

Mrs. Sugarman felt one of her migraines coming on. It always started the same way, a dull, nagging ache in the center of her forehead. And she was out of her Percocet. She knew that her primary care doctor wouldn't give her a refill. She was going to find another doctor, a more sympathetic one, one who knew about pain management with pills.

But in the meantime it would be difficult to get through the day without some sort of relief.

She overheard Addison Fiore in the teacher's room talking about having undergone a root canal. The doctor had given her some Percocet because he had dug so deeply into her gums. Addison was bragging, as she waved the bottle around, that she hadn't taken a single one because she had such a high tolerance for pain—a young obnoxious teacher, she also had a high tolerance for *causing* pain.

Mrs. Sugarman thought about how hard it would be to actually take a few of those pills out of Addison's purse. Addison would hardly miss them. Glancing at the cafeteria schedule, Mrs. Sugarman read that Addison was on lunch duty today and she wondered what Addison did with her purse, while she watched her second graders jump rope.

FOUR

ROBERT RYAN REYNOLDS was startled out of a deep sleep by the sound of a horn blaring. He tossed his dirty blanket aside and attempted to stretch on the cold, hard ground, but his muscles were stiff and his bones were tired.

He reached for the bottle of gin beside him. Empty. He couldn't remember finishing it. That was a pity. Alcohol was meant to be savored and enjoyed, not gulped down until you managed to black out.

Although maybe that was for the best.

It took him three tries before he managed to hoist himself up, surging forward and when he did, he sank down again. His head felt as though it was about to explode. What he needed to do was get some food in his system, maybe a breakfast sandwich from McDonald's.

He dug into his pants pocket. His hand emerged sticky and blackened, holding a few coins. His eyesight was going but he knew that it wasn't much. He finally managed to count it, coming up with thirty seven cents. *Wouldn't buy nothing.*

Maybe his best friend would lend him a dollar or two, his only friend, Tracy. But he couldn't go to her, not like this. She didn't like it when he drank, when he spent his money on liquor and then begged for cash to buy food.

Robert had been homeless for what seemed like his entire life, although it started when he was seventeen. He ran away first to New York City, then to Miami, to San Francisco, Seattle, Denver, ending up in this small town.

His mother died when he was twelve. He never met his father but his Aunt Millie told him everything there was to know. His father was a bigamist and an alcoholic. Robert's aunt would mumble under her breath that the "apples don't fall from the tree," and Robert knew exactly what she meant. He started drinking when he was twelve and he never stopped, not for long. Like most alcoholics, he would do anything, just for a nip. He once slugged a liquor clerk who refused to sell him a bottle of whiskey. That landed him in Juvie for twelve months and on probation for two years.

His Aunt Millie tried, she really did. She scraped enough money together to send him to rehab but he sneaked a bottle in and later he escaped to a friend's house, where he stayed for two days, before he was thrown out. She found mentors and teachers to talk to Robert, but you can't talk someone out of a bad gene. She said the rosary and she made countless novenas.

He didn't doubt that Aunt Millie was relieved when he was finally gone for good. He heard through the grapevine that she died of some rare disease soon after he hit the streets. Her death saddened him, partly because he knew he could never go home again.

Yep, he was born nothing and he was going to stay nothing. That was just the hand he was dealt.

But Tracy, Tracy was different. Tracy was classy, a lady who just happened to fall on bad times. Her husband murdered and no way to support herself, she landed on the streets.

And he knew just where to find her. She hung out in the church, praying and thinking. But that was okay. He had his own hiding place—the basement of St. Polycarp School.

FIVE

AMELIA JOHNSON SAT in the waiting room of the superintendent's office, her stomach slightly aflutter. She had dressed for the occasion in a black pants suit with a black silk blouse. She knew that Mrs. Hopwood would be appalled at what she would view as a bland, uninspiring outfit, but Mrs. Johnson felt powerful and confident when wearing black—a color Mrs. Hopwood told her to avoid because she was African American and it washed her out.

It was early Monday morning and she was meeting with Sister Mary Grace. Although Mrs. Johnson had always considered herself to be formidable, fifteen years of Catholic School education had left her with a fear of the church's hierarchy.

A seventh grade teacher at St. Polycarp, Mrs. Johnson had been appointed interim principal of the school in the fall, when Mrs. Logan left so suddenly. At first Mrs. Johnson was thrilled with the promotion. She especially liked the fact that she would have some power over the new teachers whom her predecessor had hired. And she was happy to be out of the classroom, which she thought would give her a more flexible schedule—necessary because she had two six year old twins.

But things did not go as planned.

For one thing, the new teachers, Addison, Casey and Dylan, actually tried to sabotage her. Void of re-

spect, they always turned in their lesson plans late—
on Google Docs, not on paper—which Mrs. Johnson
preferred. They frequently skipped meetings, called in
sick without any warning whatsoever and talked with
comical disgust behind her back. And that was only the
tip of the iceberg.

While dealing with preteens could be daunting, com-
municating with the parents of all of the students—from
nervous kindergarteners to eighth graders preparing
for high school—was a nightmare. She tried her best
to placate them, even though a portion of them hardly
paid the necessary tuition.

The diocese topped it off—bullying her into completing an endless amount of paperwork—which she
was woefully behind in—thwarting her efforts with
a mass of red tape and frequent observations, which
went no place at all. They were obsessed with state
standards and the core curriculum so they could keep
up with the public schools. Mrs. Johnson thought this
competition was ludicrous. Teaching to the test was
all that it amounted to, while Mrs. Johnson believed
in a strong math program, the fundamentals of gram-
mar—thanks to Mrs. Hopwood's urging—cursive writing and, above all, a firm religious training steeped in
the Catholic tradition.

Mrs. Johnson had a pretty good idea of why this
meeting had been called. Since the diocese had not
begun to search for a replacement principal, they would
no doubt offer it to Mrs. Johnson on a permanent basis.
Mrs. Johnson had been up half the night rehearsing the
speech she would give to Sister Mary Grace. While she
was grateful for the opportunity to serve as head of St.
Polycarp, and while she enjoyed it thoroughly—she

would go to confession this weekend—teaching was her passion and she longed to return to her classroom. The school librarian, who had replaced Mrs. Johnson, could go back to her first love, which was clearly books. Mrs. Johnson would demand—no maybe ask politely— to be included in the interview process for a new principal which would prevent the hiring of another Mrs. Logan. Since Mrs. Johnson had been at St. Polycarp a number of years, serving under a number of principals, and was now one herself, the diocese would no doubt be happy for her input.

"Sister Mary Grace will see you now." The school secretary stood—a bent over woman dressed entirely in beige, with copper brown hair—reminding Mrs. Johnson of a cashew.

Mrs. Johnson flashed a smile. She knew how important it was to be nice to the office help because sometimes they wielded power although the same could not be said for Mrs. Turnipseed, the school secretary at St. Polycarp.

Mrs. Johnson marched in and immediately felt herself at a disadvantage. She had only met Sister Mary Grace once and she had forgotten how tall the nun was. She was situated behind a massive desk, which seemed to be on some sort of pedestal. Sister instructed Mrs. Johnson to have a seat in a rather small chair, making Mrs. Johnson feel childlike and unimportant, as she teetered on the edge.

"How are you today, Mrs. Johnson?"

"I'm fine. Please call me Amelia."

Sister Mary Grace moved her lips in a weak grin and right at that moment Mrs. Johnson knew that—for some unfathomable reason—the superintendent did not like her. Perhaps it had to do with the murders at St. Polycarp but that could hardly be laid on Mrs. Johnson's doorstep. She hadn't been the one who hired all those psychotic people.

"Do you have any idea of what this meeting is about?" Sister challenged her.

"As a matter of fact, I do. I have to tell you, Sister, how much I have enjoyed being the principal at St. Polycarp. It's been an enriching experience. I have learned so much and I have grown as an educator. I am grateful and humbled by your faith in me. But moving forward, I would like to return to my classroom. Children are my passion and I think I could serve the diocese and our Lord better there. That being said, I would be happy to be included in the interviewing process. I have some ideas of how to make the transition smoother for the person who will follow me."

For a long moment Sister Mary Grace did not reply, although she looked as though she didn't think much of the suggestions.

The chilly silence was unsettling.

Could they force her to stay on as the principal?

"Well, thank you for saying all of that." Sister Mary Grace hardly appeared grateful—rather suspicious and antagonistic. "But the truth of the matter is that there is no possible way you could become a permanent principal at St. Polycarp or any other school for that matter. You don't have a Masters in Administration or any Masters at all as far as I can see." Sister then looked down at her desk and scowled darkly.

"So I should just return to my seventh grade class in September?" Mrs. Johnson asked in a scared, high-pitched voice.

"I'm afraid not."

Suddenly the room started to spin and fear flooded through her. She felt as though she was floating through a bad dream, her head spinning with questions. "Are you firing me?" she managed to utter.

"Well, yes and no. Actually, the diocese is planning to close St. Polycarp on July 1st."

"Why?"

"I'm glad you asked that. Have you been keeping track of the finances at your school by yourself?"

"Well, no. A man who delivers hot dogs to the cafeteria has been helping me." She saw Sister frown so Mrs. Johnson added quickly, "He is a certified accountant but he hasn't been able to get a job." A terrible thought crossed her mind and, before thinking, she blurted out, "He hasn't been embezzling, has he?"

"I certainly hope not," Sister said in a clipped voice, "because that certainly would not speak well of you. But unfortunately, it's more serious than that. You have been operating with a deficit of four thousand dollars a month for the last five months. Tuitions have not been paid by many of your families. The Ortiz family hasn't paid anything since Mrs. Logan left."

"I know that. But Mr. Ortiz is in prison for a crime he claims he didn't commit. However, he is due for parole any day now and they promise to catch up."

"That might be a good excuse for Mr. Ortiz, but he is hardly the only one behind. A fourth of your families are in arrears. Then there's the matter of attendance where your teachers are concerned. The rate of absenteeism is unacceptable."

"I understand." Mrs. Johnson thought it best if she agreed as much as possible. "These young teachers Mrs.

Logan hired have no respect for authority, or for the school. They tell me at the last minute…"

"If your staff is defiant, then it's up to you as a principal to rein them in. And what about this Mrs. Hooper, who was out an entire week?"

"Mrs. Hopwood had some problems with her son. She had to go to Asia to bring him back, but everything has settled down and…"

"Substitute teachers cost a great deal of money. And you have done absolutely nothing about fund-raising."

"You mean selling those chocolate bars?"

"Any effort made on your part would have been appreciated. Then there is the reputation of the school. With all these murders…"

Mrs. Johnson decided it was time to defend herself and the school. "Well, that can hardly be blamed on me and besides they were solved."

"It is not a question of blame. It is a question of dealing with harsh reality. A school has to be self-supporting and hopefully have enough left over to help with some of the diocese's programs. We cannot continue to pour money into a sinking ship." Sister Mary Grace took a deep breath and her tone softened. "Times have changed. Parishioners are fewer and fewer. The scarcity of nuns means that we have to hire mostly lay teachers, who demand steady salary increases and go on strike for the least little thing. Most of the students who attend our schools aren't even Catholic, so there's a lack of commitment."

"I understand all of that," Mrs. Johnson said, and, deciding to be proactive, she added, "Is there any way at all that I can turn this situation around?"

Sister Mary Grace shook her head and admitted it

was doubtful. "Not unless you have twenty thousand dollars," she said.

"How about ten?"

Sister Mary Grace shrugged.

"Five?" Mrs. Johnson added hopefully.

"It's not just the money," Sister Mary Grace said. "You have to understand, running a school is a business. And the bottom line is that the school has to continue to be profitable. So," she was back to the surly voice again, "I would suggest you call a meeting of your staff to get them up to speed and to encourage them to start applying for jobs in the fall. It's already the end of April, so they should get right on this. With all the Catholic schools which are scheduled to close, and you will be happy to know that St. Polycarp is not alone, there will be fewer and fewer openings. The positions will, no doubt, go to the people who have the necessary educational credits."

"And what about experience? Does that not count at all?" Mrs. Johnson could not keep the bitterness out of her own tone.

"Of course. Thank you for coming in." Sister Mary Grace stood up and, towering over Mrs. Johnson, extended her arm, giving Mrs. Johnson a limp handshake. "Oh, by the way," she added. "Just so you know, in the next couple of months, you may have some visitors in the school."

Mrs. Johnson hated visitors in the school.

"We have had a few offers from the state to rent the building in September. They're interested in converting the school into a methadone clinic."

I can't let this happen, Mrs. Johnson told herself, as she floated out of the office. *I can't let this happen.*

SIX

TRACY HOLTZ ENTERED St. Polycarp church cautiously. Luckily for her, it was deserted. Sometimes the children went to early Mass, sometimes the priest was hearing confessions, sometimes the portly housekeeper at the rectory would come to clean the altar and put fresh flowers in front of the statue of Our Lady of Fatima and sometimes the teacher, who always wore a brightly colored coat, would come in and light a candle.

No one paid her much mind.

No one except the teacher with the different colored coats.

Tracy had tried her best to be invisible. She was always dressed in black which was easy enough to do—that was her only outfit. With her black hair, twinged with gray, and her black sunglasses and her black hat, she could almost disappear into one of the dimly lit pews.

But the teacher with the different colored coats actually stared at her.

Tracy could only hope that she didn't go and blab to the priest and Tracy would have to find another place to spend her time.

She knew that Robert had found a way to sneak into the basement of the school, but she thought that was risky. It was clearly trespassing, where anyone should be welcome in a church.

But now that it was spring, it wasn't so bad. The winter was the worst. With the plummeting temperatures, the rain, the sleet, the snow, a body could freeze to death right there in the street. A sad and lonely way to die.

But she wouldn't die alone.

Of course there were shelters, but that would hardly work. They wouldn't let her bring her best friend in, and she could never, ever leave him behind. The truth was if it was between him and her surviving, hands down she would choose him. That's why before the end came, she had to find him a home, with someone who would love and care for him.

For he was the only thing that mattered right now, the little black and white dog, which lay under her feet in the pew.

SEVEN

Mrs. Hopwood had decided to tell Mrs. Johnson that she needed to have Tuesday off the moment Mrs. Johnson came in. She knew that her request would be met with a sneer but really what was one to do?

She burst into the principal's office and announced in an off-hand manner, "I need to be absent on Tuesday morning."

Mrs. Johnson looked tired and irritated. "It's out of the question."

"I have to." Mrs. Hopwood was careful, not to let her voice turn whiny. "There's been a death in my family." A flash of sympathy crossed Mrs. Johnson's face. "My Aunt Eunice."

The sympathy evaporated. "You don't have an Aunt Eunice."

"I do. I did. I have to go. She left me money in her will."

Mrs. Hopwood watched Mrs. Johnson's eyes widened. "How much money?"

"I don't know—several thousand." Mrs. Hopwood decided to sit down, now that the shock of her request had worn off. "Why?"

"Would you consider donating it to St. Polycarp?"

Mrs. Hopwood leaped up, miffed by the suggestion. "Absolutely not! Why would I do such a thing?"

"Because," Mrs. Johnson's voice lowered, "we are

in dire financial straits. The meeting with Sister Mary Grace did not go well. Forget about me being principal next year. She made it quite clear that, because of my lack of education, I wouldn't be considered for the job, even if such a job did exist. They're planning to close this school as of July 1st."

Mrs. Hopwood slumped down in her chair. "They say that every year."

"No, they're serious. Unless we can find a way to raise money, at the very least five thousand dollars."

"Maybe we can have a bake sale," Mrs. Hopwood said cheerfully. Mrs. Hopwood loved bake sales—the brownies, the chocolate chip cakes, the scones.

"I don't think so. Sister Mary Grace was also concerned about how much we're spending on substitute teachers…"

"Mrs. Hopwood," Daniela Bustos interrupted breathlessly, his eyes dancing with glee, "you have to come to the art room. Melissa Ortiz is crying again because Skylar said her father is a murderer and shouldn't be released from prison."

Mrs. Hopwood drew a deep breath. As far as she was concerned George Ortiz was a murderer and poor Melissa would be better off if he stayed locked up. Besides it was her only prep for the next three days. What was wrong with the art teacher who couldn't handle a teary eyed preteen? She rose slowly.

"We will talk later," Mrs. Johnson said.

Mrs. Hopwood decided to avoid Mrs. Johnson for the rest of the day.

AUNT EUNICE'S FUNERAL was not well attended. Of course, Mrs. Hopwood was present, as were Mrs. Hopwood's sisters, Roseanne and Gina, and her two brothers, David and Michael, the lawyer for the estate and the undertaker.

Roseanne gave a lovely eulogy. Mrs. Hopwood was flabbergasted by the number of facts Roseanne had learned in the brief time she cared for Aunt Eunice, since the family barely knew her growing up. Evidently Aunt Eunice was known for her impeccable fashion sense. She had a great interest in the homeless and often donated food and clothing to the cause. She had actually served in World War II in Paris. So—for a brief instant—Mrs. Hopwood was sorry that they hadn't made the connection, but it was obviously too late now.

As soon as the Mass was over, Mrs. Hopwood approached the lawyer and asked rather bluntly—she didn't have much time for niceties since Mrs. Johnson expected her to resume her duties quickly—when she could expect her inheritance.

Roseanne hissed and the lawyer glared at her.

"Not until the estate is settled. Your aunt left some bills, which need to be paid before we can disperse the money. We also have to conduct a search and make certain there are no other apparent heirs, which we don't know about."

What Mrs. Hopwood *did* know was, like everything else, this was going to be a battle.

"ALL RIGHT," ROSEANNE SAID to Mrs. Hopwood as they stood in Aunt Eunice's attic on Saturday morning. "I am leaving you two different color bags. One bag is black, that's for all the things you might want to trash."

Mrs. Hopwood was looking around at the small attic, all the boxes and the broken furniture, thinking that truly the best thing would be to trash it all, just throw it in the dumpster out back.

"The white bag is for everything you want to keep or donate to a charity. Of course, you have to get it there." Roseanne was quite bossy, used to giving orders to kindergartens and the elderly.

"I have a good mind to throw it all away," Mrs. Hopwood uttered, feeling overwhelmed by the enormity of the task.

"Don't do that. While Gina was cleaning the cellar, she found a reverse glass painting of the Last Supper and an old edition of the Bible. She's donating both of them to the church."

"Lucky for her," Mrs. Hopwood mumbled sarcastically.

"She also found a set of silverware, sterling I might add. I'll be downstairs if you need me. Oh," Roseanne said, almost as an afterthought, "let me know if you see any mice. We have some traps downstairs."

"Mice!" Mrs. Hopwood screeched. "I am petrified of mice, you know that. If I see any mice, I am out of here."

But Roseanne was out of there, already scrambling down the stairs to clean out the kitchen.

Mrs. Hopwood surveyed the attic, which was stuffed to the brim, with what looked like junk—a broken bird cage, three vacuums, two electric fans, four rotary phones, a lawn mower, a cot, stacks and stacks of books, cardboard boxes with photo albums spilling out, a cracked mirror, plastic flowers and an axe.

She plopped down on the floor and pulled one of the boxes towards her. The album was covered with dust. Mrs. Hopwood opened it and began to cough. The pictures were neatly bound, one of Aunt Eunice and Uncle

Vito—who was Mrs. Hopwood's grandmother's brother. Aunt Eunice was pretty in her day, a tall redhead with bright, bulging green eyes, although the color in the picture was fading. They were standing in front of a shop.

Mrs. Hopwood threw everything in the box right into the black trash bag, without even bothering to read any of the papers.

She worked silently and resentfully for almost an hour—making very little headway—when she noticed a trunk in the corner.

This is ridiculous, she thought. *We really should pay someone to do this. I don't care if the money comes out of my measly inheritance. It's not fair. And I'm telling that to Roseanne.*

She rose, dusted off her forest green tweed pants, and decided to open the trunk, before she spoke to Roseanne. No doubt it would be crammed with moth eaten clothes, but that would only give more credence to her argument.

Of course, the trunk did not open easily. While fumbling with the stiff lock, she chipped her newly manicured Ballet Slippers nail polish and hurt her shoulder hoisting the lid.

But it was worth it.

When Mrs. Hopwood saw what was inside, she began to tremble, dazed and thunderstruck.

The trunk was jammed packed with beautiful vintage clothes—tea length full skirts with petticoats underneath, shirtwaist dresses cinched with leather belts, poodle skirts, peplum jackets, floral dresses with matching cardigans, polka dots and madras outfits, a yellow coat, trimmed in black, sweaters with little lace collars, fitted sheaths with sweetheart necks, suits with

straight skirts and matching jackets, all in the most daz-
zling colors, cobalt blue, scarlet red, emerald green,
sunshine yellow. The wardrobe reminded Mrs. Hopwood of *Rear Window*, or *Breakfast at Tiffany's*. Mrs.
Hopwood found it incredible that the clothes were in
impeccable condition, packed in tissue paper, although
there was a slight smell of moth balls, which Mrs. Hopwood could easily cure.

They all had price tags on them ranging from twenty
five dollars to over a hundred. Mrs. Hopwood could
only guess what they might be worth today.

There was a red velvet box at the bottom of the clothing and Mrs. Hopwood's heart lurched when she opened
it and saw the jewelry it contained—Art Deco pins
in the shape of fans, silver butterfly cuffs, dangling
earrings green and black and silver, chokers with jade
stones, a watch set in rhinestones.

On the side of the trunk were five handbags, a struc-
tured floral bag, a bright blue one trimmed in gold like
a little suitcase, a mint green one with a copper leaf for
an opening, a saddle bag in three shades of brown and a
Kelly-style bag in Mrs. Hopwood's favorite color, violet.

Mrs. Hopwood searched through each and every bag,
but they all appeared empty except for one, where she
found a small golden compact—the name Dagny engraved in sequins. She placed it gently in the jewelry
box.

Holding her breath, her heart pounding furiously, she
lifted out a peacock blue sheath and put it against her.
It looked as though it just might fit. All right, it might
be a trifle big, and a little long, but with vintage clothing like this, size could not possibly be a consideration.

Her cell phone rang the familiar Alfred Hitchcock

tune. It took Mrs. Hopwood several minutes to find it—
turned out it was under a broken sewing machine. Her
stomach plummeted when she saw it was her husband,
Monte, who was her ride home.

"You almost done there?" he asked. "I want to go
to the gym."

"I'll be done in half an hour." She heard her husband
sigh. Patience was not one of his strong points. "Could
you do me a favor?"

"What kind of a favor?" he asked suspiciously.

"Could you empty out the trunk of the car?"

He didn't respond. Mrs. Hopwood couldn't decide if
that was good or bad. Finally he asked stiffly, "What
are you talking about?"

"Well, I was cleaning out the attic and I opened a
trunk and Monte, you never saw such an array of beautiful vintage clothing. I won't have to buy a single thing
for the next year in a half…"

"No."

"What do you mean no?"

"You are not bringing some old lady's clothing into
this house."

"You don't understand, they're vintage. They're
worth money. They don't make clothes like this anymore…"

"Then sell them and use the money to hire someone
to organize your closets. You're a hoarder, Julia, and you
need help. You have completely taken over every closet
in the house. Do you realize that most of my clothes are
in the garage and I have a few coats in the shed? Do
you think this behavior is normal?"

"I'll throw things out."

"You always say that but you never do. Hoarding evidently runs in your family."

"Aunt Eunice wasn't a blood relative."

"I don't care who she was, those clothes are not coming in this house. I've had enough, Julia. And I mean it. If you bring those clothes into the house, I'll burn them, I swear."

He hung up.

Mrs. Hopwood was feeling very discouraged. Monte was irritated with her again. Lately, he seemed to be snapping at her often and with very little reason. Anyway, she wanted these clothes. She needed these clothes.

She looked down at her phone.

Time to call her best friend.

EIGHT

MELISSA ORTIZ SANK down on her bed and reached under her mattress, retrieving a small leather notebook.

She had won it in class, a short story contest, writing about a child, who learned that her brother had committed a horrible crime. The prize Mrs. Hopwood gave her was well appreciated. Melissa never had a notebook as nice as this one.

Mrs. Hopwood said that it was important to write down your goals, and to review them daily. Melissa had copied a quote Mrs. Hopwood wrote on the board. "If you can see it, you can be it." And Melissa knew exactly what she wanted to be.

I want to be a great writer, like J. K. Rowlings. I want to write for children, to entertain them, to inspire them and to make them believe that no matter what their circumstances are as a child, they can grow up to be rich and famous.

I want to be just like Mrs. Hopwood. I want to wear beautiful clothes, a fresh, new outfit every day, with no repeats. I want to have matching jewelry and walk around in pretty high heel shoes. I want to have silky, thick, wavy hair like hers and the way she does, I want to smell like a garden. And I will have a husband and a son, who adores me.

"Melissa?"

Melissa slammed her notebook when her mother entered the room.

"What's that?" Her mother was dressed in her waitress uniform, a black mini skirt, a low cut white blouse, and high ankle strapped shoes. She worked in a Gentlemen's Club, serving drinks and jockeying for meager tips.

"Nothing." Melissa stashed the notebook in her backpack. "Just something for school."

"I gotta go in early—to set up. Ginger's out again." A few seconds passed and then she blurted out, "You know your father is up for parole this week."

Her mother had mentioned that before but to Melissa it didn't seem quite real, because her father didn't seem quite real. He had gone to jail when Melissa was a newborn and any contact she had with him was at a prison table.

He frightened Melissa, an angry man with huge biceps tattooed in obscene pictures, a man smelling of sweat, who gazed hungrily at her with dark eyes.

Her mother paused for a second. "Are you okay, Melissa? How are you feeling?"

"I'm fine, Mom."

"You're not tired or anything."

"No!"

"Muscles not aching?"

"No, stop!" Melissa had inherited Hemochronmatosis from her mother, a disease which meant that she had too much iron in her blood. But she hadn't had any symptoms for years. It didn't stop her mother from worrying, though and when her mother worried, it reminded Melissa that she wasn't quite like anyone else.

"I hate to ask you to do this," her mother said in a,

tense tiny voice, "but you may have to give up your room."

"What?" Melissa looked around at her tiny space, the size of a broom closet, but it was all hers.

"When your father comes home." Her mother sounded embarrassed as she leaned towards Melissa. Melissa saw the way her make-up—two shades darker than her pale—pasty complexion stuck in her pores and streaked down her neck. Mrs. Hopwood's make-up was dewy and light and her cheekbones glowed. "Your father is going to want his privacy after all his years in prison. So you're going to have to share a room with me."

"With you?"

"Unless you'd rather share with Adam." Adam was Melissa's brother. They seldom spoke.

Melissa didn't respond.

"I'm gotta get going." Her mother bent down to kiss Melissa on the cheek, smearing her slash of scarlet lipstick. Melissa smelled the cheap musky perfume.

"Don't stay up too late," her mother warned as she shuffled out the door. She stopped suddenly and added. "You know there's a possibility that your father may not make parole."

Melissa didn't say what she was thinking. *I hope he doesn't.* Because she wouldn't feel safe, as long as he was free.

NINE

"WHERE ARE YOU?"

The desperation in Mrs. Hopwood's voice immediately put Mrs. Johnson on guard. "I'm just leaving the baseball field, after watching the twins play. I have to tell you that they're the backbone of the team. I wouldn't be surprised if they end up being professional players."

"They're six years old. Listen, you have to do me a favor."

"What sort of favor?" Mrs. Johnson was wary as she rifled through her handbag for her car keys.

"I need for you to come and pick me up at my Aunt Eunice's. It's not far, right on Franklin Street. And if you can, bring the van."

"That's not possible." Mrs. Johnson was irritated by the request because she thought in spite of her protests, she was probably going to get roped into doing the favor. "I'm meeting Peter and the twins at Alfredo's for pizza. He has the van. I thought Montgomery was picking you up."

"Well, here's the thing." Mrs. Johnson hated it when Mrs. Hopwood said, "here's the thing" because it always involved a long, complicated, convoluted explanation. "Evidently Aunt Eunice used to have a shop, where she sold used clothing, which, of course, now is vintage clothing. You wouldn't believe what I found in one of the trunks. The most exquisite dresses and skirts and blouses and jewelry, and five handbags, well, four, because I took one. And Monte, well, he refuses to let me bring the stuff in the house. He actually had the nerve to call me a hoarder."

"You *are* a hoarder, Julia."

Mrs. Hopwood was undeterred. "Whatever. So I was thinking that maybe, just maybe, you could store the clothing and the bags and the jewelry, in your cellar, in that nice little space you have near your boiler. And then every morning you could bring me an outfit, your choice, and I could change in the teachers' room and then I could change back at the end of the day and that way Monte would never suspect that I'm wearing the clothes and he couldn't accuse me of hoarding because I'm not the one who is actually doing the hoarding. Of course, it would be really great if you could text me in the morning to let me know which outfit you choose and, then that way, I could make sure that I bring in the matching accessories."

For a moment Mrs. Johnson was speechless. When she finally found her voice, she lashed out. "Have you lost your mind?!" She was screaming so loudly that a group of parents on the losing team, who stared at her every time she clapped for her twins, were now glaring at her. She lowered her voice. "You don't think I have enough to do in the morning, trying to get the boys ready for school, prepping myself to come in to St. Polycarp and deal with a hostile staff when I'm worried about losing my job in the fall, and now my back is killing me."

"What's wrong with your back?"

"I'm in horrible pain, probably from lifting the twins.

You have asked me to do some insane things, some dangerous things, but this—this!"

"All right, all right, calm down."

Mrs. Johnson did not like to be told to calm down when she had every reason to be irate. And where were her darn keys? She hated this handbag.

"No one seems to realize how valuable this merchandise is, especially the jewelry. There are price tags on everything and even in those days, they were high end."

"Then why don't you," Mrs. Johnson had finally located her key ring, stuck to the bottom of her purse, "for once in your life do something for someone else and sell all the clothing and jewelry and donate the profits to St. Polycarp?"

Mrs. Hopwood was silent. Mrs. Johnson suspected she had gone too far.

"That was unkind." Mrs. Hopwood was clearly hurt.

"I'm sorry. I'm just really overwhelmed. I've got to go."

"No! Don't hang up. I just got a brilliant idea. Why don't we have a fashion show? You know the upper school girls think that they're models already and they would love to strut down the runway wearing Aunt Eunice's clothes."

"And how exactly does this hair brain scheme make money for St. Polycarp?"

"We can hold an auction and sell the clothing right off of their backs."

Mrs. Johnson hesitated, which gave Mrs. Hopwood the opportunity to jump right in.

"I'll do all the work. You won't have to do a single thing, except come and get me and the clothing right now. You have to admit, I might be a little shaky when it comes to the metric system and world geography, but one thing I do know is fashion. And there's then Sister Grace Maria."

"Sister Mary Grace"

"When she sees how much money we made and how hard we're trying, she's sure to reevaluate her plans for September."

"Well, maybe." Mrs. Johnson was thinking of all the things which could go wrong.

"You won't regret it," Mrs. Hopwood promised.

"I already do."

REGRET WAS THE first thing Mrs. Johnson felt when she saw Mrs. Hopwood standing beside the dumpster flanked by white trash bags. Mrs. Hopwood had talked her into storing Aunt Eunice's clothing at St. Polycarp since in Mrs. Hopwood's grand scheme—they would benefit the school. In spite of her aching back, Mrs. Johnson was forced to get out of the car and help Mrs. Hopwood hoist the bags into the trunk, onto the back seat and in between the passenger's seat and the driver's seat.

"I didn't finish the attic," Mrs. Hopwood said brightly. "I have to go back. Maybe I'll find more stuff." She glanced at her watch.

"Do you think you can hold these purses on your lap?" Mrs. Johnson was having a hard time seeing out the front window.

Mrs. Hopwood grabbed the trash bag, where it overturned, spilling out the handbags, sliding onto the floor, onto Mrs. Hopwood's lap and onto Mrs. Johnson's leg.

"I can't drive this way." Mrs. Johnson looked down at a pretty brown saddle purse.

"I wonder why there were no shoes," Mrs. Hopwood

said thoughtfully as she scooped up all the purses, turned around and threw them on the floor of the back seat.

"How much do you think you will sell that brown handbag for?" Mrs. Johnson found herself asking before she had a chance to think about it.

"I don't know. I thought we could double everything on the price tags. I think," Mrs. Hopwood rose, knelt on the seat and leaned back, "the price on it is…"

"Don't do that!" Mrs. Johnson warned. "In the first place you should be wearing a seat belt."

"It says seventy-five dollars, so I guess we could let it go at one hundred and fifty."

"That's a lot of money. Please sit down and put your seat belt on. The parents at St. Polycarp are struggling. They can't afford those prices."

"Oh, no. We're not going to just invite our parents. We're going to invite the entire town, all those rich people on Blueberry Hill. They'll go crazy when they see these clothes. We can do a whole promo. Save our school." Mrs. Hopwood looked at her watch.

"Why do you keep checking the time? I'm the one who's in a rush."

"I'm not checking the time," Mrs. Hopwood said rather irritably. "This is my new apple watch. I can get messages, measure how much I walk…"

"You never walk."

"And even dial 911."

"I want that bag," Mrs. Johnson blurted out. "But I can't afford to pay a hundred and fifty dollars."

"So just take it. You know, there was another trunk in the corner. I bet that had the shoes in it."

"I don't feel good about it."

"The shoes?"

"No, taking the bag for nothing. What if I pay fifty dollars?"

"Sold!" Mrs. Hopwood said cheerfully. "You see, we're already making money."

MRS. HOPWOOD INSISTED on dragging the clothes down into the basement and since it was Saturday, and the school was closed, there was no Mr. Salisbury to help. Mrs. Johnson's back ached with every trip.

Mrs. Hopwood wrinkled her nose. "There's a bad smell in here."

Mrs. Johnson sniffed the air, looking at the old pipes, which winded around at grotesque angles. "I don't smell anything." She was anxious to get out of there. She had never really felt at home in the dark, dank, damp basement with its cement floor and mold covered walls. "Well, maybe."

"Oh my God!" Mrs. Hopwood shrieked and then skedaddled to the staircase.

Mrs. Johnson's heart raced. "Did you see a mouse?"

Mrs. Hopwood shook her head.

"A rat?"

"I think," her voice lowered, "I think that there is someone hiding behind the boiler. I saw a shadow."

Mrs. Johnson glanced at the enormous boiler, which stood like a sentinel in the middle of the dungeon. "It's just your imagination. But let's go. It's the weekend. I don't need to be at school."

"Me neither," Mrs. Hopwood said as she flew up the narrow, wooden stairs.

TEN

ALMOST CAUGHT. But really, what choice did he have but to hide behind the boiler when those two gabby women came clamoring down the stairs, dragging a lot of old clothes with them?

Luckily his years of never having enough food kept him skinny, which came in handy if he had to hide. As soon as he was sure they left the building, he'd head towards the cafeteria. Sometimes he could find a loaf of bread, which hadn't been locked up.

Meanwhile those nice clothes would make a comfortable bed.

Hopefully, he wouldn't have an accident on them in the middle of the night.

ELEVEN

"DOCTOR NAYMAN'S OFFICE."

"Yes, this is Nancy Sugarman. I'd like to speak to Doctor Nayman."

"Doctor Nayman is with a patient. Is this an emergency?"

"No. I'm afraid by mistake—purely by accident— the Percocet the doctor prescribed fell down the toilet. You know how hard those child proof vials are to open. They really should give you an option for people like me, who don't have children. Anyway, I was struggling to get the cap off of the bottle, and I was in the bathroom, and whoosh, the entire bottle landed face down in the water. I suppose I could have put my hand in there and tried to retrieve some of the pills…"

"Could you hold on, please? Someone is calling on the other line."

Mrs. Sugarman really couldn't hold on. The seventh graders were in music until nine fifteen and, any moment, they were going to come stomping in. She tried calling the office at eight thirty and again at nine, but all she got was the answering machine. You would think that a doctor's office would open at eight for people who had to work.

"So what is your problem?" The receptionist was back on the phone.

"I need Doctor Nayman to renew my prescription for

Percocet. And while he's at it, he could really give me a higher dose. The dose I'm taking now doesn't seem to be doing much." It occurred to Mrs. Sugarman that maybe the receptionist could call the prescription in herself and there would be no need for Mrs. Sugarman to get involved with the doctor. "I'll give you the number of the pharmacy."

"Tell me where I can reach you and I'll have the doctor phone you when he's free."

When he was free would probably be right in the middle of algebra class. But unfortunately, Mrs. Sugarman was out of choices.

SHE KEPT HER cell phone on the entire time. Luckily Mrs. Johnson had no silly rule about phones in the classroom. On the contrary, she encouraged teachers to keep their cell phones where they could see them, and sometimes she sent text messages to the staff.

At 3:10 the doctor still hadn't called her back, which was a good thing, because at least she would be able to talk in privacy. But then the fire bell rang, an unexpected drill, and, because it was so close to dismissal time, the students were divided on whether or not to take their backpacks with them.

"If you're already packed up, you can," Mrs. Sugarman said. "But just hurry into line, please." She grabbed her cell phone and held it tightly. And then the rumbling began.

"I don't have to take my backpack. I already did my math homework."

"We have math homework?"

"I can't find my backpack. I think someone stole it."

"It's in the trashcan, you nitwit."

"Please, students, fall into line."

It was chaos going down the stairs, and, if it had been a real fire, her class would have perished.

After the children were counted, and half of them left, and half of them returned to the classroom, the doctor finally phoned. Mrs. Sugarman found a quiet corner near the office.

"What seems to be the problem?" Doctor Nayman sounded grumpy.

"Thank you for calling me back. I dropped the bottle of Percocet you prescribed for me right into the toilet. I'm so clumsy and now I need more."

"I understand that's what happened." The doctor's voice was clipped and cold—and unconvinced. "What you must understand is that Percocet is a narcotic and therefore under strict regulation. I can't, in good conscience, renew your prescription three weeks later. If you're really uncomfortable, you could try taking a couple of extra strength Excedrin."

"Extra strength Excedrin!" A kindergarten parent flashed a forced smile at Mrs. Sugarman, and she lowered her voice. "I don't think you understand how much my head hurts. It's like a hot, sharp pain, that doesn't go away." Except it wasn't really her head right now, but her stomach from all the tension.

"If the pain is intense…"

"It is!"

"Then maybe it's time we schedule an MRI."

"I can't. In the first place, I'm claustrophobic."

"There are open MRIs."

"And in the second place, I'm very busy with school and the state exams."

Addison Fiore came strutting down the hall.

"Maybe," Doctor Nayman said in exasperation, "I could give you a prescription."

Mrs. Sugarman's heart leaped.

"For a pain management session."

"No, thanks." Mrs. Sugarman watched as Addison plunked her handbag on the counter and stepped in, heading for Mrs. Johnson's office.

"If there is nothing else?"

"Nothing else." Mrs. Sugarman hung up on the useless doctor.

The halls had thinned out, the voices had faltered, and there it was, staring at her in the face, the handbag she had been hoping to dip into for several days. This was her opportunity and she edged closer to the counter.

Who knew if the pills Addison had bragged about were still there?

And just as Mrs. Sugarman was about to do the deed, Jason Briggs, one of Mrs. Sugarman's seventh grade students, came creeping down the hall. He was a nice enough young man, but some of the other students avoided him, because according to teacher gossip, his older brother was a drug dealer.

"What are you doing in the building?" Mrs. Sugarman snapped.

"Forgot my backpack," he mumbled and, as he turned around, displayed it, and almost hit Mrs. Sugarman in the face.

The moment was lost. Addison emerged and grabbed her handbag, while Mrs. Sugarman watched Jason, who was leisurely drinking from the water fountain.

Meanwhile Addison was chatting with Casey, about collaborating on a project. Mrs. Sugarman was just about to go upstairs, straighten out her classroom, when she saw Addison put down her handbag again, rummage through it, and take out her wallet.

"I have a meeting with a parent," she told Casey, "and I'm going to need some coffee. Do you want anything?"

"I'm out of here," Casey said, "but I'll walk to the corner with you."

Was Addison going to leave her handbag on the counter?

No.

Instead Addison took one look at Jason, who was loitering at the water fountain, zipped it up and carried it behind the counter, placing it on Miss Turnipseed's desk. Mrs. Turnipseed, the school secretary, had taken the afternoon off, something about trying to straighten out her social security. Then Addison turned around and, gabbing merrily with Casey, sprang out of the building.

Mrs. Sugarman hated merry people.

She was just about to tell Jason to move along when Jason began to stroll down the hall and slowly, very slowly, he disappeared from sight.

Mrs. Sugarman had no idea about how much time she had. At any moment, Mrs. Johnson could come barreling out of her office.

It was now or never.

Quickly, but not so quickly as to arise suspicion if anyone was watching, Mrs. Sugarman ambled behind the counter to Miss Turnipseed's desk. She could hear Mrs. Johnson on the phone, trying to secure a stage for some production—probably the spring concert where the entire school sang passé Broadway songs out of tune, although she had heard rumors that had been canceled.

She unzipped the purse, hoping she didn't have to fumble around. And she didn't. Right away she spotted the vial of pills. She grabbed them, zipped the purse back up, and scrambled out of the area.

Mrs. Sugarman had been saved.

TWELVE

"CLASS, I HAVE some very exciting news." Mrs. Hopwood stood in front of her fifth grade class.

"You're quitting?" David shouted out.

"One more word out of you and you're going straight down to Mrs. Johnson."

That shut David up. He was afraid of Mrs. Johnson, who wasn't beyond calling the parents of wayward students and demanding that they come and get their children immediately. The parents, most of them interrupted from their jobs, were furious.

"As you may know," Mrs. Hopwood continued, "St. Polycarp is experiencing some financial problems." She wasn't sure if she should have shared that fact with the students, so she quickly added. "I have found a way to raise money."

"Selling candy bars?"

"Greeting cards?"

"No one sends greeting cards anymore. You just write on their timeline on Facebook."

"Nothing like that. We're going to have a fashion show."

The slumped, bored girls sat up straighter and became wide-eyed.

"I am going to choose models from the fifth grade, the sixth, the seventh and the eighth. The girls will be modeling very high end, expensive, vintage clothes."

"Can I be a model?"

"I think you have to be thin."

"I am a model. I did a print ad for the Gap."

"That was three years ago."

"What fun is that for us?" Roberto moaned. "We can't be models."

"That's true, but I'm going to need a lot of boys to take pictures of each of the items, and then someone has to arrange the photos in a booklet, so people can bid. Also we will need boys to help with the staging and the lighting."

'I have a brand new camera."

"My father owns a printing company."

"I will choose," Mrs. Hopwood raised her voice, "only well behaved children to participate."

"I guess that leaves me out."

"It is never too late to change your behavior. I will be watching all of you."

Mrs. Hopwood had no doubt that the rest of the school year would be smooth sailing.

SHE GLANCED AT her watch, which sent a message to stand. If Mrs. Johnson had her way, Mrs. Hopwood would probably be standing all day. It was almost ten after three. Mrs. Johnson always gave her a heads up when there was going to be a fire alarm, since Mrs. Hopwood needed time to change out of her spike heels and put on her fire drill shoes.

Otherwise, Mrs. Hopwood would hold up the entire second floor as she wobbled down the stairs.

When the siren blared, some of the students grabbed their backpacks, anticipating leaving for the day. So when Mrs. Hopwood returned to the classroom, it was in complete disarray. She almost tripped over one that was unzipped in the aisle.

Curious at which student had been so careless, she bent down. A red leather notebook tumbled out.

She recognized it immediately.

Mrs. Hopwood was a nosy parker and she wondered if Melissa Ortiz—who was an amazing writer—was actually using the notebook to create a short story.

So Mrs. Hopwood began to read.

"YOU SHOULD HAVE seen it!" she told Mrs. Johnson. "She wrote that I smelled like a garden and she wanted to be just like me when she grew up, to wear lots of nice clothes. That puts a lot of pressure on me, because I'm running out of nice clothes."

"You shouldn't have read it." Mrs. Johnson was barely paying attention, sitting behind a massive desk, staring at her laptop. "It's called breaking and entering."

"I didn't break anything." Mrs. Hopwood plopped down on a chair. "Nor did I enter. This is a school and, in a school, there is no expectation of privacy. I watch *Law & Order.*"

"I watch *Law & Order* too." Mrs. Johnson muttered distractedly. "And that only applies to an open area, like a desk, or a bookcase."

"The backpack was open and the notebook practically fell out."

"Neither one of us knows what we're talking about." Mrs. Johnson leaned back in her chair. "I feel bad for Melissa. Her father has been in jail for twelve years on a manslaughter charge. He's up for parole. The poor girl is probably on pins and needles, praying for his release. Listen, about those clothes in the basement. They're all scrunched up in the corner and they're very wrinkled. They need to be ironed."

"I don't iron."

"I know that." Mrs. Johnson looked in disapproval at Mrs. Hopwood's wrinkled yellow linen skirt. "Maybe we could have the models take the clothes home they will be wearing and ask them to do the ironing."

Mrs. Hopwood thought that was risky and said so. "I'm going to include my class. I already told them"

"You told them!" Mrs. Johnson almost leaped out of her chair. "You shouldn't have done that. Not until I discussed it with the staff."

"When are you going to call a meeting? What are you waiting for?"

"You just can't call a meeting." Mrs. Johnson sat back down and put her head in her hand. "You know how these teachers are. If you ask them to stay an extra fifteen minutes, you have to give them three days' notice."

"You were one of those teachers a few months ago," Mrs. Hopwood reminded her. "You know that floral handbag?"

"No." Mrs. Johnson had returned to her laptop.

"I think it fell out of the bag when we were transporting the clothes. I looked in the cellar and it's not there. Unless it's still in your car."

"I'll look when I have a minute. Maybe on June 21st."

"I'm off." Mrs. Hopwood rose and stretched. "I'm going to church to light a candle. Let me ask you this. Did you ever see that woman in church? She's dressed all in black and she sits in a side pew."

"Maybe."

"She might be dangerous."

"The church isn't our responsibility. If you're really concerned, tell Father Bartholomew."

"He's deaf and he's blind. She might be dangerous."

Mrs. Johnson looked up. "Under the right circumstances we can all be dangerous. We both learned that."

THIRTEEN

"LET ME DO all the talking," Mrs. Johnson instructed Mrs. Hopwood as the climbed the stairs, leading to the rectory. Mrs. Johnson did not know why but she harbored a strong suspicion that Father Bartholomew didn't like Mrs. Hopwood.

"You better talk loudly. He's as deaf as a doornail."

"What's a doornail?"

Mrs. Hopwood admitted that she had no idea.

There was no reason to ring the bell. Father Bartholomew met them at the door. He was a short man, stooped over, with a wild mane of white hair and, small, angry, sharp eyes.

He smelled like tobacco and oregano.

He pointed, stony faced, to a small cell-like room and the teachers sat on tiny, straight back chairs. Mrs. Johnson was more comfortable in the confessional.

"I don't know if you're aware of it, Father," Mrs. Johnson began in a booming voice "But there are rumors that St. Polycarp School might close in the fall."

"What are you talking about? Rumors? There are no rumors!" Father Bartholomew hollered back. "I know you met with Sister Mary Grace. If you ladies had managed the school better," he glared at Mrs. Hopwood, as though she was personally responsible for the dwindling enrollment, "this might not have happened."

Mrs. Hopwood was not one to be wronged and to

stand silent. "We have a way to fix it. We're going to have a fashion show."

"A what?" He bent his face towards her.

Mrs. Johnson kicked Mrs. Hopwood with her clog. "A fashion show, Father. We're going to have the students model some clothing and then we're going to auction off those clothes."

It was difficult for Mrs. Johnson to know whether or not the priest thought this was a good idea. He was still peering at Mrs. Hopwood and his irritated gaze had traveled to her red and white necklace, which descended straight down into her ample cleavage.

"Are you going to be showing any breasts?" Father Bartholomew asked.

"Of course not."

"What about thighs?"

Mrs. Johnson heaved a deep sigh, wishing she was someplace else, anyplace else. "Father, these are vintage clothes."

"What?" He cupped his ear and leaned towards Mrs. Johnson.

"Old fashion," Mrs. Hopwood shouted. "Would you like to see the ad I designed?"

Father Bartholomew didn't answer, maybe because Mrs. Hopwood had asked the question in a normal tone of voice. Mrs. Hopwood obviously thought his silence indicated an affirmative answer. It took her several minutes to find the actual promotional ad, which necessitated emptying out her entire bucket bag, a flowered cosmetic case, a neon yellow wallet, an empty bottle of perfume, a half of a protein bar, a pair of crimson flats and a bent license plate—Mrs. Johnson would ask her about the license plate some other time.

"What is this?" Father Bartholomew looked at the program with genuine puzzlement, as though it was written in Chinese.

"The promotional ad for the fashion show." Mrs. Johnson thought that maybe some of the proceeds could be spent on a hearing aid for the priest.

"Who is this?" Father Bartholomew pointed a bony finger to the picture of the compact with the name Dagny etched in sequins.

"I found that compact in one of the handbags and I decided it was so pretty, I want it to be our logo," Mrs. Hopwood said proudly.

"Who is this Dagny?" Father Bartholomew repeated.

Mrs. Johnson was too exhausted to provide any explanation, so she turned to Mrs. Hopwood, who also looked petered out. "It's not a real person. I mean, it might have been, or still is, I guess she could be alive, we don't know for sure…"

Father Bartholomew turned towards Mrs. Johnson. "What is she talking about?"

"I think this woman was named after Dagny Taggart from Atlas Shrugged…"

"I know that book. It's a thousand pages, explaining the benefits of capitalism. Capitalism has ruined this country!"

"But that has nothing to do with our fashion show," Mrs. Hopwood argued.

"Of course it does! What are you having the fashion show for, if not to make money?!"

"For the poor." Mrs. Johnson had no intention of getting involved in a political debate. "Father, we would like to ask you a favor. Could you put this ad in the Sunday bulletin? St. Polycarp has some very wealthy parishioners and we're hoping that they will buy some of the clothing."

"I got nothing to do with that. Mary Jones is the one you need to speak to."

"Do you have her contact information?"

"What?"

"How do we get in touch with her?" Mrs. Hopwood bellowed.

"Do you go to Mass every Sunday?" He directed the question to Mrs. Hopwood who lowered her eyes in shame. Mrs. Johnson knew that her Mass going was limited to holy days and holidays.

"I'm there every Sunday," Mrs. Johnson said.

"Well, then you don't read our bulletins. If you did, you would know that at the bottom, there are instructions for people who have something meaningful to contribute."

"I think I have one at home." Mrs. Johnson stood. "Thank you for your time, Father."

Mrs. Hopwood gave a weak smile as she rose. "That was painful," she whispered in Mrs. Johnson's ear as they headed for the front door.

"It certainly was," Father Bartholomew snapped.

MRS. HOPWOOD CALLED Mrs. Johnson promptly on Sunday morning.

"I went to church…"

"I didn't see you there," Mrs. Johnson said.

"I'm very upset with the way that Mary Jones displayed my ad. I went with the specific purpose of grabbing a few brochures…"

"And then you left?" Mrs. Johnson had always thought

it was shabby, here her friend was a Catholic school teacher, and did not regularly attend Mass.

Mrs. Hopwood had to admit that was true. "But just so you know the picture of Dagny's compact, my pretty logo, was crooked," she babbled on. "Also Mary Jones had taken it upon herself to add her own headline—*Attire from the Attic*. That sounds as if the clothes being modeled and sold are moth ridden and moldy. And to make matters worse, this Mary Jones got a hold of a picture of me, a bad picture I might add, a horrible hair day and no lipstick, and put my name beside it, Julie Hopwood. You know no one calls me Julie!"

"Well, at least we got the word out," Mrs. Johnson tried to comfort her.

"With a lot of misinformation," Mrs. Hopwood grumbled.

FOURTEEN

IT WAS THAT teacher again—the one with all the different colored coats. Tracy had been keeping count and she was up to sixteen.

Today the teacher was wearing a white coat splashed with lilacs. She was wobbling in lavender high heels and she was carrying a mint green handbag. She looked like a breath of spring.

Tracy figured that she must be very rich but also very troubled, because she came almost every day to light a candle in front of the St. Jude statue. She didn't stay very long, just whispered a prayer.

It seemed to Tracy that just before she left, she always glanced in Tracy's direction.

That was exactly what happened except this time the teacher was staring at the floral purse which Tracy hugged to her chest.

Then the teacher tottered over.

Tracy bolted upright and broke into a sweat. "I didn't steal it!" She meant to shout but she hadn't spoken to anyone for so long that her voice came out raspy and hoarse, her breath rattling. "I found it in the street in front of the school. It was empty, like someone probably took out the wallet, and the credit cards, and the keys and the ID."

The woman seemed confused, which was often the case when people spoke to Tracy. Their reactions vacillated between fear and disgust and pity. "That handbag belonged to my Aunt Eunice."

"Well, here, you can have it back." Tracy shoved the purse into the woman's startled face, and then remembered that she had three dollars in there, cash a young boy had given her when he saw her sleeping in the street.

"My aunt is dead."

A wave of alarm shot through Tracy. "I didn't kill her and I didn't steal her bag."

"Of course not. You can have the purse. We were just going to auction it off at the school," the woman hesitated, "to help the less fortunate."

"Like me?"

The woman didn't answer. Instead she fumbled in her own purse, took out a yellow wallet, grabbed a ten dollar bill and handed the money to Tracy. "It's bad luck to give someone a wallet or a handbag without some money in it." She rolled up the bill and plunked it inside the floral bag.

At that precise moment, Sugar Daddy jumped up and began to bark.

"Calm down," Tracy ordered, and then she turned towards the woman. "He's mine too!"

The woman just nodded and she inched towards Sugar Daddy, patting him gently on the head.

A dog lover. Tracy liked her.

And then she was gone, leaving the faint scent of lily of the valley behind.

FIFTEEN

HE FELL ASLEEP and when he woke, he saw something he hadn't seen before. He had slept with the clothes covering him, and on the bottom of all those garments were two handbags. Now that perked him up quite a bit, because there was always the possibility that money could be buried inside and maybe even a bit of jewelry.

Someone had left a dim overhead bulb lit, so he could see slightly. He dug his hand inside of each purse and then came out with a piece of paper. He was in the middle of trying to read it—he never was very good at reading—when he noticed a shadow in the corner.

His eyesight might not be good but there was nothing wrong with his hearing.

So he heard a voice asking him to drop what was in his hand.

It was an odd voice, not easily recognizable, and for a moment he thought he imagined it. He looked down at the paper and it seemed to contain a name, Dagny Danvers. Something else, something smudged.

A hand reached towards him.

And then Robert thought, that maybe, just maybe, this piece of paper was something valuable, something he might be able to sell.

He wasn't about to give it up, not when he could use it to get himself some money.

"No way," he said, aware that his voice quivered

from too much liquor and too many cigarettes. "You ain't getting it."

Now the person was in front of him and all Robert could see were these cold gray eyes, before he was pushed down. He fell into a pile of clothing, which really didn't hurt one bit. It took him a minute or two but he was able to crawl back up.

"You're going to be sorry," he said in what he hoped was a crazy voice. "I'm going to tell everyone what you did to me. And I'm going to sue you."

He might be a little crazy but this person was crazier.

A heavy object coming right towards him. Before he could cry out, before he could say, "take it, go ahead" he felt an incredible pain and then some material over his face. He couldn't breathe, when he heard someone coming down the stairs, actually whistling.

He had been saved.

Maybe not.

Another incredible pain, this time at the back of his head.

Movement. The person was dragging him behind the boiler.

The person was leaving and all Robert had to do was move, or cry out.

Except he couldn't.

He couldn't, because he was falling, falling into darkness, as he dropped the piece of paper that had gotten him killed.

SIXTEEN

Mrs. Johnson had no sooner arrived in her office on a dark, cloudy Wednesday morning, when Addison Fiore marched in behind her.

"Amelia, can I talk to you for a moment?"

Mrs. Johnson, numb with fatigue, wanted to say no, not until I have my coffee and my buttered bagel, not until I check my e-mail and look over my daily calendar. But Addison was a troublemaker, so Mrs. Johnson just waved her towards an empty seat.

"Someone stole my Percocet."

"Your what?"

"The prescription the dentist gave me for my root canal."

"Antibiotics?"

"No, they're pain killers."

Mrs. Johnson didn't know quite what to say, so she just mumbled something that she and Mrs. Hopwood frequently said—sometimes to each other—when they weren't really sorry and didn't want to get involved, "I'm sorry for your troubles."

"Someone in this school is responsible for my troubles! And stealing drugs is a felony."

"Actually, if it's a small amount of drugs, it could be a misdemeanor."

Addison was obviously not interested in Mrs. Johnson's legal knowledge. "I think I know who took my pills. Jason Briggs."

"Jason Briggs?" Mrs. Johnson had taught him briefly when Mrs. Sugarman's seventh grade class had been hers, earlier in the year. Jason was a nice, quiet, cooperative boy, although he was a slowpoke.

"I left my purse here yesterday for two minutes while I ran across the street to get a cup of coffee and an apple. He was hanging around the water fountain, watching my every move."

"That doesn't…"

"One of the teachers told me, I don't want to say who and get her in trouble for gossiping, but someone told me that Jason's older brother was selling drugs. I think Jason took my pills and gave them to his brother to get rid of them on the street."

Mrs. Johnson thought it was best to nip this in the bud. "He was arrested, not convicted."

"Only for lack of evidence." Addison looked at the clock. "I think you should question him."

"I'll see what I can do." Mrs. Johnson did not intend to do anything except maybe send an e-mail to the staff, warning teachers not to keep their values in open view. And maybe she would ask Mrs. Sugarman to keep her eye on Jason.

By the time she got to her coffee it was cold.

"I won't keep you long," Mrs. Johnson told Mrs. Sugarman. "I know you're on a prep and I'm aware of how valuable this time can be."

"Excuse me." Miss Turnipseed crept into the office. Mrs. Johnson frowned when she saw the fur piece that Miss Turnipseed wore around her neck almost touching her bluntly cut, slightly lopsided fringed gray hair. It looked like a dead rat. "But Doctor Winters just called to confirm your appointment today at three thirty. And someone was looking for you before."

"No doubt. Someone is always looking for me. Tell Doctor Winters I'll be there. Could you close my door on the way out?"

Miss Turnipseed frowned. The need for privacy, however, had nothing to do with her but the parade of teachers who loitered outside Mrs. Johnson's office hoping to pass on wild stories.

"I'm having some problems with my back," Mrs. Johnson confided. "The doctor will probably just pump me up with pain killers. And speaking of pain killers, Addison's Percocets are missing."

Immediately Mrs. Sugarman became flustered and began to sputter. "What does that have to do with me?"

"Nothing, of course, it has to do with one of your students, Jason Briggs. Addison saw him hanging around the front desk when she left her purse there yesterday."

"Well," Mrs. Sugarman paused. "I did see him waiting in the hall for no good reason. Not that I think he would take anything. Why would he?"

Mrs. Johnson thought it best that she ignored that question. "Just keep an eye on him, would you? It's really important that all of the teachers secure their valuables out of sight. That's all."

Mrs. Sugarman lingered by the door. "I saw you bring in a lot of clothes with Mrs. Hopwood. They seem so pretty. Are you giving them away?"

"Oh no, they're vintage, quite valuable. The school is going to have a fashion show and auction them off. They're already tagged and will probably triple the price."

"Do you think I could buy something? At cost?"

Mrs. Johnson hesitated. Mrs. Sugarman was a short, stout woman. It was doubtful if anything would fit. Besides, the school needed money desperately.

As though she could read her mind, Mrs. Sugarman blurted out, "I was in the basement and happened to see a stunning blue handbag. I really would love to own it."

"I guess it's all right," Mrs. Johnson said reluctantly. "It will cost you about fifty dollars."

"Great! I'll drop off a check at the end of the day. And don't worry, I'll be watching Jason."

"You do that."

After Mrs. Sugarman left, Mrs. Johnson wrote an email to the staff, informing them that there would be a brief meeting after school. She could hear the moans minutes later.

SEVENTEEN

MELISSA WAS SO NERVOUS, she could barely get through the day. Mrs. Hopwood had asked her to please stay after school. There was a matter she wanted to discuss. It was the first time her teacher had ever singled her out and Melissa could only surmise that she was in terrible trouble.

It had to be the spelling test, which Melissa knew that she had failed miserably. The actual mark didn't matter. Her mother didn't care about things like that. But the thought that Melissa had disappointed Mrs. Hopwood filled her with dread. She would have to promise that she would do better next time.

The day dragged by. After the dismissal bell, Melissa lingered by her desk. Mrs. Hopwood was texting someone on her phone and, for a moment, Melissa wondered if she had forgotten.

Melissa approached her cautiously and then blurted, "I'm sorry about the spelling test. I didn't have time to study."

"The spelling test?" Mrs. Hopwood looked confused. "I didn't correct them yet." Now Melissa felt like a fool. "I can't spell to save my life, hardly seems necessary with spell check. Anyway, that's not what I wanted to talk to you about. How would you like to be a model in the fashion show?"

"Oh my God! I would love to!" Melissa could almost hear her heart leap.

"Great. Why don't you come with me now and pick something out. You'll have a choice because you're the first model chosen. Unfortunately, the clothes are being stored down in the cellar, and, unfortunately, they're a little on the wrinkled side. You will have to iron your outfit."

Melissa followed Mrs. Hopwood down two flights of stairs, noticing the little red bow on the back of her black and white checkered heels, her carefully blown dried hair with a few strands of curls by her neck, and her scent, flowery and expensive.

The clothes were piled, helter skelter, in a great big pile. Mrs. Hopwood rifled through a few, explaining that they would first have to find her size. Melissa spotted a lime green dress and she knew that green was one of Mrs. Hopwood favorite colors.

"Might be a trifle bit big, maybe we could pin it." Mrs. Hopwood looked down at the price tag. "Seventy-five dollars. I bet it's worth at least triple that now. Oh, look, here's a matching purse." She walked over to the boiler and picked up a green handbag with a copper leaf closure. "I don't know what these purses are doing here. They were neatly on top of the clothing." She looked around. "And I wonder what happened to the blue one. Oh well. Why don't you take the green one? You can wear it on the runway. Pick out two outfits. You'll be modeling three."

"A lot of clothes here," Melissa said, in an attempt to make conversation. She wasn't going to say anything about the smell, but it was almost as though something had died down in the basement, like a rat. She chose a yellow skirt and a polka dot blouse, and then a fitted scarlet dress. She felt as though she was walking in some sort of dream. Mrs. Hopwood had actually given her first choice of the outfits to model. "I'll take very good care of these," she promised, as she leaped to her feet. "I'll return them in excellent condition." *Although she wasn't quite sure where she was going to find an iron.*

When Melissa rose, she saw the corner of what looked like a filthy red jacket sticking out from behind the boiler. She thought it odd and was just about to comment when Mrs. Hopwood's watch began to ping. "Oh my God! I'm supposed to be at a staff meeting. Mrs. Johnson is going to kill me!"

She flashed a quick smile at Melissa and then she was off, Melissa trailing behind her.

EIGHTEEN

"WHERE HAVE YOU BEEN?!" Mrs. Johnson, ruffled and tense, demanded the moment Mrs. Hopwood walked into the staff meeting.

Mrs. Hopwood flopped down in a chair with a slight groan, a little miffed that she was being chastised in front of everyone. "I was speaking to one of the students about modeling in the fashion show."

"We were just discussing the fashion show. I was trying to explain the details but you know more than I do."

"May I speak?" Addison's hand shot in the air. "I know Julia was the one who came up with what may or may not be a good idea, but I don't quite understand why she gets to be the person in charge. I mean, shouldn't we vote or have a committee decide?"

Mrs. Hopwood had never liked Addison since she stole Mrs. Hopwood's second grade class right from under her. And Mrs. Hopwood had waited for months for an opportunity, so she sprang up in her seat. "I'll tell you why I'm in charge. I'm in charge because every piece of that vintage clothing, some of them quite expensive, was willed to me by my Aunt Eunice. I could have done the selfish thing and sold the items myself and kept the profit, but I'm not a selfish person." She glared at Mrs. Johnson. "And that's why I'm in charge."

Addison slumped down in her chair, his face slightly flushed.

The rest of the meeting went smoothly, settling a date for the fashion show, assigning tasks to various teachers. Mrs. Hopwood would have loved to have left Addison out but since no such thing was possible, she asked her to work on set design. From the looks that Addison and Casey exchanged, it was obvious that Addison was not pleased.

Mrs. Johnson, who never cared for lengthy meetings as a teacher, cared for them less as a principal, so they finished quickly. But there were always those teachers who lingered to gossip, jabbering brightly, asking ridiculous questions like Dylan—Addison's friend and fourth grade teacher—who wondered if she could buy some of the items at cost.

Mrs. Hopwood was appalled. "Absolutely not. We're doing this to make money."

"How come Mrs. Sugarman got that nice blue purse?"

"Mrs. Johnson said it was all right," Mrs. Sugarman admitted sheepishly.

The moment that Mrs. Hopwood was alone in Mrs. Johnson's office she demanded an explanation.

"I DIDN'T SEE the harm in it." Mrs. Johnson said and a wave of pity ran over Mrs. Hopwood, as she noticed how worn her friend was. "There are other purses."

"Well, actually there aren't," Mrs. Hopwood said. "I let Melissa Ortiz take one home, she's modeling."

Mrs. Johnson snorted.

"And that homeless woman in the church? She found the flowered one in the street. I told her she could keep it. And I gave her ten dollars."

"Dare I ask why?"

"Because I felt sorry for her. She looks like a crumpled, old, broken, black umbrella. And because you told me that I never do anything for anyone else."

"Oh my God! I suppose I will hear that until one of us dies."

"By the way," Mrs. Hopwood put her hands on her hips, "I did not appreciate the way you spoke to me in front of the staff."

"You were fifteen minutes late to a meeting you called. Look everyone knows we're friends, so I have to be very careful not to show favoritism. God, I hate this job."

"Cheer up. You're not going to have it that much longer."

MRS. HOPWOOD ARRIVED home to a quiet house. Alexander was still at college and her husband, Montgomery, hadn't come home from work—a perfect time for research.

She wanted to learn all she could about Melissa's father.

She googled Ortiz and murder and one name in the area came up. George Ortiz.

Mrs. Hopwood read each newspaper article eagerly.

The facts of the case were simply this—on February 14th, twelve years ago, Victor Holtz was gunned down in an alley behind his home. Nosey neighbors confirmed that George Ortiz's wife, Winifred, was having an affair with Holtz. According to one neighbor, loud voices had broken out in the alley—that she couldn't identify—then minutes later she heard gunshots. She called the police.

Following an anonymous tip, the detectives found the gun used in the shooting on the roof of Ortiz's apartment, buried in a drain pipe. The gun was registered to George Ortiz.

Ortiz denied being the killer, but finally with the advice of his public defender he admitted that it was a crime of passion and the charges were reduced to manslaughter. He was given fifteen years with a chance from parole.

And his chance was coming up.

Mrs. Hopwood could only hope that he would soon be home and Melissa could start to smile again.

NINETEEN

MRS. SUGARMAN CLOSED her eyes. It was eight ten in the morning, she was sitting in her classroom and she was already in such agonizing pain. She wasn't sure how she could possibly make it through the day.

It wasn't just her usual migraine, now she had a nagging toothache. It started as a dull pain, but last night it woke her from a sound sleep. She needed something strong to make it all go away and she was fresh out of her pills.

A rumbling on the stairs forced her to snap open her eyes. Her gaze fell on the bright blue purse she stashed on the bottom of the book shelf.

It was hideous.

Something that Mrs. Hopwood would wear, loud and gawky. Didn't Mrs. Hopwood realize that after a certain age, it was best not to draw attention to yourself?

Mrs. Sugarman had no intention of keeping the handbag. She couldn't imagine wearing it under any circumstances. What she intended was to try and sell it on e-bay. She paid fifty dollars for it. She would sell it for triple that.

Prescription drugs were expensive.

Still she was shocked when she opened the purse and found something in the zippered compartment. It looked like a pill box with the initials DD on it. Her heart quickened at the thought that the pills inside might be useful, even if they were old and dried up. But alas, the little gold box was empty. She threw it in her desk drawer.

She heard Addison's voice in the hall, chatting with Casey. Mrs. Sugarman managed to stand and trudge to her doorway.

"Addison, I wonder if you could help me."

Addison did not look as though she wanted to be helpful.

"I woke up with a nagging toothache. My own dentist retired," she lied. The last dentist Mrs. Sugarman had visited was fifteen years ago. He was Chester's third cousin, an alarmist, who kept insisting that if Mrs. Sugarman didn't have her gums scrapped, she would soon be toothless. "I heard you say in the teacher's room that you had an excellent dentist."

Addison shot Mrs. Sugarman a puzzled look, probably because she had never said such a thing.

But Mrs. Sugarman forged ahead. "So could you give me a recommendation?"

"I go to Doctor Fenway on Northampton Street, next to Friendly's. But I doubt that he can take you on such a short notice. He's awfully busy."

"Well, I can certainly try, can't I?'"

SHE GOT AN appointment for four o'clock. She had hoped that it would be earlier so she would have an excuse to leave school. The waiting room was packed and smelled of Novocain as she was serenaded by Frank Sinatra, crooning about something stupid. Mrs. Sugarman took a seat at the end of a small sofa, managing to take out a math test, which she decided to correct. It was long overdue and a few parents had already complained to

Mrs. Johnson that they seldom received exam papers back from her.

She found Shane Caffrey's paper first, quickly scrawled a hundred on it, and used it as a guide. She was half way through the correcting, when she noticed something odd.

Jason Briggs got a ninety. He had answered two problems incorrectly, both by careless mistakes.

Jason Briggs never got a ninety, or even an eighty, or seventy.

A few papers down the mystery was solved. He had copied the answers from Sophia Kogan, right down to the errors.

St. Polycarp had a zero tolerance for cheating and Mrs. Sugarman knew that if she reported the incident to Mrs. Johnson, Mrs. Johnson would have no choice but to suspend Jason.

Whenever Mrs. Sugarman thought about Jason, she felt a stab of guilt for not defending him more vigorously when Addison accused him of stealing her pills. She decided to speak to him privately and to warn him that if ever did such a thing again, she would have to take the matter to the principal.

ONCE THE DENTIST agreed to see her, Mrs. Sugarman collapsed in the chair and wasted no time describing her symptoms. She sat bored and uninterested, when the dentist viewed the X-ray on a large screen, hovering in the corner.

"There's a lot of decay." He pointed to a tooth in the lower part of her mouth, attempting to show her the amount of damage, as though she didn't believe him, as though she knew or cared about what he was saying. "You're going to need a root canal." He delivered this news with a grave, solemn voice as though he was announcing that she should have exploratory surgery. "Probably a crown and a post. I can't start this today. I just managed to squeeze you in. What I can do is give you a script for antibiotics. The tooth is not infected yet, but you might want to keep them on hand, just in case, it gets worse."

"Of course." Mrs. Sugarman ripped off the bib which was sticky with drool and caught her distorted reflection, eyes bloodshot, pink face puffy, in the stainless steel water holder. "As I explained I'm in quite a bit of pain. I would like a prescription so I can be comfortable. Perhaps Percocet ?" she asked hopefully.

A look of disapproval crossed the dentist's flat, bland face. "I would suggest," he said dryly, "that you try something over the counter, maybe Advil, or extra strength Tylenol."

"I don't know if I told you," which wasn't true, Mrs. Sugarman knew very well, everything she had said, "but I suffer from horrible migraine headaches. So unfortunately, I've already built up a tolerance for the non-prescription pain killers."

"Why don't you take one of your headache pills then?" he asked in a hard voice.

"I don't have any left." Mrs. Sugarman held on to the arm rest and drew herself up very slowly. She knew that she was losing the argument and it was time to try a different tactic. "Addison Fiore recommended you. We teach together in a Catholic School." She thought the fact that she was an instructor in a religious school would make him think that she was a God fearing, upright citizen.

The dentist's expression was unblinking, venomous.

"She told me you gave her Percocet," Mrs. Sugarman added.

"That's true." The dentist stood his ground and drew a deep breath. "But her issue was entirely different. For one thing she came in with an abscessed tooth. Her mouth was swollen and she could barely chew. The root canal I performed was on a back molar and involves several roots and several visits." The dentist turned around, snapped off his plastic gloves and began to wash his hands. "I suggest you make an appointment as soon as possible before the tooth gets any worse."

Mrs. Sugarman was tempted to ask, "Then will I get some Percocet" but instead she just marched into the reception area.

"That will be a hundred and fifty dollars," the receptionist said brightly as she grinned with crooked, yellow teeth.

"I was only in there for fifteen minutes!" Mrs. Sugarman protested.

The cheery attitude began to vanish, as the receptionist shrugged, holding her lumpy cardigan around her hunched shoulders.

"How much is this entire procedure going to cost me?" Mrs. Sugarman demanded. "For the root canal and the crown and the post."

"Well…"

"I have a right to know," she yelled, not troubling to keep her voice down.

"It depends."

"Give me a range."

"Anywhere from two thousand to thirty five hundred."

"I can't afford that!" Mrs. Sugarman took out her checkbook with the measly balance.

"We take credit cards." The receptionist pointed to a sign where imprints of colored cards were displayed boldly.

"I'm maxed out."

The receptionist had no recourse but to wait patiently while Mrs. Sugarman made out a check. *When she got home, she would stop payment on it. After all, the dentist hadn't really done a darn thing, except expose her to unnecessary radiation.*

"I'll be in touch," Mrs. Sugarman lied as she threw the check at the receptionist.

"Do you want a receipt?" The receptionist called after her.

No, Mrs. Sugarman did not want a receipt. What she wanted was some Percocet.

And then it hit here, with the same sharp pain which radiated down her jaw. There was something she could do.

That was to talk to Jason Briggs.

TWENTY

SHE WAS BACK AGAIN, the woman with the many coats. Only this time she wasn't wearing a coat at all, but a peach stripped dress and a peach polka dot sweater.

And she wasn't alone. She was with that pretty African American teacher, who always looked annoyed.

"Look, she's carrying the floral purse I gave her and it's stuffed to the brim, probably with all of her earthly belongings. Should we say something to her?"

"Absolutely not. What makes you think she even wants to talk to us? She's entitled to her privacy."

For some reason the two teachers were conversing in very audible whispers, as though she couldn't hear them, as though she was invisible.

"Maybe she's hungry and we could buy her a sandwich. Or ask Pearl if there are any leftover chicken nuggets in the cafeteria. And what about her poor little dog? He must be starving. I think I have a protein bar in my handbag."

"I saw that protein bar. What do you want to do? Poison them?"

"Maybe she's not homeless at all. Maybe she's the victim of an abusive husband and she's hiding from him. Or maybe there's been a recent death in her family and she comes here to mourn. Maybe she needs to think things through."

"What you need to do is start tagging those clothing, so we can put the photos in the program."

"I have Melissa and a few girls doing that after school tomorrow. She's going to bring back the outfits I gave her so we can take pictures."

"Just light your candle, say your little prayer, so we can get out of here."

The voices drifted off as they strode out of sight.

And Tracy sat, part of her, wishing that they had stayed a little longer. Their cheerful chatter was company, making her feel less lonely. She wondered what happened to Robert. She hadn't seen him around lately. She had a feeling that he would end up badly, drinking the way he did. His hopeless attitude didn't help, although God knows he had every reason to despair.

Tracy wished that those two teachers had left that protein bar.

TWENTY-ONE

ALTHOUGH IT SEEMED like a good idea at the time, producing a fashion show was turning out to be more work than Mrs. Hopwood had anticipated. Even though she had formed committees, she was doing most of the labor herself. True, her fifth grade students were helping her with the organization and the publicity—away from the classroom the children were absolutely delightful, but then again Mrs. Hopwood had only chosen the comatose ones—still they needed a teacher to supervise and to stay late.

Mrs. Hopwood did not like to stay late.

She was getting no help whatsoever from Mrs. Johnson, but she could hardly complain since she had promised that she would do most of the work herself. These days Mrs. Johnson often sat in her office with the door closed. Mrs. Hopwood might have believed it was school business, until she happened to overhear a snippet of conversation and she realized it was about her twin boys.

"She's been on the phone all morning, poor thing," Miss Turnipseed whispered, "I think there has been some trouble at school. Jeffrey Joseph…"

"It's Jeffrey James."

"Well, anyway, one of them assaulted a classmate for no apparent reason."

Mrs. Hopwood was betting that Mrs. Johnson would find an apparent reason. "Would you tell her I'd like to talk to her?"

"Right now, she's very busy." Miss Turnipseed had never been a fan of Mrs. Johnson's in the fall, but the moment Mrs. Johnson was appointed interim principal, her loyalties had shifted. Now she defended Mrs. Johnson with the devotion of a pit bull.

Mrs. Hopwood trudged back to her classroom. A perfect spring day, the gym teacher—a well-built man with a hook nose, heavy mournful eyes, protruding ears, closely cropped black hair but great biceps—had asked Mrs. Hopwood if he could keep the children out a bit longer than the allotted time.

Mrs. Hopwood answered that the children could stay outside as long as possible.

She slumped down in her chair and clicked on her e-mail with some hesitancy. No telling who would be complaining.

Three emails. The first was from Mrs. Simmons who wanted Mrs. Hopwood to know that Sunset could not do any homework tonight because she was going to a Jack and Jill party.

Mrs. Johnson sent the second e-mail, which was a reminder to turn off the lights in the classroom as well as the computers, as she was trying to save on the electricity bill.

And then there was the third e-mail, from someone who called himself Stronghold 0211

I go to church regular at St. Polycarp. I saw the ad you ran in the church bulletin. I take care of my mother, who is an invalid and she loves vintage items.

But she especially likes pocketbooks. I wondered if you had any. I would be willing to pay you anything you ask because it would make her very happy.

The email made Mrs. Hopwood very happy. Obviously the ad was working. Here a complete stranger wanted to buy the vintage items and even stated that price was no object.

Mrs. Hopwood wasted no time answering.

Thank you so much for reaching out. Actually we did have five handbags, but they were given to three teachers, a student and a needy woman. However, we are in the process of tagging and photographing the many lovely pieces of clothing as well as some stunning jewelry. I am certain that you will be able to find something beautiful to give to your mother.

Mrs. Hopwood pressed send and almost immediately received a reply.

Could you please give me the names of the teachers, the student and the needy woman? I would be more than happy to buy the handbags from them and I would be willing to double what they paid.

Now Mrs. Hopwood thought this was most peculiar. No way was she going to give out the names of Mrs. Johnson, Mrs. Sugarman or herself, and certainly not Melissa—she had already decided that Melissa could keep the handbag. And she didn't even know the name of the homeless woman.

Should she even bother to answer?

Well, she couldn't because just then the students burst into the room. The fresh air seemed to have invigorated them and Mrs. Hopwood knew that she was in for a long afternoon.

AT THREE FIFTEEN Mrs. Hopwood raced to the copy machine before any of the teachers could monopolize it. First in line, Mrs. Sugarman was right behind her, gasping with impatience.

Too bad.

She smelled Mrs. Johnson before she actually saw her turning the corner, a mixture of chocolate, hair spray and musk. Before Mrs. Hopwood had a chance to open her mouth, Mrs. Johnson spoke.

"I'm in a hurry. I have to go to talk to the twins' teacher."

Mrs. Hopwood thought it best to keep silent on that subject. "I think you should know I got an email from a parishioner who saw our ad and wants to buy some of the vintage items."

"Good."

"But he really wanted handbags for his mother. I had to explain that they were all gone." Mrs. Hopwood jammed a pile of papers into the feeder. "Then he wrote back wanting the name of the people who had the purses. He even said he'd pay double."

"You didn't tell him, did you?"

The word searches were coming out all wrinkled. "Of course not. Nobody would consider selling them."

"I certainly wouldn't," Mrs. Sugarman piped in from behind.

'Gotta go." Mrs. Johnson zoomed away.

"Shoes!" Mrs. Hopwood shouted after her. "I think that there is an entire trunk of shoes in that attic."

And then the machine stopped.

"You broke it again," Mrs. Sugarman moaned.

"I'll tell Miss Turnipseed." Mrs. Hopwood had no intention of getting her yellow sheath dirty.

Except Miss Turnipseed had already gone.

TWENTY-TWO

"IT WOULD BE nice if you came with me this weekend to see your father."

Her mother managed a smile and Melissa noticed that her bright fuchsia lipstick had migrated to her gray teeth. "I think he would like it very much if you were there, showing support."

"I can't. I've been helping Mrs. Hopwood after school so I'm behind in some of my homework."

"Yes, I wanted to talk to you about that." Melissa felt a wave of disgust as her mother sank down on the sagging bed.

"What do you mean?"

"Don't you think it's weird that all of a sudden Mrs. Hopwood has taken an interest in you?"

"I still don't know you what you mean."

"She never paid any attention to you before and now she's giving you clothes and a handbag…"

Melissa wanted desperately to get up and walk out, go to the bathroom, but her mother was blocking her escape. "She didn't give me anything. I'm modeling for the fashion show. I told you that."

"You're a little heavy to be a model."

Melissa looked down at her science notes again and pretended to be reading.

"I'll tell you what it is. It's about your father. She's read that he's getting out of prison and she's nosy. I read all about her on Google. She and that principal are nothing but troublemakers. Do you have any idea how many murders she's been involved in? Well, more than your father."

"She didn't commit any murders, Mom."

"Neither did he. Look, I felt terrible confessing to the police your father wasn't home the night of the murders, and I didn't know what time he came in, but the cops trapped me. They didn't tell me why they were asking about that night. So by the time I had answered the question, it was too late." Her mother stood, peering down at Melissa for several minutes. Melissa stared back with what she hoped was a chilling detachment.

"Just be careful, that's all, baby."

Melissa wanted to say that her mother was the one who needed to be careful.

TWENTY-THREE

What happened? Apparently, Mrs. Hopwood could not wait to text Mrs. Johnson.

It's a long story. Basically, Garland and Jeffrey James were the last two contenders in the lower school spelling bee. Garland, who is known to be a bully, was taunting poor Jeffrey James and actually pushed him. My boys know that they are never supposed to hit a girl, so he had to find some other way to defend himself.

What did he do?

They were cutting out spring flowers and Jeffrey James was using the teacher's scissors, since he is so responsible.

And?

He cut off one of Garland's braids. Her mother was hysterical. You would think that Jeffrey James had decapitated her daughter. She was going on and on about how Garland was going to have to compete in the spelling bee with a boy's haircut. Turns out the principal—who unlike me doesn't even make an effort to be fair—banned Jeffrey James from the spelling bee so Garland is going to win by default.

Are you going to punish him? He needs to take responsibility for his actions.

This is coming from the mother of the year.

That's mean.

Hey, I never judged Alex and God knows I could have. Got to go. Pizza is here.

BECAUSE MRS. JOHNSON had left early the day before, she was way behind in her paperwork. So she managed to come in early, hoping for peace and quiet.

That hope was shattered when Addison, looking surly, came crashing through her door at 7:30.

"I need to talk to you." Addison took two stomping steps towards Mrs. Johnson. "I have a complaint."

"No surprise there." Mrs. Johnson could not resist the barb.

"It's about one of your teachers."

Mrs. Johnson could only hope that it wasn't Mrs. Hopwood.

"It's about Mrs. Sugarman. Do you know what she did?" Mrs. Johnson wanted to say that she was of the firm opinion that teachers should settle their differences between them but, before she opened her mouth, Addison leaned forward and, with furious contempt, pointed her pale pink manicure finger in Mrs. Johnson's direction. "She asked me the name of my dentist. I could hardly refuse to give it to her. I have to say I knew the moment we met that there was something not quite right about her. She's not even a real teacher, she's a librarian."

"Well, actually…"

"So she made an appointment. My dentist called me very upset. She tried to bully him into giving her some drugs for pain."

"Maybe she was in pain."

"That's not all. He charged her for a consolation. She wrote out a check and then she had the nerve to stop payment on it!"

Mrs. Johnson released a great sigh. "Don't you think that this is really between Mrs. Sugarman and the dentist?"

"No! Because I'm the one who recommended him and it reflects badly on me!"

"I don't know what you expect me to do." Mrs. Johnson was watching her e-mails multiply. "Whatever happened occurred off of school property and I have no jurisdiction…"

"I would think," Addison eyes burnt with anger, "that you would want to know the sort of people you have working for you. And it reflects badly on the school."

"I didn't hire Mrs. Sugarman and I couldn't fire her even if I wanted to. In the fall, God willing, that the school is still open, Mrs. Sugarman will return to the library, where she is more than qualified. In the meantime, what we all need to do is present a united front. We can do this by cooperating with Mrs. Hopwood to make sure that the fashion show is a success. When Sister Mary Grace realizes how hard we've worked, she is more likely to keep St. Polycarp up and running."

Addison looked unimpressed with what Mrs. Johnson had considered to be an inspirational speech. "You should know that I am not planning to return to St. Polycarp in the fall. The private school I attended as a student has an opening for a third grade teacher and I've been hired there. It's much more in line with my educational philosophy and my value system."

Mrs. Johnson's heart gave a slight leap. "We'll be sorry to lose you."

A look of disbelief swept over Addison's face.

Mrs. Johnson vowed to go to confession on Saturday.

"I NEED YOU to do me a favor." Mrs. Hopwood poked her face in minutes later. She was wearing a neon orange rain coat although it was seventy degrees and there wasn't a cloud in the sky.

Mrs. Johnson must have looked bewildered because Mrs. Hopwood quickly said, "It's going to storm this afternoon. Don't you ever watch the weather?"

"No time."

"What did she want?"

"Who?"

"Addison. I saw her leave your office."

Mrs. Johnson had neither the time nor the energy to go into specifics. "She's not returning next year. She got a job in a private school."

"Oh goody. Anyway on Saturday I'm going to return to my Aunt Eunice's house to gather the shoes. Monte is bringing me but then he has to go to work. I need you to pick me up and put the shoes in your car. We can carry them in on Monday morning."

Resentment flooded Mrs. Johnson. "I can't. It's the start of baseball season. Besides, shoes are not a good idea."

"Why would you say that?" Mrs. Hopwood was trying to tangle herself from her raincoat, while holding her tangerine colored bucket handbag.

"Because—unlike handbags—shoes are specific. Anyone can use a handbag, and clothes can be made to fit, you know all about that." She couldn't resist the scowl when she caught a glimpse of a rather tightly fitted bandage dress in coral, which Mrs. Hopwood had obviously made to fit. "But shoes either work or they don't."

"So what am I supposed to do with them? Throw them out? Even if we charge a minimal amount, it's still money in our pocket."

Mrs. Johnson said what she always said, when she was being bullied into doing something she rather not do, but she didn't want to admit defeat aloud. "I'll see what I can do."

"How did it work out?"

Mrs. Johnson glanced down at her ten new e-mails. "What?"

"With Jeffrey James."

"He's devastated about being cut from the spelling bee. Peter and I feel as though that's punishment enough."

Mrs. Hopwood frowned, expressing disapproval.

Actually it was another lie. Mrs. Johnson had heard Jeffrey James tell his brother that he was relieved that he wouldn't be competing because the entire process made him nervous. And if he had to be in the spelling bee, he was going to miss on purpose.

Mrs. Johnson would definitely have to go to confession.

"AMELIA, CAN I speak to you for a moment?"

Mrs. Johnson did not want to speak to anyone for a moment. She had to leave early for a doctor's appointment and there were e-mails to answer, parents to meet, forms to fill out…

"Actually, now is not a good time."

"This won't take long, I promise." Mrs. Sugarman sat herself right down on the padded chair across from Mrs. Johnson's desk. Mrs. Johnson wondered, if perhaps she switched the seat to something less comfortable, whether people wouldn't force themselves into her office. "I need to ask you a question." Mrs. Johnson noticed that beads of sweat had broken out on Mrs. Sugarman's forehead. "I wonder if I could possibly have an advance on my salary. This month has been hard on me. I've had a lot of unexpected expenses."

"Is that why you stopped payment on the check you wrote to the dentist?" Mrs. Johnson asked.

Mrs. Sugarman bounced up, grabbed a tissue from Mrs. Johnson's desk, wiped the perspiration off her face, and then leaned forward in an aggressive manner. "Who told you that? That bitch, Addison?"

Mrs. Johnson decided not to answer.

"Just so you know, he was a horrible dentist. He did nothing." Mrs. Sugarman sank down in the chair and crumpled the tissue in her hand. "He barely spent ten minutes with me. I'm thinking of reporting him to the better business bureau. Maybe," her voice faltered as her eyes watered, "if I told you why I need the advance. My baby sister, she's quite a bit younger than me, she has a daughter, who was born slightly retarded. I can't tell you how she was bullied for years. She's a senior in high school now, and this nice, kind boy asked her to the prom. My sister is a single mother. Her husband left her after Tiffany was born. I offered to buy Tiffany

the prom dress. It would mean so much to her! I priced
them and they run about two hundred and fifty dollars."

"That's really nice of you, but as you know, Nancy,
St. Polycarp is under a lot of scrutiny from the diocese. They're looking into our finances. They think,"
Mrs. Johnson lowered her voice, "they think that we
have been squandering money, especially on substitute teachers."

"I'm not one of the teachers who are chronically absent." Mrs. Sugarman assumed a hard, cold, harsh tone.

"Of course not. And I didn't mean to imply that you
are. Nevertheless, if I were to give you an advance on
your salary, it just wouldn't look right. However, I think
I might be able to help you."

"Oh, I would be so grateful! And I promise I'll pay
you back at the end of the month when I get my check."

Mrs. Johnson intended to crash that illusion lickety-
split. "No, I didn't mean that *I* would lend you the
money. I'm really not in a position to do that. With the
twins' tuition and all…" She stopped herself. It wasn't
necessary for her to make excuses to her employees.
"What I can do is let you take one of those beautiful
vintage dresses for your niece."

The look of appreciation vanished from Mrs. Sugarman's face. "It's not that I want to appear ungrateful, but
it's only that my niece is quite young, barely seventeen,
and those dresses, well they're quite old."

"I know it appears that way. But vintage is hot, par-
tially because it can't be imitated." At least that was
what Mrs. Hopwood often said. "We laid out quite
an assortment down in the cellar, of colors and sizes.
You're free to choose something for your niece."

"Thank you." Mrs. Sugarman hoisted herself from the chair by gripping the arms.

Mrs. Johnson waited until she left the room and then she closed the door behind her. How on earth was she supposed to run a school when she was constantly being interrupted?

She sank down in her own chair, took a sip of her ice cold coffee, looked in disgust at her hard bagel and threw it into the trash.

Scanning her e-mail—if she got one more notification about curriculum regulations or testing, she was going to unsubscribe. Let the next principal figure it out.

If there was going to be a next principal.

She noted that Mrs. Hopwood had sent an e-mail to all the parents. Wishing that Mrs. Hopwood had cleared it first with her—after all, Mrs. Hopwood wouldn't dare do something like that if Father Felix was still in charge—she read the note.

As you know, St. Polycarp is about to have our first fashion show.

This is a very exciting time. Catalogs will soon be available with details on how to go about bidding and the suggested prices for each item.

Mrs. Johnson had no doubt that the price of the printing would come out of St. Polycarp's meager budget. She could only hope that, at the very least, they would break even when the bidding ended on those old clothes.

I will also be setting up a google document, where you can record your bids and I will e-mail you instructions when I'm done. You can either bid at that time or wait until the fashion show, when your beautiful daughters will be modeling the clothing and jewelry.

Even though some of the teachers have been helpful, I could use some volunteers.

Mrs. Johnson knew that this statement was going to enflame the staff.

I'm going to need ladies to help the models dress and undress backstage. I also need volunteers to display the clothing prior to the actual show, someone to help me sort all the bids and someone to make arrangements for the winners to pick up the items.

I would appreciate any help you could give me to make sure that our beloved St. Polycarp stays open for years to come.

Well, Mrs. Hopwood was certainly doing everything in her power to make sure that the fashion show was going to be a smashing success. And Mrs. Johnson only wished that she could do more to help her friend, but running a school was sapping up all of her energy.

And by the time the fashion show was over, it would probably sap all of Mrs. Hopwood's energy as well.

TWENTY-FOUR

MRS. SUGARMAN HAD never considered herself to be a lucky person and as time went on she became more and more convinced that the stars were lined up against her. She was fresh out of pills and Jason Briggs was absent for the next couple of days.

She breathed a sigh of relief when he finally came in, although he looked rather irritated when she asked him to miss the start of gym, because she needed to speak to him.

In spite of her beating heart and her pounding headache, she was well prepared.

"What's this about?" Jason asked, as he swayed from one foot to another.

She whipped out the Math test.

"A." He grinned. "I guess studying really pays off."

"It did for Sophia Kogan. But not for you."

He stared guiltily.

"I also corrected the spelling tests from last week. You got the same words wrong as Sophia. The chances of that happening, well, it's minimal."

Jason dropped his head in shame.

"You know that St. Polycarp has a zero tolerance for cheating. If I should report this to Mrs. Johnson, it will result in a mandatory suspension."

"Please Mrs. Sugarman, don't say anything. My brother, Logan, he's been in a lot of trouble. I know that this is going to sound crazy, but I'm it, the family's hope. They want me to get good marks, to go to college, to become a doctor or a lawyer." He laughed weakly. "They haven't figured it out yet, but I'm not very smart."

Mrs. Sugarman thought that a little stroking would not be a bad thing. "You're smart enough, Jason, if you really studied."

He shook his head in disbelief.

"All right." She made it sound as though the decision was difficult, although she had the perfect opening when Jason had brought up the subject of his brother. "I won't say anything, as long as you promise it will never happen again."

"Thank you! Thank you!"

"About your brother…"

"My brother?" He nervously rocked from side to side.

"Not many people know this, and I'm telling it to you in the strictest confidence, but I decided to go back to school and get a degree in social work. People might think, at her age? But you're never too old to be the person you might have been."

Jason nodded without any enthusiasm.

"Anyway, my area of study will be young men, who at some point in their lives took a wrong turn. Men like your brother."

"My brother?" he repeated.

"I wonder if it would be possible to reach out to him. I really think I could learn a lot and do him some good in the process, maybe help turn his life around. If you could just give me his number…"

Jason hesitated for several long seconds and then said, "I don't know about that. My brother, he doesn't like talking to strange people. Lots of social workers have tried to help him, but he's not interested. And if he knew I was discussing him with a teacher, well, he's got a real bad temper."

"Your brother wouldn't have to know that we were in the least way connected. I would tell him I got his contact information from the court system. Does he know I'm your teacher?"

"Are you kidding? He doesn't even know what grade I'm in."

"There you go," Mrs. Sugarman said cheerfully.

"I don't know." Jason shifted from one foot to another.

Mrs. Sugarman let her eyes settle on the spelling test and then gave him one, long, desperate look.

"I guess it would be all right. Just don't mention me. Promise?"

"Promise."

As soon as her class went down to lunch, Mrs. Sugarman tried the number that Jason had given her. But the only answer was a robotic recording, and the message wasn't something she wanted to leave. She would have to try again.

Mrs. Hopwood was on lunch duty so Mrs. Sugarman took the opportunity to hustle into Mrs. Hopwood's classroom. She had to find that email, the person who would pay double for a handbag. She was hoping Mrs. Hopwood left her computer on because she was quite careless that way. Mrs. Sugarman had to wait several minutes because Dylan was meeting with a parent and they could easily see her enter a classroom which wasn't her own.

No password was required. All Mrs. Sugarman needed to do was click off the screen saver—which was a picture of a sullen teenager, probably Mrs. Hopwood's son—and Mrs. Hopwood's e-mail magically appeared. This was going to be easier than Mrs. Sugarman thought.

The email from the eager buyer had arrived several days ago, so Mrs. Sugarman scrolled down, past several e-mails from parents, one from Mrs. Johnson, several from J.Crew, Victoria Secret, Banana Republic and one from Alex.

But nothing from anyone wanting to buy purses.

It occurred to Mrs. Sugarman that maybe Mrs. Hopwood had deleted it.

She heard a clamor on the stairs. How could the students possibly be returning to the classroom when the lunch period was barely half way over?

A clap of thunder shook the window panes.

Great. Rain meant indoor recess. She clicked off and headed downstairs to the dark basement.

MRS. SUGARMAN WAS prepared to grab the most expensive dress she could find. But as much as she wanted the money, she couldn't possibly stay down there. The odor was disgusting. There was no doubt in her mind that something or somebody had died in the walls. She grabbed the first dress she saw, a black lace, trimmed in red, something a waitress would wear in a cheap Italian restaurant. But a designer label was sewed in and it had an old price tag on it, which read one hundred and fifty dollars. Mrs. Sugarman figured that it had probably doubled in price. She returned to her classroom, just as the students came barreling up the stairs.

She scrawled a note to Mr. Salisbury, telling him
that he should check the cellar because something was
definitely amiss there and then sent it down with two
troublesome boys, hoping they would get lost and not
return anytime soon.

They did and, when they came back twenty minutes
later, they made up a lame excuse that they couldn't find
the janitor and then they finally learned that he was sick
and hadn't come in.

For one moment Mrs. Sugarman wondered if the old
man had dropped dead in the cellar and that was the
source of that disgusting smell.

Well, she had her own problems.

She tried Logan and decided to leave a message,
which asked him to return her call because she was
going to make it worthwhile.

And then she waited.

FOR TWO DAYS Mrs. Sugarman carried her cell phone,
everywhere she went, including the bathroom, which
she was visiting quite a bit. Withdrawing from her
pills played havoc with her stomach, not to mention
the sweating and the nausea. She kept the volume on
her phone turned up high while she slept because she
thought that drug dealers probably called in the middle of the night.

On one hand, she was praying that Logan would call
soon. On the other hand, she had to find a way to get
the money, because Logan wasn't the sort of man who
would take credit.

It was time to visit the vintage shop with the two
items to sell and she expected to be paid five hundred

dollars, enough for several rounds of pills. So immediately after school, she headed for *Tristen's Treasures*.

"WHAT YOU GOT?" The thin man behind the counter wore a dirty tee shirt. His arms were decorated with tattoos of cows and his droopy eyes were bloodshot, something sticky was dangling from his bushy mustache.

Mrs. Sugarman had packed both items carefully in a shopping bag and she took out the dress first, flattening it against the counter.

While Mr. Tristen examined the dress, Mrs. Sugarman looked around at her competition, which was scanty. Racks of pedal pushers—*who wore pedal pushers anymore*—dresses in neutral colors which were long and large, peep toed shoes with boxy heels, unstructured bags thrown half hazard into a straw basket, and, in a glass case, under the counter, an assortment of inexpensive jewelry, colorful beads, button earrings, seasonal bracelets and one faded looking cameo.

She looked up when Mr. Tristen said dully, "Can't do much with this."

"What do you mean? It's vintage!" She was aware that her voice was shrill and shocked.

"Lady, everything here is vintage. Look." He turned the dress inside out and pointed to some white spots under the sleeves. "Deodorant."

"But no one will see these spots," she argued.

"The buyer will. You wouldn't believe how fussy people are. And smell this." He shoved the dress under Mrs. Sugarman's nose.

She caught a whiff of that disgusting basement odor. "Well, it's old," she mumbled.

"This is more than old. It's as if someone had been

buried in it. One thing is for sure. The dress is going to have to be dry cleaned so I gotta deduct that from the price. What else you got?"

She slammed the purse down, fighting the impulse to snap.

Mr. Tristen glanced at it, then he lifted it up. "Heavy."

"That's because it's well made. You can see yourself it's trimmed in gold, like a little suitcase."

"But the gold is scratched. Besides blue purses don't sell so good." He ran his small hands over the leather. "Okay, I'll give you two hundred dollars for both items."

Mrs. Sugarman felt her stomach cramp and her face redden as she was overcome with a burst of heat. "Two hundred dollars! That's ridiculous. The last vintage shop offered me two hundred dollars just for the purse!"

"Then I suggest you return to that shop. I can only give you what I can sell it for and still make a small profit."

"How about two hundred and fifty?"

He shook his head. "Two hundred is my final offer."

It was his only offer. But what choice did she have?

He gave her two hundred dollar bills and, when she protested—Logan might not take such large bills, thinking that they were counterfeit, and maybe they were— he told her to go to the bank.

Well, maybe two hundred would be enough.

TWENTY-FIVE

Mrs. Hopwood was disappointed when she had a chance to rival through the trunk and examine the shoes. Mrs. Johnson was right. They were going to be a hard sell.

Most of them were quite small in size and rather dated. Stacked, chucky heels, in neutral colors, brown, black, navy and gray, lots of peep toes and some of them were badly scuffed. A pretty pair of blue shoes peeked through the rubble but they were a half a size too big. She was tempted to throw all of them in the dumpster, but maybe she could sort them by size and raffle them off as a group.

She glanced at her watch. Mrs. Johnson wasn't coming for another fifteen minutes. Was there anything else of value in the attic?

From two floors below, Mrs. Hopwood heard a toilet flush.

For a moment, Mrs. Hopwood held her breath. She had thought that she was alone in the house. Then she realized that Roseanne must have come over.

Mrs. Hopwood had entered through the kitchen. It was obvious that Roseanne hadn't gotten around to emptying out that room. The cabinets were full of expired food, dusty glasses, and chipped dishes. The realtor wanted everything out of the house, so it looked pristine and new. At this rate, it would be a year before the house was sold, which would delay settling the estate. Who knew when Mrs. Hopwood would ever see her inheritance?

She was just about to call down to her sister, when her cell phone rang and the picture of Roseanne flashed on the screen.

"You'll never guess where I am."

"Probably not. Listen, Maria needs to know if you still want her to do the Green Ion on your hair."

"The what?"

"The Green Ion. You said you wanted to give it a try because you know how frizzy your hair gets with the summer humidity. Anyway, she is booked solid for the next month, and in July she's going on a second honeymoon. Bev is going to take the babies. But if you want Amanda or Carrie to do it, there's no problem."

Mrs. Hopwood heard footsteps in the front hall. "Why don't we discuss this upstairs?"

"Upstairs where? Gina, your highlights are beautiful!"

Mrs. Hopwood felt her stomach jolt. "Are you with Gina?"

"Yes, because you know how she is. She refuses to drive to Feeding Hills, which is so crazy. It's mostly back roads…"

The footsteps traveled to the stairway.

"Where are you?" Mrs. Hopwood asked frantically.

"At Salon 322. Why? Where are you?"

"I'm at Aunt Eunice's in the attic. And someone is downstairs. I heard a toilet flush and now he's climbing up the stairs! I smell him too! Musky!"

"Didn't you lock the door behind you?"

"I came through the back. Oh my God, my purse is in the kitchen!"

"Listen, hang up right now and call 911."

"I can't," she said in a shaky voice. "I'm too scared."

"What are you? Barbara Stanwyck in *Sorry Wrong Number*? Never mind, I'll call for you."

She left Mrs. Hopwood with a dial tone.

With every nerve in her body tightening, Mrs. Hopwood looked around desperately for someplace to hide. Behind the trunk?

The footsteps were getting closer. There was a way to dial 911 on her apple watch, but she wasn't sure where the button was and she was too nervous to look for it.

She ran over to the window and tried to get it open. No time. She released a bloodcurdling scream and, as her knees buckled, she sank to the floor.

The footsteps halted, pounding down the stairs, and Mrs. Hopwood heard the front door rattle and slam. Looking out the window, she got a glimpse of a figure dressed in black, running across the front yard.

She didn't move a muscle until she saw a police car pull up in the driveway.

Mrs. Johnson was right behind them.

"Ma'am, are you able to let us in?" A masculine voice rang out as he hammered on the front door.

Mrs. Hopwood raced down the stairs and was relieved when she saw two burly officers step into the house.

"What happened?" Mrs. Johnson pushed past them and entered into the hall.

"Well, I came here to get some of my aunt's property. She's dead. Anyway, I heard a toilet flush and then footsteps downstairs." Mrs. Hopwood was aware that she was rambling, but she was unable to slow down.

"I thought it was my sister, Roseanne. Then she called me on the phone. I still thought she was downstairs but then she started to talk crazy, about ion treatments and highlights and I knew she was at Salon 322. She hung up and called you. But then when I heard him climbing the stairs, I screamed rather loudly. He might have got scared because I heard him go out the front door and I saw him running across the lawn."

"Could you identify him?" The policeman, whose tag read Officer Bennis, rubbed his bald head.

"No, he was dressed in black."

The other cop, who had a mop of black hair and an unruly moustache, and identified himself as Officer Wheeler, examined the front door. "There's no sign of a forced entry."

"He probably came in the back door," Mrs. Hopwood said sheepishly. "And I left my purse on the table."

"Tell me, you didn't lock the door," Mrs. Johnson said.

"All right, you two ladies wait here while we go inside and have a look."

The moment they were out of sight Mrs. Johnson started. "What were you thinking, leaving the door open?"

"I was thinking that this is a nice neighborhood, where everyone has bird feeders in their backyard and picket fences in the front yard, and where neighbors bring each other home baked blueberries muffins in a basket, wrapped in pretty towels…"

"There are no safe neighborhoods anymore. You should know that! Because of you, I'm going to miss Justin Joseph, who is pitching in the second half of the game."

"He's only five. They'll be other games."

"He's six!"

"Ma'am," Bennis poked his head from the kitchen. "We found your purse in the backyard, turned inside out, the contents scattered on the lawn. You want to identify it and tell us if anything is missing?"

"I can't believe this!" Mrs. Hopwood lamented, feeling very much like a victim.

"Neither can I," Mrs. Johnson said.

MRS. HOPWOOD FOUND her scarlet purse in the dirt with the paisley lining exposed. Her zebra wallet was nearby. She grabbed it, looked inside, and then exclaimed, "He took my money!"

"How much money are we talking about?" Officer Wheeler twirled his bushy moustache.

"Three dollars."

"Three dollars!" Mrs. Johnson yelled. "I'm missing my sons' baseball game for three lousy dollars?"

"What about credit cards?" Officer Bennis asked.

"I only carry American Express and it's still here. What if he copied the number down?"

Officer Bennis stooped down and gave Mrs. Hopwood her house keys, her Juicy Fruit gum, her make-up bag and a pill box.

Mrs. Hopwood immediately checked her make-up bag, making sure that the thief hadn't stolen her brand new MAC lipstick. It was still there.

"It's obvious what happened." Officer Bennis stood up and wiped the dirt off the front of his pants. "The robber was casing the houses, saw that the door was open and noticed your purse on the counter. He took the opportunity to get some quick cash."

"No doubt disappointed," Mrs. Johnson mumbled.

"He did more than that," Mrs. Hopwood insisted. "He used the toilet."

"Probably thought no one was home," Wheeler said. "No car in the driveway. When you screamed, he realized his mistake and he took off. If you want, you can go down to the precinct and fill out a report."

"For three dollars?" Mrs. Johnson asked.

"No, I'm good," Mrs. Hopwood lied.

"I FEEL AS though I've been violated," Mrs. Hopwood said as she dragged the trash bag full of shoes out of Mrs. Johnson's car. "Could you give me a hand, carrying this inside the school?"

"I can't. I told you, I have a bad back."

"I thought you were going to make a doctor's appointment." Mrs. Hopwood dropped the bag on the pavement in front of the school and noticed a small hole visible at the bottom.

"I did. I'm going for an MRI. I probably have a ruptured disc from carrying the twins around."

"You're still lugging them around at their age?"

"Don't go there. Do you mind using your keys? Mine are at the bottom of my backpack."

MRS. HOPWOOD DID MIND. She almost tripped over the plastic bag. But she was tired of arguing and she wanted to go home.

She reached inside her handbag and unzipped the small compartment. It gave her the willies thinking about the person who put his hands inside. She would never feel the same about the handbag again.

The zipper compartment was empty.

"They're not here. I always keep them here."

Mrs. Johnson released a sigh of disgust, and gave her a very cold look.

"I know what must have happened. The police didn't see them hidden in the grass, maybe under the lilac brush."

"Well, I'm not going back there." Mrs. Johnson plunked her backpack on the concrete. "They're just keys. No one can connect them to St. Polycarp, even if someone finds them."

Mrs. Hopwood lowered her eyes and her stomach lurched.

"No one can connect them to St. Polycarp, even if someone finds them," Mrs. Johnson repeated.

"You know those cheesy key rings they gave out a few years ago for Catholic School Week, the ones engraved with the school's name on it?"

"I knew I should have never given you those keys!"

"You didn't. Father Felix gave them to us when we were coming in early to work on development."

"That was a good time." Mrs. Johnson grabbed her key and rammed it into the lock. "No responsibilities, I just did what I was told. No Sister Mary Grace breathing down my back. It was a good year."

"I think two people got murdered that year."

"I'll tell you this." Mrs. Johnson threw the door open. "I'm not the one, who's going down on her hands and knees and searching in the dirt. You better pray to St. Anthony that you find them."

"I think that St. Anthony is only for lost things, not stolen things."

"Well, then pray to St. Jude then, or St. Therese. Just find those damn keys!"

Mrs. Hopwood didn't respond, nor was she about to

bring the shoes all the way down to the basement on her own. She'd ask Mrs. Salisbury to help her. She just threw the broken plastic bag in the back of her classroom. And then she went back to Aunt Eunice's house to search for the keys.

THEY WEREN'T THERE. Mrs. Hopwood soiled her red and yellow plaid pants and ruined the heels of her yellow shoes, but she found no keys.

Mrs. Johnson stood and watched her, leaning against a tree, and complaining about her back as her face screwed up in irritation. "I'm not going to change the locks on all three doors until I'm sure that the keys are lost."

"They're lost." Mrs. Hopwood rose, wishing that there was a place to wipe her hands. "Can I go inside and wash my hands?"

"You know what I think? I think that you never had those keys in that purse."

"I always put them in the zipper compartment," Mrs. Hopwood insisted.

"Except you never use the same purse twice. What you should do is go home and figure out when you last used the keys and what handbag you were carrying that day. And if going inside to wash your hands means you have to dig through your purse to find your aunt's keys, forget it. I just want to go home. And you should go too. I'm betting you'll find the school keys there."

Mrs. Hopwood did not say what she was thinking. *You'd lose.*

"WHAT ARE YOU DOING?" Monte asked when he saw their bed covered with a multitude of handbags, all shapes and all sizes. "Are you giving them away?" he asked hopefully.

"No, I'm looking for the keys to St. Polycarp. My purse was stolen. They got my cash."

"How much?" He threw his arms open.

"Three dollars."

He lost interest and was leaving the room.

"The thief might have taken the keys to St. Polycarp," she called after him.

He stopped at the threshold. "What would a thief want in that school?"

"Computer and all the vintage clothing you wouldn't let me keep. They're some nice pictures…"

"Never mind. I'm so sick and tired of hearing about the drama in that school."

He walked away, leaving Mrs. Hopwood feeling somewhat hurt that he cared so little about what was such a big part of her life.

And now the thief had access to that life.

Because the keys were nowhere to be found.

TWENTY-SIX

ANOTHER DAY WENT by and still no call from Logan. Mrs. Sugarman resisted the urge to call him. If he thought she was anxious, if he thought she was a desperate drug addict, he might double the prices of the pills. Like all drug dealers, she had no doubt that he was a greedy, unethical person.

And just when she thought again about how unlucky a person she was, she saw Miss Turnipseed walking down the hall, carrying a stack of catalogs. Because Miss Turnipseed was an older woman, Mrs. Sugarman rather liked her. It was nice to see someone elderly— older than Mrs. Sugarman—who took pride in her work and seemed to possess good judgment and conservative values.

"Let me take those from you." Mrs. Sugarman held out her hands.

"No, that's all right. I have to distribute these to all the teachers. They're too bulky to put in the mail slots. What's annoying is most of the teachers order their supplies online and anyway," she dropped her voice and moved a bit closer—Mrs. Sugarman could smell peppermint on her breath, "Mrs. Johnson is going to send out a memo, telling teachers that they shouldn't order anything for the fall, because the school might not be reopening."

"I can deliver half of these, to the teachers upstairs. Save you a trip."

"Well, that's very nice of you, dear." Miss Turnipseed put the catalogs on a chair and began to check them off as though she was saying the rosary. When she handed them to Mrs. Sugarman, she stared at her for a moment. "Are you sure you want to do this? I wasn't going to say anything but you don't look well. Are you coming down with something?"

"I was." Mrs. Sugarman grabbed the catalogs. "But I'll soon be on the road to recovery."

Mrs. Sugarman wasn't such a dear. She had seen Mrs. Hopwood in Mrs. Johnson's office and there was no reason why she shouldn't take advantage of the opportunity.

If she was quick.

And she was quick.

Mrs. Hopwood's computer was on and, while Mrs. Sugarman listened for the clicky clack of high heels on the staircase, she scrolled down to trash.

Mrs. Hopwood had lots of trash.

Mostly clothing companies, offering her all sorts of sales and coupons, but here was exactly what Mrs. Sugarman was searching for—an e-mail from Stronghold 0211@ gmail. com.

She grabbed a catalog and a pencil and wrote the address down.

Some other women, not as clever as she, would figure that they already sold the vintage purse, so what possible good would it be to know the e-mail address now?

But Mrs. Sugarman had a different agenda. She could

e-mail the man and sell him another vintage purse—she had lots of old pocketbooks. Who could possibly know what Mrs. Hopwood had given her? She would ask for a hundred dollars and that would make up for the paltry sum she had received from that cheap Mr. Tristen.

Just as she clicked off, Mrs. Sugarman looked up and noticed a pudgy girl standing in the doorway, eying her. Then Mrs. Hopwood came tottering in, leading a gaggle of noisy students.

"I… I… I," Mrs. Sugarman stuttered. "I want to talk to you. I was going to leave you a note."

Mrs. Hopwood looked suspicious but Mrs. Sugarman thought that was probably her usual expression, since Mrs. Hopwood had already been in a few dubious and dangerous situations.

"I wanted to know what I could do to help you with the fashion show."

"I already assigned you to a committee." Mrs. Hopwood eyed her students with exasperation, a paper airplane missing her by inches. "All right! Everyone in their seats. Word search time. First one finished gets a huge candy bar."

The students skidded back to their seats.

"I know," Mrs. Sugarman blurted out, "and I don't like to complain. But I would have to work with Addison and to be perfectly honest, we don't really get along."

For a moment Mrs. Sugarman thought that maybe Mrs. Hopwood was going to say something negative about Addison but the moment passed, and all Mrs. Hopwood mumbled was that she would have to think about it.

As her heart raced and she began to sweat, Mrs. Sugarman knew that her life depended on getting in touch with Logan Briggs. If he didn't call by tonight, she was going to call him.

Because she really needed those pills.

MRS. SUGARMAN FINALLY reached Logan later that evening.

"Yeah, what do you want?"

The greeting was so curt, so unexpected that Mrs. Sugarman was momentarily stricken speechless. The carefully rehearsed pitch flew from her mind as she heard the labored breathing at the other end of the phone. "Is this Logan Briggs?"

"Who wants to know?"

Mrs. Sugarman was not about to give out her name. "I need some prescription drugs."

"Lady, you got the wrong number."

"No, please, please, don't hang up. I got your number from your brother, Jason."

Hesitation. "He wouldn't do that."

"Well, you see, he didn't know why I wanted your number. He thought I was going to help you, as a social worker would. Right now, I'm in terrible pain and the doctor is a sadist. I need some way to dull it."

"Listen, I don't know you from Eve. And my brother, he's kinda stupid. You could be an undercover cop, trying to catch me in a sting."

"No." A spasm of fear ripped through her—Logan was her last hope. "My name is Nancy Sugarman. I'm Jason's homeroom teacher. You can look me up in the St. Polycarp website. Well, it might say librarian there, because I used to be the librarian but in the fall…"

"I don't give a damn about school politics." Logan cut her off in the middle of her rambling.

"No, of course not. Why would you?" She knew that she was babbling. "Can you help me out?"

Another long pause. Had he hung up?

"Please, I'm willing to pay top dollar."

"What do you need?"

"Percocet, Vicodin, any of them will do."

"I'm not sure what I can get a hold of. And if I do, it's going to run you about fifteen dollars a pill."

Fifteen dollars? That was rather steep. Of course, Logan didn't take credit cards. "All right, I'll take ten pills."

"Ten pills? What are you kidding? I don't get out of bed for less than two bills."

"All right then." Mrs. Sugarman was doing the math in her head. "I'll take fifteen then." When Logan didn't answer right away, Mrs. Sugarman added, "I could turn out to be a very good customer, make you a lot of money."

"Yeah, that's what they all say. Then they end up in a slab. I got your number. I'll be in touch."

TWENTY-SEVEN

IT WAS IRONIC, her sitting her in a church, and the teacher, who had been so nice to her, thinking that she was praying, when instead she was planning. Planning on something that God would not approve.

Everyone knew that life wasn't fair. That was something that mothers told their children from an early age, at the first complaint. But shouldn't someone or something be around to balance the scales?

Tracy didn't believe in karma, letting the universe take care of sinners. Some sinners led happy lives and died peaceful deaths in their beds, while their victims suffered terribly. Oh yes, God would even it out.

But Tracy was too impatient to wait for God.

THEY HADN'T A lot of money, but Victor really wanted children. So when Tracy found out that they couldn't have any, Victor was despondent. Tracy suggested a pet, but Victor claimed that he was allergic to fur. So when Sugar Daddy crossed her path, shaking, shivering and starving, she decided that whatever happened she was going to keep him. Although he turned out to be a far better companion than Victor had ever been, Tracy wondered if she was a good master. If she really loved Sugar Daddy, she would try to find him a real home. He didn't deserve to be on the street.

Victor wasn't the perfect husband. He had a hair trigger temper but Tracy had learned how to slither around it. He wasn't much for conversation and he wasn't ambitious. They would have gone on for years the same way.

Until that horrible woman ruined it all.

Winifred Ortiz.

So if someone should ask Tracy how she ended up homeless, she wouldn't hesitate to tell them the name of the woman who had ruined her life.

Winifred Ortiz.

They had met at the apartment of some fortune teller, who had gotten in touch with Victor's dead mother. The dead mother had never liked Tracy and she had always encouraged Victor to find someone else. It turned out that the someone else lived in the same building as the soothsayer. Tracy wasn't sure of the exact day the affair started. It was the little things at first. Victor doing so much inventory until late into the night, the freshly new underwear he bought, the more expensive cologne, the way he wouldn't meet her eyes.

I can live with this, Tracy had thought, *because whoever she is, he will grow tired of her, or more likely, she of him, and life will go on for both of us.*

Maybe Victor would feel guilty and their bond would grow tighter. After all, she had to take some responsibility for his straying. She hadn't given him enough attention, made him feel special, so when he met the other woman, who fussed, and found him worthy of admiration, it was only natural that a relationship would develop.

And it did seem to be working. The night he died, he called her to tell her he was going to be late. But he had some very good news. Maybe he found a new job. Maybe they were going to move away.

She never found out what that good news was.

She'd never forget the faces of the two policemen, who came to her door. They didn't spare words, got right to the point, like a sword through her heart. "Your husband has been murdered."

The ensuing days elapsed like scenes from a nightmare. The jealous husband had lost control and shot Victor once in the head.

Once was all it took.

At first he denied it, but later decided to plea it out. Twenty years.

Except it had only been twelve and George Ortiz was about to be released on parole.

Hardly aware of the danger which awaited him.

TWENTY-EIGHT

"Mrs. Hopwood?"

"Oh Melissa, would you mind waiting until I finish this text to my son?"

Melissa wished that she didn't have to wait. For one thing by the time she got down to the cafeteria the tater tots might be gone. For another, it had taken quite a bit of nerve to approach Mrs. Hopwood and now her heart was hammering so hard that all she wanted to do was run away.

"So what's up?" Mrs. Hopwood smiled and Melissa couldn't help but wonder how she kept her lipstick so pink and so shiny after an entire morning of teaching.

"I don't know if I should say anything. I don't want you to think that I'm a snitch."

"Is this about a student?" Mrs. Hopwood glanced at her phone. Melissa thought she was probably checking for a reply.

"No, it's about a teacher."

Mrs. Hopwood looked up in interest.

"Remember yesterday?"

Mrs. Hopwood nodded, slightly bewildered.

"I saw Mrs. Sugarman at your desk."

"Oh that. She was looking for a piece of paper to write me a note about the fashion show."

"No. She was reading your email."

Mrs. Hopwood seemed wary and then Melissa knew that she had made a mistake. Sometimes adults didn't want to know certain things because then they were expected to take some sort of action. So all Melissa had done was to put Mrs. Hopwood in a difficult position.

"Well," Mrs. Hopwood finally spoke, "my computer was on and my e-mail was visible. Mrs. Sugarman probably couldn't resist taking a peek. I can't fault her for that." She leaned forward and Melissa could smell the flowery scent. "The truth is that I'm kind of nosy myself."

Melissa did not want to appear like a fool, so she stood her ground. "No, it was more than that. She actually clicked on your computer and then when she saw me standing by the door, she clicked off. She had a real guilty look on her face."

"Well, thank you for telling me that, Melissa." Except Mrs. Hopwood didn't look thankful. She looked irritated and confused.

I should have minded my own business, Melissa thought. *Mrs. Sugarman never did anything to me and Mrs. Hopwood was probably better off not knowing.*

"Melissa, I know that this is a troubling time for you. So if you ever want to talk," Mrs. Hopwood scribbled a phone number on a piece of note paper, with the name Julia embossed in gold lettering, "feel free to call me."

"Thank you." Melissa folded the paper and crammed it into her skirt pocket and then wrote her own number on a piece of scrap paper. "Just in case," she added.

Mrs. Hopwood nodded in an abstract sort of way and stuffed the paper into her yellow tote bag.

Melissa doubted that she would ever use it.

WHEN MELISSA ARRIVED HOME, she found her brother, Adam, in the kitchen.

The siblings never had very much to say to each other. Even as small children, they seldom played together. Melissa especially disliked his friends, particularly Logan Briggs, who was a well-known drug dealer.

But jammed in that narrow kitchen, Melissa felt compelled to speak. "So did you see him?"

Adam nodded as he pulled open the refrigerator door, ripped open a carton of milk and began drinking. Melissa was searching in the cabinet for cookies, but stopped when she saw an army of ants march into the box of saltines.

"He's getting out, you know." Adam broke off a piece of cheese and stuffed it into his mouth. He slammed the refrigerator door but it didn't close all the way because of a broken spring. "Course he has to say that he did it and he's sorry. Otherwise they won't let him come home."

Melissa was eying a brown banana.

"You don't want him to come home, do you?" Adam stared at her with his father's eyes.

"He doesn't like me," Melissa mumbled.

"That's ridiculous. You know he didn't do it. Listen," he lowered his voice when he heard footsteps on the stairs, "I know all about the argument and the gun and the no alibi. But Papa swears the gun was planted and he couldn't have argued with Victor because he wasn't in the alley that night. The important thing is that he served his time. He's coming home and he's going to take us to the Dominican Republic for a nice vacation and then he's going to get us out of this rat trap, move us to the other end of town. We can change schools. No one will know who we are."

Melissa felt as though someone had slapped her. "I don't want to change schools. I'm happy at St. Polycarp."

The door burst open and Melissa's mother stumbled in, carrying bags of groceries. No one offered to help her as she staggered to the table.

"The potato chips were on sale." She seemed downright jubilant. "I even got some sour crème dip and some day-old donuts. Root beer, too." She began emptying the plastic bags.

Adam grabbed the chips and ripped open the bag with his teeth.

"You're going to be happy when I tell you this, Melissa." Melissa couldn't imagine her mother saying anything which would make her happy. "I got a message from Julie."

"Who's Julie?"

"You know, your teacher."

"What did she want?" Melissa asked breathlessly, hardly able to get the words out.

"She was asking for volunteers to help with the fashion show. I figured you're one of the models..."

Adam snickered. "Her a model?" He pointed a grimy finger. "She's too fat."

"The least I can do is help out," Melissa's mom threw some hamburger meat into the freezer. "It's not like we can buy any of the clothes."

Melissa knew what she wanted to say. "What makes you think they're going to want help from the wife of a murderer?"

But instead she said nothing, just retreated to her room where she could be alone—at least for a few precious minutes.

TWENTY-NINE

THE MOMENT THAT Mrs. Hopwood walked into her house, she knew something was very wrong. It wasn't that anything was out of place, at least not that she could see. But her living room seemed different somehow and a strange smell filled the air, driftwood, coconut and that touch of musk—very familiar.

She debated on going upstairs, but Monte would be home any minute and what else could she do? Cower downstairs and try to explain to him? She'd rather run into the robber.

She wasn't going to be fearful. She grabbed the blow dryer off the coffee table—a blow dryer she seldom used because it was too heavy to manipulate—but it was perfect for whacking someone on the side of the head.

Unless, of course, he was carrying a gun.

She crept up the stairs.

The door to the master bedroom was open, just as she left it, a hastily made up bed, her coffee cup on the bedside table, the sweater she decided against thrown on the chaise in front of the fireplace which was never lit because Mrs. Hopwood was petrified of fire.

Alex's door was slightly ajar. Mrs. Hopwood always avoided going in there. If something was amiss or missing she would never know.

Neither would Alex.

The door to the pocketbook room was closed. She never closed it. Was someone hiding in there?

She heard a car pull up in the driveway. In a moment Monte would come bursting through the front door and demand to know what she was cooking for dinner. And the fact that she had no plans, well, the intruder better beware.

She flung the door open and released a gasp of surprise when she spotted her purses strewed on the single twin bed, on the desk near her laptop, on the peach wall to wall carpeting, on the floor of the open closet.

Monte was clambering up the stairs and she stood, paralyzed.

He stopped, stared, nudged her aside and then asked, "What the hell were you looking for?"

"You think I did this? Someone broke into our house. I'm calling the police."

She pushed him out of the way, grabbed the land line from the bedroom and dialed 911. Monte followed her inside, shaking his head, his irritation mounting. "What have you gotten us into?"

OFFICER BENNIS AND Officer Wheeler didn't seem very interested in her plight—maybe because they had met before under similar circumstances.

Mrs. Hopwood and her husband waited in the living room, Mrs. Hopwood, telling Officer Bennis what happened, Mr. Hopwood pacing back and forth, huffing and puffing, as though all of this was just a horrible inconvenience.

Officer Wheeler had left the room, wandering upstairs and downstairs at a snail's pace. "Someone jimmied open the patio door," he said. "If I were you, I'd get a better lock."

"What do you think they want?" Monte directed the question at his wife.

Officer Wheeler answered that they were probably searching for cash.

"Why me?" Mrs. Hopwood asked. "I don't have any money. I'm poor."

Montgomery stared at her, annoyed, as though admitting that they were not well off was a blight against his manhood.

"That's all relative." Bennis collapsed on the sofa, as though this was a social visit. "What exactly do you do, Mrs. Hopwood, job wise, I mean?"

"She teaches in an inner city school," Monte answered for her.

"Well, there you are." Wheeler said, as though the mystery had been solved. "Look through your handbags and let us know if anything of value is missing." He glanced down at his cell, which was blasting a tune from Rocky. "We have to go." He glanced at his partner. "We got another call."

"A robbery?" Mrs. Hopwood was hoping there was a rash of them and this was nothing personal.

"No, just a bunch of neighbors complaining about a man, who is about to make parole."

"George Ortiz?" Mrs. Hopwood asked.

Six eyes turned in her direction. "What do you know about that?" Wheeler finally spoke.

"His daughter is one of my students. Do you think there might be a connection?"

"I can't see it." Bennis rose slowly. "My guess is the robber realizes now that you have nothing much worth stealing and he won't be back again. But, of course, if anything suspicious happens, don't hesitate to call."

"I'll walk you out," Monte stalked away and Mrs. Hopwood knew that he was just trying to escape from the scene of the crime.

"WHY ARE YOU WHISPERING?"

"Because I'm in the bathroom. Monte went out to get us a pizza and he may be back any moment. He's angry, like this whole thing is my fault."

"Well, maybe if you didn't flash all those pretty clothes…"

"Oh please! I've been flashing my pretty clothes for years and nobody's tried to rob me or go through my purses. Just because I happen to have a lot of twenty dollar dresses I bought from Penney's with a coupon, it doesn't make me a victim. No, Amelia, it's more than that. I think it has something to do with the fashion show and the vintage clothing."

"Justin Joseph, sit down and study your spelling words. You're not going to fail another test because you can't memorize a few simple words!"

"Someone wants something in those handbags."

"No, not in front of the television. Sit in the corner, facing the wall, where they'll be no distractions."

"Amelia, are you listening to me?" Mrs. Hopwood asked, not bothering to hide her frustration.

"Yes, I'm listening to you, even though what you're saying makes no sense at all. How would anyone know what you have?"

"What are you talking about? Everyone knows! I sent that e-mail to the parents…"

"About that e-mail…"

"And I announced it in the church bulletin."

"Yes, you did all that. But you never said you had any handbags. You never mentioned them because you had given them all away."

Mrs. Hopwood was silent. She was not about to concede, not when the feeling in her bones was so strong and her insides were churning so badly.

"Besides, let's just say for argument's sake—Justin Joseph, I'm watching you—that someone hid something in a handbag twenty years ago, maybe a key to a safe deposit box, or a map directions to a hidden treasure. He would know what handbag he put it in. He wouldn't have to look through all of your handbags."

"But what if he wasn't the person who put it there?"

"How did he even know that you had some vintage handbags? He couldn't have seen you with them. You threw them in the big trash bag with a bunch of clothing and then we carried them into the car. We didn't look at them again until we were inside the school."

"You're right. The only people who knew I had the handbags were the people I gave the handbags to. Mrs. Sugarman has been acting very peculiar. Melissa said she saw her reading my e-mail. And that homeless woman, we don't know anything about her."

"Please! Justin Joseph, I'm testing you in two minutes and you better know those words! The people you gave the handbags to would hardly be searching for them because they already have them. And why would a robber wait twenty years if he knew that somehow your Aunt Eunice might have the handbag he was looking for? There's just no way to connect the dots. I've got to go. And thanks for asking about my doctor's appointment for my back."

Mrs. Hopwood heard the phone click.

She should have asked about Mrs. Johnson's MRI but, after all, she had just been robbed, and Mrs. Johnson hung up so swiftly that Mrs. Hopwood didn't even have a chance to tell her something important.

That something important was that the robber hadn't looked in all of her handbags, because the nice ones, the more recent ones, were not in the pocketbook room at all. They were wrapped in tissue paper and placed under her bed in the master bedroom, so they didn't get mangled with the others.

She needed a broom to drag them forward and it took her several minutes to locate the lavender vintage bag. Mrs. Hopwood hadn't used it yet because, even empty, it was heavy.

She undid the lock with the little key, which hung from the strap. She unzipped the side compartment, and found nothing. The purple lining was intact, so if something was hidden there, she couldn't find it.

She heard the front door slam. Monte was home and she was betting it was going to be a silent supper.

THIRTY

"WHAT'S GOING ON HERE?"

Mrs. Johnson walked into Mrs. Hopwood's classroom and saw chaos. Some of the students were drawing on the Smartboard, some of the girls were on the floor surrounded by photographs, a few students were playing cards and seemed to be gambling with chips, some students were doing word searches and a few were playing with iPads. One pupil sat in the back of the room, eating cheese doodles, two girls by his side shrieking with laughter.

"We're trying to finish up the catalog. It's due at the printer's tonight."

"They're not all working on the catalog." Mrs. Johnson did not want to venture from the threshold of the room. She was afraid she would step on a body.

"They have free time."

"At ten in the morning?"

Mrs. Hopwood said what turned out to be her usual refrain. "I have no help."

"Well, you also have an observation."

"Now?"

"Now. Didn't you get my voicemail?"

"I did but I deleted it because it wasn't clear. One of your twins was wailing in the background."

"You have an observation." Mrs. Johnson thought it important that she sound firm.

"Now?" Mrs. Hopwood repeated.

"Now."

"Well, obviously that's not possible."

A chubby girl with frizzy blonde hair, broken glasses and a bland puffy face, approached Mrs. Hopwood. "Do you want the photos grouped by color or by price?"

"Um," Mrs. Hopwood hesitated, "I think by color." She turned towards Mrs. Johnson. "Come back tomorrow," she said in a dismissive tone.

Mrs. Johnson had had enough. She took Mrs. Hopwood by the sleeve of her neon green cardigan and dragged her into the hall, while a few of the students looked astonished.

"I can't come back tomorrow. I have a principal's meeting, which will probably last all day. You know as well as I do, Julia, that you would never have pulled something like this when Father Felix was in charge, or Mrs. Logan…"

"Her!"

"You would have been prepared."

"That's because they were real principals. By your own admission, you're not qualified."

"Nevertheless, I have the position now and I need to observe you."

"All right," Mrs. Hopwood sighed. "I guess I could get something ready this afternoon."

"I'm busy this afternoon. I have back to back meetings, mostly with parents. I'll be back at eleven thirty." She didn't think it would be prudent to tell Mrs. Hopwood that one of those parents was Melissa Ortiz's mother. "And please try to make an effort."

Mrs. Hopwood shrugged. "As Diane Keaton said in Baby Boom, just don't expect too much."

MRS. JOHNSON DIDN'T expect too much and she didn't get too much. Mrs. Hopwood delivered a lesson in language arts, reviewing adverbs, substituting them for strong verbs, but there was no hook at the beginning of the lesson and no wrap up at the end.

And no enthusiasm from either Mrs. Hopwood or her students—in fact the students looked angry—probably upset because their free time had been interrupted with actual learning. No one raised his hand and one of the boys was actually dozing in the back.

Mrs. Johnson didn't know how she could possibly write it up. If she said something negative, Mrs. Hopwood would, no doubt, refuse to sign it. Besides, all the observations were filed in a teacher's portfolio and could affect the ability to get a job in the future. At any rate, it would be read by the new principal of St. Polycarp, if one would be forthcoming.

God, she hated this job.

And she was about to hate it more when Mrs. Ortiz walked in.

"HAVE A SEAT, Mrs. Ortiz."

"Thank you." The tense woman, who sat opposite of Mrs. Johnson, clutched her stained brown tote bag over her chest and leaned back into the chair. She wore too much make-up, which wasn't clearly blended, creating unflattering lines on her aging face. Her frizzy brown hair with gray roots was carelessly thrown on top of her head. She was dressed in black and her pants strained at the waist, exposing a roll of white flesh underneath her beige slightly soiled blouse.

Mrs. Johnson felt sorry for her. "What can I do for you?"

"I'm here to talk about Melissa. She doesn't know it yet but her father made parole this morning. He'll be coming home at the end of the week."

Mrs. Johnson was unsure if that news was good or bad, but she did manage to mumble, "Wonderful."

"It will be a period of adjustment for everyone, especially for Melissa. I think she has mixed feelings, so if she should fall behind in her studies…"

"Shouldn't you be having this conversation with Mrs. Hopwood?"

"About Mrs. Hopwood…"

Mrs. Johnson released an audible sigh, mentally preparing herself for what was about to come.

"She seems to be taking quite an interest in my daughter. She even gave my daughter her cell number."

"Mrs. Hopwood takes an interest in all of her students."

"But this interest is sudden."

"I'm not sure what you're implying, Mrs. Ortiz."

"Let me be honest with you."

Mrs. Johnson had lived long enough to know that the statement, let me be honest with you, was never followed by a happy conversation.

"I think that Mrs. Hopwood's interest has something to do with my husband's release from prison."

"And why would Mrs. Hopwood care about your husband's release from prison?"

"Because she's nosy." Before Mrs. Johnson could argue the point, which might be hard to do since Mrs. Hopwood *was* nosy, Mrs. Ortiz continued in an angry tone. "I wouldn't be surprised if she was working part time for one of those scandal sheets."

"Mrs. Ortiz," Mrs. Johnson leaned forward and

stared into Mrs. Ortiz's beady gray eyes, "with all due respect, Mrs. Hopwood is a dedicated, hardworking teacher," *although not lately,* "who has a very full life outside of school, a husband and a son," *who didn't live at home but managed to get in a lot of trouble in college* "and she simply would not have time to work a part time job."

"Well," Mrs. Ortiz shook her head in defeat, "I will tell you this. I don't think she's a good influence on my daughter."

Mrs. Johnson didn't know how to respond to this statement so she just mumbled, "I'm sorry you feel that way."

"All those colorful clothes and jewelry. Mrs. Hopwood is obviously a very materialistic person. We're trying to teach Melissa good values, the only thing that matters is the person inside, that she should do the right thing, the moral thing" Mrs. Johnson couldn't help but think—*like her father* "and every day she's distracted, wondering what Mrs. Hopwood is going to wear."

"Mrs. Ortiz—" Mrs. Johnson interrupted, trying to contain her fury and her disgust—after all, this complaint was from a woman who hadn't paid tuition in months "—it's almost the end of April. There's about eight weeks left of school. Next year Melissa will have a completely different teacher…"

"I don't think Melissa is coming back here next year. My husband is moving us to the other side of town."

"Melissa is a lovely girl. She'll be missed. Now, if you will excuse me," Mrs. Johnson stood, "I have a lot of work to do."

Reluctantly Mrs. Ortiz rose. "Oh by the way," she said. "I volunteered to help Mrs. Hopwood with the fashion show. I think it's only right that I take an interest in my daughter's education."

"I'm sure Mrs. Hopwood will be grateful," she replied in a flat, distant voice.

"I'm not doing it for her." With that nasty remark, Mrs. Ortiz stomped out of the office.

God, Mrs. Johnson thought, *I hate this job.*

THIRTY-ONE

So HE WAS getting out.

She had seen a newspaper in one of those contraptions, where you put fifty cents in and pull down the door, grabbing a copy. But Tracy didn't have fifty cents. She didn't have a dime, so all she could do was peer through the glass. And the headlines told the story of the release of George Ortiz.

She didn't have a dime and she was hungry. Some woman had given her five dollars yesterday but she spent it on a double cheeseburger—which she shared with Sugar Daddy—a bottled water for him, an order of fries and a small coffee. The small coffee was a mistake. It played havoc with her stomach and sent her straight to the ladies' room. She was there for a while when an employee came barging in and shouted at her through the stall.

"As soon as you're finished with your business, you got to leave. And get that mangy dog out of here."

"It's a service dog. I suffer from depression."

"Right now I'm the one who is suffering. We can't have you stinking up the bathroom."

The bathroom stunk plenty without her, but she left anyway, wishing she could sit a little longer, like a normal person.

The coffee kept her up all night, although she always slept fitfully under the bridge. In the winter social work-

ers would come round them up, like stray dogs, and
force them into shelters where she didn't dare close her
eyes. Now she plum refused to go because they wouldn't
let her bring Sugar Daddy. They said they would put
him in an animal shelter but she knew once they were
separated, she'd never get him back. And it wasn't like
they would find him a good home. They would probably gas him in no time. No way was Tracy going to
let that happen.

SHE CLOSED HER eyes and drifted off, her head against the
cold, hard pew. She dreamed of happier times, growing
up by the ocean before her mother died and she had to
move in with her grandmother.

A cold, hard, critical woman, she had never cared
for Tracy's father and reminded Tracy daily that she
was just like him, stupid and ugly, without an ounce
of common sense.

Maybe she was right and that's who Tracy was.

And maybe that's why Victor went looking in other
places, which got him killed.

Maybe if Tracy had had a sibling, a kind sister, or
even a cousin, someone would have taken her in, off the
streets, giving her a home, found her a job. But some
things were just destined to be.

And where was Robert all this time? It wasn't like
there was anyone to ask. But she missed him, the only
person she met who understood how hard life could be
living in the streets.

People came and went, mostly quickly. They'd kneel
down in front of a statue, say a quick prayer, bless themselves, then dash off to their own lives. One rather large
man entered huffing and puffing, approached the altar

and stood there for a few moments. Then he dug into his pocket and pulled out a bill. He went over to the poor slot. But he didn't put the money in.

Instead he placed the bill on top. And just before he left he glanced her way.

Once she heard his footsteps receding, she rose slowly, her legs swollen and stiff. She stumbled over to the corner of the church and saw the twenty dollar bill.

God bless him, she thought.

She crumbled up the bill and stuffed it into her flowered purse. She and Sugar Daddy would eat good tonight.

IT WAS LATE afternoon and colder than it had been in the morning. Tracy vaguely recalled that a poet once wrote that April was the cruelest month. For Tracy they were all cruel months.

On the way to the corner store—she was planning to buy a tuna sandwich, a cup of tea and maybe a large black and white cookie for dessert—she saw her.

Winifred Ortiz, coming from St. Polycarp School.

She had aged, grown heavier and the sexy vibe from years ago now just looked sloppy. But still she strutted down the street, as though she were entitled, as though she wasn't the wife of a murderer.

Tracy was walking in her direction and she stopped and stared severely at Winifred.

"I don't have any money. Sorry." Winifred shoved past her.

Tracy took the black hood off of her head, waiting for some recognition.

"I said I don't have any money!"

"You don't know me, do you?"

"Nope." And Winifred didn't want to know her, because she didn't even give her a second glance.

But Tracy kept following her, close behind, until Winifred whirled around and threatened to call a cop.

"And you know plenty about cops, don't you?" Tracy fired at her.

The expression on Winifred's face changed from anger to awareness. "You're Victor's wife."

"I *was* Victor's wife before your husband murdered him."

"Yeah," Winifred had started walking again. "That was a long time ago."

"Not for me. For me time has stood still."

"He paid his debt. Sometimes," Winifred's voice softened, "you gotta let go."

"Never," Tracy said and she would have added more but she saw Mrs. Hopwood coming towards them.

So she turned right around and she just walked away.

THIRTY-TWO

MRS. HOPWOOD WAS most surprised when she saw the homeless woman talking to a stranger in the street as she clutched the purse in front of her.

The thing that was rather puzzling was that they both stared at her, as though they knew her—well, the homeless woman did, kind of. And they stopped talking when she approached, parting apprehensively to let her pass.

But that was just the first of three very bizarre occurrences as she made her way home.

It was a cool April evening and Mrs. Hopwood had always been partial to cool weather. She could layer on clothes—more pretty things to wear. She didn't sweat—her hair remained frizz free—and it was easier to exercise. The walk home was less than a mile and it was already daylight savings time. Runners littered the curbs, mothers wheeled wailing toddlers from the park—an ice cream truck was parked on the corner of Franklin and Sycamore playing a happy tune.

Right there on Franklin Street she received the second shock. In the window of a rundown thrift store sat the bright blue bag she had given to Mrs. Sugarman.

Mrs. Hopwood was not one to notice details—not the easily forgotten ones like ingredients in a food. Faces tended to blend together, and she couldn't tell one location from another. But when it came to fashion, she could discern the smallest difference in size, shape, and prints.

And this was definitely the bag.

She marched in.

The man behind the counter was watching some sort of sports program on TV—sports were some of the details Mrs. Hopwood hardly noticed.

"I'm interested in that blue handbag in the window."

"Oh yeah." He grabbed the remote, clicking it to mute. "That's some beauty. Just got it in yesterday. Belonged to some woman's great grandmother. Perfect condition."

"And this woman did she have grayish spiked hair?"

"Could be."

"Well, that purse wasn't hers to sell. It's part of the vintage collection I inherited from my Aunt Eunice. It's all going to go on sale on May 13th at St. Polycarp, the profits to benefit the school. Maybe you'd like to come and bid on some of the merchandise."

"Maybe. But listen," he made a wide sweep with his flabby thin arms, "all this vintage stuff, it's all from someone's Grandma Millie or Aunt Nettie. Besides, possession is nine tenths of the law, so now I got the purse, it's mine. I'll tell you what I'll do since you look like a nice lady and it's for charity. I bought it for two hundred and fifty dollars. I'll sell it to you for three hundred."

"Three hundred dollars? For a handbag that's mine?" she asked in amazement.

He rubbed his dirty beard. "Hey, I just got your word that it's yours."

Mrs. Hopwood knew a losing battle when she fought one. "Will you take a check?"

He pointed to a sign, which had been scrawled on the wall. No Checks, No Credit, No Refunds, No Exchanges.

"I'm a Catholic School Teacher," she argued.

"Well, so was your friend. And according to you, she had no right to sell me the handbag. Sorry. You don't have a credit card?"

Mrs. Hopwood did not want to put anything more on her credit card. She was already overextended. Well, she'd make the school pay her back as soon as the purse was sold. She whipped out her American Express.

"Master Card and Visa only."

Feeling slightly ill, Mrs. Hopwood took out her Master Card.

THREE HUNDRED DOLLARS LATER, Mrs. Hopwood dragged home the heavy blue purse. Coupled with the school bag, she was so exhausted she considered taking the bus. But no bus was forthcoming so she trudged on.

Bending down in her front yard to pick up the evening paper, a wave of dizziness passed through her. But when she glanced at the headlines, the dizziness intensified and her stomach gave a weird lurch, as though she was on an elevator descending in a bumpy manner.

The two people Mrs. Hopwood had seen on the street, the homeless woman and the stranger had made the front page of the newspaper.

Mrs. Hopwood took the paper inside, sank on the couch, and read the article about George Ortiz's release from prison. The stranger she couldn't identify was hardly a stranger. She was Melissa Ortiz's mother. And the homeless woman? She was married to the victim.

The photographs were old and black and white taken

at the time of the murder. But the women were easily recognizable.

Without even taking off her crimson colored coat, Mrs. Hopwood reached for the phone.

"Is this about your observation?"

"My what?"

"Your observation."

"Hell, no. I don't care about that. Have you seen the newspaper?"

"Like I really have time to sit down and read a paper. Boys, you are supposed to be doing your math homework."

"There's an article about George Ortiz. He made parole."

"I know. His wife came in to see me."

Mrs. Hopwood felt her throat tighten. "What did she want?"

"She wanted to know why you are suddenly taking an interest in Melissa. She thinks it's because you want the scoop on her husband."

"Oh God! I think I ran into her in the street. Was she a heavyset woman, wearing too much make-up? She was talking to the homeless woman, whose name is Tracy, so we can stop calling her the homeless woman."

"Don't erase so hard and you won't get holes in the paper! I'm tired of giving you fresh paper!"

Mrs. Hopwood thought that she hadn't had a normal conversation with Mrs. Johnson since she had given birth.

"Then when I was walking home I went by the vintage shop, you know the one I mean, on Franklin? And what do you think I saw in the window?"

'I'm too tired to guess."

"The blue handbag I gave to Mrs. Sugarman. Evidently, she sold it for two hundred and fifty dollars."

"Really?" Mrs. Hopwood detected a slight interest in Mrs. Johnson's tone.

"I bought it back for three hundred dollars."

"Why?"

"Because it belongs with the rest of the stuff. I'll get reimbursed when it sells."

Mrs. Johnson paused and then said, "I hope you know what you're doing."

"And what's that supposed to mean?"

"Only that there is a lot going on, but nothing is actually happening."

"What I'm doing is trying to save the school, Amelia." Mrs. Hopwood looked down at her phone and noticed a voicemail. "I got to go."

Mrs. Johnson had hung up before she did.

The voicemail was from Mr. Hopwood telling her not to wait for dinner—which she had no intention of doing, since she hadn't even made dinner—because he was working late.

That made it three times in two weeks.

THIRTY-THREE

IT WAS SEVEN THIRTY in the morning and while, Mrs. Johnson was gulping down her coffee, taking huge bites of her buttered poppy seed bagel, she heard shouting in the front hall.

"I can't believe you would do such a thing! Here, out of the goodness of my heart, I gave you one of my aunt's vintage purses to use as your own, and you upped and sold it! I don't understand."

Mrs. Johnson entered the hall and saw an embarrassed Mrs. Sugarman cowering in the corner. "No, you wouldn't understand because you're healthy."

"Because I'm wealthy? I'm not wealthy!" Mrs. Hopwood protested.

"I think she said healthy," Mrs. Johnson said.

"Can't you tell that I'm sick?" The question was directed at Mrs. Hopwood but Mrs. Sugarman was staring at Mrs. Johnson. And Mrs. Johnson had to admit that Mrs. Sugarman didn't look well, pale, exhausted, clammy, sweaty. Dark shadows appeared under her reddened eyes. And there was a bad odor coming from her.

"I'm sorry you're not well," Mrs. Hopwood's voice softened just a touch with what sounded like a tentative apology. "But what does that have to do with selling my purse?"

"I needed money to buy my medication."

"What kind of medication?" Mrs. Hopwood sounded suspicious. "We have medical insurance."

"Not that kind of medication." Mr. Sugarman's hands were twitching slightly. "I have a very rare disease and the drugs are experimental. Insurance won't cover them."

"What is your sickness?" Mrs. Johnson was rather nosy herself. "Can't your family help you?"

"I don't have any family. And I'd rather not talk about my sickness. I just try to take one day at a time."

Mrs. Sugarman turned slowly and holding on to the barrister wobbled up the staircase.

"You didn't have to yell," Mrs. Johnson said.

"Something is not right about her," Mrs. Hopwood responded and quickly looked at her watch. "I'm going across the street for coffee."

"Your children will be swarming into the classroom at any minute."

"I got time. You want something?"

"I want a million things," Mrs. Johnson said, "but you can't get me any of them."

MRS. HOPWOOD WAS running a meeting after school with all the parent volunteers and the one cafeteria lady, Pearl. Mrs. Johnson thought she should be there to learn just what was going on, although she didn't have high expectations.

But she was pleasantly impressed when she saw that the meeting was well run and Mrs. Hopwood seemed to have everything under control, which couldn't be said for her classroom.

"I'll need for all fourteen of you to be behind the stage," she told them. "We have fifty-two outfits and fourteen models. Each of you will be assigned to a model. Your model will have to change three times. You're to help the models in and out of the clothing. Once the model undresses, you are to put the outfit on one of the padded hangers and place it on the rack. Students will wheel the rack out at intervals and hang the outfit under each description so buyers will be able to bid. I will send you all an email confirming this conversation. But in the meantime, are there any questions?"

"I have a question. I'm Melissa Ortiz's mother."

"Oh yes." Mrs. Hopwood nodded. "Melissa is a lovely girl."

"I want to see my daughter actually do the modeling."

"I understand that. But I really need the volunteers to be backstage."

"Why can't I be one of the people handing out the programs?"

"We have students to do that. Maybe your husband can take a video."

Everyone was silent, staring at Mrs. Ortiz.

"Is he coming?" Pearl narrowed her blue eyes.

"Yes, of course, he's coming." Mrs. Ortiz's face contorted with fury. "Why wouldn't he be coming? He's Melissa's father."

"Okay." Mrs. Hopwood quickly got a hold of the situation. "Make sure I have everyone's e-mail before you leave."

"I'd like to say a few words." Mrs. Johnson stepped up to the front of the room, ignoring Mrs. Hopwood's frown. "I just want to thank you all for volunteering. This fashion show means a lot to the future of St. Polycarp. So again, please understand how very grateful we are."

Reluctantly the women rose.

"Looks like things are going well," Mrs. Johnson said as soon as the volunteers vacated the room.

"You seem surprised," Mrs. Hopwood said with some relish.

"Relieved," Mrs. Johnson said.

MRS. JOHNSON WAS feeling nauseous, probably from the pain killer she had taken before lunch. A ginger pill—one of Mrs. Hopwood's rare good tips—was in order.

She entered her office and saw right away that her purse was missing.

It wasn't in the usual place, on the window sill, which perhaps wasn't too smart. She had told all the teachers to secure their values and here she was leaving hers in plain sight.

"Miss Turnipseed," she crossed the threshold and spoke to the school secretary, who was enjoying a cup of tea and some shortbread cookies—no doubt stolen from the cafeteria while Pearl looked the other way, "have you seen my handbag? You know the one I mean, the gray one?"

"No." Miss Turnipseed looked annoyed, and Mrs. Johnson didn't know if it was because she had been interrupted or because she felt as though she had been accused.

"Has anyone been in my office?"

Miss Turnipseed scrunched up her face in thought. "Now that you mention it, Mrs. Sugarman came in. She left an article for you she thought you might enjoy."

Mrs. Johnson went back into her office and glanced

at her desk. An article debating the benefits of cooperative education had been ripped out of a magazine and Mrs. Sugarman had attached a brief note.

Thought you might find this interesting.

Well, maybe Mrs. Johnson might, if she was still teaching and if she hoped to teach in the future. Right now cooperative learning was the very last thing on her mind. What she did find interesting was that Mrs. Sugarman, who never cared one iota about educational philosophy, used this article as an excuse to rob Mrs. Johnson.

Mrs. Johnson sank in her chair. She had a thief in the midst. Suddenly it all made sense, Mrs. Hopwood's purses, the missing keys to the school...

But what was Mrs. Johnson to do with this information? She had to confront Mrs. Sugarman, maybe even dismiss her on the spot. A scandal like this would certainly be the last nail in the school's coffin.

She couldn't put it off.

Wearily she rose and made her way to the second floor, passing the teacher's room.

And there it sat, right on the table, her gray purse.

Had she left it there, when she took her pills at noon? Was that possible?

A burst of relief washed over her. Mystery solved.

Except when she opened her purse, her pills were gone.

THIRTY-FOUR

THERE WAS LITTLE doubt in Melissa's mind that this was the worst day in her short and miserable life. The thought that her mother was going to be involved with Mrs. Hopwood filled her with dread.

Melissa was ashamed of her mother, mortified by her behavior. Married to a murderer, whom she cheated on and caused the death of an innocent man, and now she was welcoming home with open arms a killer, well, what kid wouldn't be ashamed?

Melissa took her time, walking home and trudged up the rickety steps of her tenement, into the dimly lit hallway, to the third floor. Appalled, she found her front door decorated with yellow streamers and a huge *Welcome Home* sign.

"So today's the day."

She whirled around to find Mr. Peroy, the super, and the soothsayer, standing behind her. His watery gray eyes mocked her and when he smiled she noticed that he was missing teeth on the bottom of his mouth.

"Yep, today is the day. And I can tell, you ain't thrilled."

Melissa rummaged through her backpack for her keys, struggling not to look at him. "My father served his time." She repeated the line she heard uttered so often by her mother.

"Bet you're wishing it was more time. Someone

should tell the neighborhood that a murderer is living in their midst."

"I'm sure you got that covered, Mr. Peroy." She flung the front door open and slammed it shut with such force that the Welcome Home Sign fell to the floor.

She waited a few moments and then looked out of the peephole. Mr. Penroy had left, she could hear his heavy footsteps on the stairs. She opened the door and picked up the Welcome Home sign. She crumpled it into tiny pieces and threw it into the incinerator.

"WHY DO WE have to wait so long to eat?" Adam whined. "I'm hungry now."

"You know why. It's a special dinner for your father. I explained all that. I'm going to pick him up at the bus station and we should be back around eight. I spent all morning cooking, fried chicken, French fries, broccoli and for dessert, his favorite, chocolate cake. I want everything to be special."

Including herself, Melissa thought. Her mother had dressed for the occasion, in one of her old party dresses. The problem was the stretching material was too tight, she was spilling out in the front, the orange fabric puckered around the waist, creating unflattering lumps. Melissa felt sorry for her.

"Why the long face, Melissa?" her mother asked.

"All that fried food isn't good for us."

"Your father has been in prison for twelve years. He'll be expecting a home cooked meal."

"Someone tore down your Welcome Home sign and threw it in the trash," Adam announced somewhat gleefully.

As though she didn't believe him, Melissa's mother

went to the door, opened it, and looked up and down the hall. "I think it must have been Penroy. I'm going to report him to the landlord." She closed the door and then asked Melissa when the fashion show was.

"I don't know," Melissa lied. "Why?"

"Because your father and I want to go. We want to sit right up there in the front row and cheer you on as you glide down the runway."

"Or trip down the runway." Adam grabbed a handful of peanuts.

"Adam, those are for your father!" When her mother slapped his hand, Melissa retreated into her bedroom.

Except it really wasn't her bedroom any more. Her mother had already moved in while Melissa was at school. A small cot was stuffed into the corner of the room, clothes piled up on the one chair. Her mother's make-up littered the bureau with the broken drawers. She had pushed aside Melissa's small jewelry box to make room for the lipstick tubes, the blush cases, the cold cream jars.

Melissa closed her eyes and leaned against her headboard. She wished that she could close her nose because her mother's cheap, heavy perfume was making her nauseous.

She wished that she was brave enough to run away. She entertained a daydream—Mrs. Hopwood would invite her to come and live inside a beautiful house and Melissa would escape all of this.

Well, maybe she would.

If Melissa told her how unbearable her home life was, and if Melissa made enough trouble for her father, maybe she would.

THIRTY-FIVE

MRS. HOPWOOD KNEW that she had to get rid of the shoes in the back of her classroom. For one thing, the boys kept bumping into them, breaking the bag further, and scattering the contents. Michael Waterson actually fell on a stray gray pump and cut his lip.

All Mrs. Hopwood needed now was a lawsuit.

But Mr. Salisbury was still out with some sort of horrid cold and Mrs. Hopwood couldn't possibly lift the bag by herself. And with Mrs. Johnson's bad back— not an option.

Maybe if she brought the shoes down in small stages. So after school, she decided to venture down to the dark, dank cellar to scout out the best place to store the shoes. She also wanted to make sure that none of the vintage clothes got left behind when the girls had gone down to fetch the outfits. While it was true she was standing on the stairs, while the girls complained, they completed the task quickly and carelessly.

Well, she was going to be quick about it also.

THE MOMENT SHE stepped into the basement Mrs. Hopwood knew that something was very wrong. For one thing the odor was overwhelming, so much so that she didn't dare to breathe. An army of rats must have died in the wall.

Maybe putting the shoes down her wasn't such a

good idea after all. The dust and the dirt was staining her own pink and lavender polka dot shoes.

She was just about to leave when she noticed a piece of red material sticking out in front of the boiler. The temptation not to look was overwhelming. But the rumbling above—students being dismissed—gave her a shot of courage and she approached the boiler with great trepidation. No, this couldn't be one of Aunt Eunice's garments. For one thing, it was filthy and for another? And for one another—it was attached to a long, very white arm!

Her eyes widening in horror, she glanced at the bloated, unrecognizable face. She tried to scream but no sound came out of her mouth. Instead she ran, tripping several times, scrambling up the stairs and bursting into Mrs. Johnson's office.

MRS. JOHNSON WAS on the phone, arguing about some unpaid bill and she shot Mrs. Hopwood an annoyed look.

"Yes, but you are billing us for services we never received. We had no learning specialist the entire year. The state was supposed to send us someone…"

Mrs. Hopwood slammed the door. "Hang up, it's an emergency."

Mrs. Johnson shook her head. "Of course, I am not going to pay for it. That's ridiculous."

Mrs. Hopwood decided to take matters into her own hands. She stormed over and hung up on Mrs. Johnson.

"What is the matter with you?" Mrs. Johnson's face was a mixture of shock and fury.

"There is a dead man in our cellar."

"What?"

"I found a dead man behind the boiler."

For several long moments Mrs. Johnson did not reply. Then she said in a scared, little voice, "Are you sure?"

"Do you mean are you sure I saw him? Or am I sure he's dead? Both!"

"Is it anyone we know?"

"I didn't recognize him. His face was all puffy, like he's been dead for ages. But he was dead all right."

Mrs. Johnson hid her face in her hand.

For a moment Mrs. Hopwood thought she might start to cry. "We have to get rid of him."

"Are you suggesting that we move the body?"

"Of course not. We have to call the police, but in the meantime, we have to keep this quiet."

Mrs. Johnson sat in her chair, staring, as though she was paralyzed.

"Do you hear me? If the word gets around that this man—a dead man—met his demise in our basement where we were storing the clothes, that's the end of the fashion show."

"What are you talking about?" Mrs. Johnson leaped up. "A man is dead and all you're worried about is the fashion show."

"Well, maybe you would like some bad publicity."

"What if it's Mr. Salisbury?" Mrs. Johnson said. "He might have just dropped dead down there."

"No, I don't think so. I mean, I saw his hair. It was brownish. Mr. Salisbury's hair, whatever little he has, is white."

"I can't do this anymore," Mrs. Johnson said. "I can't do this anymore. I can't do this anymore."

"Well, at the least, could you call the police?"

Mrs. Johnson just sat there, shaking her head. Mrs.

Hopwood grabbed the phone and dialed 911. "My name is Julia Hopwood. I am a teacher at the St. Polycarp School on 92 Franklin Street. There is a dead body in our basement."

THIRTY-SIX

MRS. JOHNSON KNEW that in the years to come, she would remember this as one of the worst periods in her life.

By the time the police arrived most of the teachers had already left. Thank God Addison and Casey had a Pilates class. Only Mrs. Sugarman was in her classroom and when she saw the police, she asked a lot of questions, which Mrs. Johnson simply said, she could not answer at the time.

Mrs. Hopwood led the way into the cellar and then she begged whoever would listen not to tell anyone where the body was. She went into a long explanation of how the clothes were going to be auctioned off and if anyone knew that a dead body had been found nearby, no one would feel good wearing them. The policeman—a young man who couldn't be more than twenty-five—just stared at her with a blank, uncaring expression.

The woman, stout, short, and surly, introduced herself as Officer Vogt and then pointed to the male cop, Office Healy.

Mrs. Johnson stood with Mrs. Hopwood as the police stomped over to the boiler.

"One of the homeless," Vogt said. "I've seen him around. I think his name is Robert. Could have been hiding out in the basement for a while." She turned towards the teachers and asked who was in charge.

Tentatively Mrs. Johnson raised her hand.

"Do you know if he was hiding out here?" she asked.

Mrs. Johnson was ashamed to say that she had no idea.

"Hangs around the bridge, begs money for liquor." Vogt bent down and brought up an empty bottle of gin. "Poor guy probably drank himself to death."

Mrs. Johnson heard the wailing sirens and minutes later two burly looking guys came trudging down the stairs, holding a stretcher.

"Is that it?" Mrs. Johnson asked, slightly relieved. Until she saw Mrs. Hopwood pick up a piece of paper in the corner of the cellar.

"I'll have the coroner look him over but we usually don't do autopsies when there is no reason to suspect foul play."

Suddenly Mrs. Hopwood was staring at the body and Mrs. Johnson decided she was not going to ask her what was wrong. Not in front of the police. Not ever.

"Please don't say anything about where he was found," Mrs. Hopwood pleaded with Vogt.

"Why would we?" Vogt shrugged her shoulders.

"What's going on there?" Mrs. Sugarman shrieked from the stairs. Mrs. Johnson was going to do her very best to ignore her.

"Stay where you are," an EMT worker yelled. "Coming through."

"Oh my God!" she yelled, "what happened?"

The moment the police headed for the stairs, Mrs. Hopwood stuck a piece of paper in Mrs. Johnson's face. It was a dry cleaning receipt with Dagny Danver's name on it.

"This is supposed to mean something?" Mrs. Johnson whispered, heat rising on her face.

"He had a bump on his head," Mrs. Hopwood whispered back.

"Don't even think it!" Mrs. Johnson said in a soft and deadly voice.

THIRTY-SEVEN

TRACY WAS LEAVING the church when she saw an ambulance pull up in front of the school. It was late afternoon, so they were probably not coming for one of the students. A teacher perhaps? Hopefully not, Mrs. Hopwood. Tracy knew her name now because she had found one of the brochures on the church floor. Mrs. Hopwood seemed like a kind lady, a good lady.

Tracy stood on the side, trying to be invisible, waiting.

It took a while but the door flew open and two men emerged carrying a stretcher. A stretcher with a body on it but the body was covered with a sheet, so Tracy had no idea who it was. Somehow though she had a very bad feeling. Sugar Daddy darted out and he followed the men, just as they were sliding the body into the back of the ambulance. The sheet slipped off and Tracy saw Robert.

His face was white and distorted, bloated. He had been dead for several days. Her eyes fill with tears. She always knew that he would probably end up dead, but not like this. Well, at least he had died in the school not on the cold, hard streets.

"Excuse me?" She looked up and saw a woman cop in front of her. "Do you know this man?"

Tracy could have lied, but what was the point. She

nodded. "His name was Robert Ryan Reynolds. He was sleeping in the basement of the school."

"That's what we figured." The woman looked down at Sugar Daddy. "Your dog?"

Again Tracy nodded.

For one, brief, horrible minute Tracy thought that she was going to take Sugar Daddy away but the cop just shook her head and headed for the cruiser.

Tracy went back into the church and said a silent prayer that Robert was finally at peace.

THIRTY-EIGHT

I JUST HAVE to get through the day, Mrs. Sugarman told herself. *If I can do that I'll be okay.* Logan had sent her a text late last night instructing her to meet him that evening at ten o'clock on the corner of Essex and Pine—and to have two hundred and fifty dollars in small bills.

She knew that both Mrs. Johnson and Mrs. Hopwood were angry at her. But she also knew that, for some reason, they didn't want to speak about the man who had died in the basement, although the air in the school with already thick with rumors and suspicions. Mrs. Sugarman had been at the top of the stairs. She saw the body being removed and she couldn't help but wonder if it had been there when she had picked out the dress. At this point Mrs. Sugarman was determined to keep quiet, because why cause trouble? However, if Mrs. Johnson did not give her a glowing recommendation in the fall—assuming St. Polycarp was closing—then Mrs. Sugarman would tell everyone that the clothing they had bought for a hefty price may have been covering a dirty and dead man.

SHE FLOATED THROUGH the day, giving her students written assignments, which she would probably never get around to correcting. But active teaching was not a possibility for her.

At three fifteen she sprang out of the building, and, on the way to the parking lot, she passed the church. A homeless woman with a skinny dog was sitting on the steps. Dressed in all black, she looked like the grim reaper enjoying the sunny April day.

But it wasn't her clothing that caught Mrs. Sugarman's eye. It was her purse, a pretty flowered handbag, one that looked as if it might be one from Mrs. Hopwood's vintage collection.

"Excuse me." Mrs. Sugarman climbed up a few steps.

The woman's tiny eyes—which were sunken—darted around, as though she wasn't sure whom Mrs. Sugarman was addressing.

"I can't help but admire your stunning purse." The only response was a nod. "I collect handbags myself and I'd love to buy it from you. I would give you twenty dollars."

"No." The answer was firm and final. "It was a gift."

"From Mrs. Hopwood?" No reply. "I'm a teacher at the school also. I don't know if you're aware of it, but that purse was supposed to be sold at an auction to benefit St. Polycarp. Mrs. Hopwood had a lot of clothing and purses to sell but she stored them in our cellar and some of them were ruined by a dead man, so now she's scrambling for merchandise." The woman did not look impressed, as she began to scrutinize Mrs. Sugarman. "I could give you fifty dollars for it. As much as I love pocket books, I'd return it right back to Mrs. Hopwood, and I know that she'd be grateful."

"I'd have to hear that from Mrs. Hopwood." She blew her long and greasy hair off her wide, flat face.

"Listen…"

"Pardon me." Mrs. Sugarman turned around. A heavy jawed woman, dressed in gym clothes, stood behind her and smiled feebly. She looked vaguely familiar. "I'm Mrs. Rome, Clarice's mother."

"Happy to meet you." Mrs. Sugarman extended a

sweaty hand, wishing that she could run into the church, the way the homeless woman had, with the little dog following her eagerly.

"I'm sorry we haven't met before." Mrs. Rome gave her a small smile, which quickly turned to a grimace. "My husband came to the midyear parent/teacher conference. I was in Brazil."

"No problem." Her stomach dropped and Mrs. Sugarman knew that she'd have to visit a bathroom soon. "Clarice is doing splendidly."

"Well, I wouldn't know that because I haven't seen a test paper in months. Clarice said you give them a lot of written work, but you never correct it, or return it, or go over it."

For a moment Mrs. Sugarman thought about lying, saying that Clarice perhaps had misplaced the assignments. But Mrs. Rome looked like the sort of lady who might have a lot of other parents on her side. Mrs. Sugarman wiped the perspiration off her face before responding nervously. "I am so sorry about that. I haven't been well, you know, a rare disease."

For a moment, concern crossed over on Mrs. Rome's face. "I'm sorry to hear that. And, of course, you'll be in my prayers. Nevertheless, our children deserve to be taught. Perhaps Mrs. Johnson could hire a substitute."

"No. I've been to the doctors and I'm going on medication. I'll be fine. And I'll be returning those papers in a few days."

"I certainly hope so."

"If you'll excuse me, I'm late for a meeting," Mrs. Sugarman said, as she hurried away. "I'm on the board at the Children's Hospital and I have to go over some plans for the renovations."

Mrs. Sugarman barely made it home and into her bathroom.

MRS. SUGARMAN HAD never met a drug dealer before and she thought it best that she change out of her teacher clothes, wear something casual, covered by a nondescript trench coat. The meeting place planned was in a rather seedy part of town, so she decided to take a cross body purse, keep it tightly against her chest, with the stuffed bills inside. It was while she was looking for that handbag that she came across another.

The purse was very similar to the one she had sold. It was the same ocean blue and had a similar size and shape. And she must have bought it at least ten years ago.

Mr. Stronghold had no idea what a vintage purse looked like. She could easily sell this one to him—after all it was in good condition—and he'd never be the wiser. And she would be the richer. A perfect solution.

She dragged out her laptop and worked carefully on the e-mail. She was sweating so much, her fingers kept slipping. But when she was finally finished, she was satisfied with what she had written.

Hi,
I work at St. Polycarp School and I know from Mrs. Hopwood that you are looking to acquire vintage pocketbooks. I am one of the teachers she gave a handbag to. I'd like to sell my vintage purse.

She was not lying because nowhere in the email did she indicate that she was selling the purse she had actually been given nor did she refer directly to the e-mail that he had sent to Mrs. Hopwood.

It's sky blue and in excellent condition. I would like two hundred dollars for it.

Please let me know if you're interested.

Taking pains not to use her real name, she signed it *Purse Collector*, and after reading it several times, pressed the send button.

It wasn't until she closed down her computer that she realized she hadn't been thinking straight. Of course, Mr. Stronghold would know her name, because her address was nancysugarman@StPolycarp.

But really for once she hadn't done anything wrong.

SHE WAS WALKING out the door, when she glanced down at her phone and noticed she had an email from Mr. Stronghold.

Thanks for reaching out. Is this a purse from Mrs. Hopwood's collection?

Mrs. Sugarman thought that this was very weird. Why was it only Mrs. Hopwood's purses that he was interested in? Although the purse that she was offering was hardly vintage, Stonghold didn't know that. There must be something about Mrs. Hopwood's purses that made them different.

It wouldn't hurt to lie.

Yes, of course.

Like lightning the response came.

When and where can we meet?

Mrs. Sugarman didn't think it was wise to meet him in any abandoned place. She was seeing Logan at ten.

Cozy Café was not too far. Although she wasn't sure of the clientele, at least it was well lit. She wished she could meet Mr. Stronghold before Logan, which would give her more cash to buy more pills.

Cozy Café at ten fifteen.

You got it. And this is from Mrs. Hopwood's collection. Right?

Right. It was stored in the basement. Police are questioning who saw what. I was at the top of the stairs. I'm willing to sell the purse cheap because it was around the dead man.

SHE WASN'T SURE why she wrote all that, maybe to make herself and the purse more interesting. And it wasn't as if it has been a secret. People saw a body being carried out. Well, that was the problem with e-mail. You pressed that send button and whatever you wrote disappeared into space and there wasn't a darn thing you could do about it.

Stronghold didn't write back. Probably thought that she was some sort of a nut. She grabbed the blue purse and she was on her way.

AT EVERY STOPLIGHT, she checked her phone. No response from Mr. Stronghold. Maybe he suspected it wasn't vintage. Maybe she shouldn't have said anything about the dead body. Maybe that statement gave him the willies.

She parked on the corner of the old abandoned tenements. The night had started to darken and from nowhere she heard the sound of a dog crying and large popping sounds. She hoped what she heard were firecrackers. She wouldn't do this again. She'd get clean. She'd get help.

There was no place to park in the area, so she had to leave her car several streets away. She was reluctant to leave the blue purse in the car, even though it wasn't valuable, some thief might think it contained money.

So carrying two purses, she emerged from the car and sprinted the two blocks, feeling apprehensive. Would she even recognize Logan? Maybe a thief would get her first, maybe a rapist.

As she stood there waiting, she thought about the purses. Why was Stronghold so intent on getting Mrs. Hopwood's purses? Was it because there was something in one of them? The pill box she found with the initials DD on it was hardly significant. Maybe the compact that Mrs. Hopwood displayed on the brochure had been in that purse also.

Maybe just maybe there was something hidden in the compact. It could have a fake bottom. She would have to think of a way to steal it.

Where was Logan anyway? Was he late? Was he not coming? How silly of her to think that drug dealers would be reliable.

Maybe he sent her a message. No—but she noticed that she had an email.

Her heart pounded when she saw that it was from Stronghold.

Where are you?

I'm sorry. I'm waiting for someone who is late.

I'm in a hurry. Can I come to where you are?

Now Mrs. Sugarman was torn. On one hand, she wanted the money she could get for the bogus purse, but, on the other hand, this was a deserted street. But really, if she was willing to meet a drug dealer, a man who was giving his mother vintage purses had to be safer.

I'm on the corner of Essex and Pine.

And this is definitely one of Mrs. Hopwood's purses?

Now Mrs. Sugarman was beginning to get really annoyed. Even in her muddled brain, she knew that this had nothing whatsoever to do with vintage purses and everything to do with specific purses, the purses Mrs. Hopwood had.

I told you it was. But my question to you is do you want the actual purse or something in the purse? I know there was a compact. Mrs. Hopwood had that. But I found something else. Do you want that also?

No answer.

Well, maybe Stronghold would answer her when he came.

She put the phone back in her pocket and took it out a moment later when it vibrated. But it was only an e-mail advertising a remedy for people who were going deaf.

She heard something behind her. Quickly she turned around, expecting to see Logan, or a tall, imposing man.

Instead she saw something quite different, someone somewhat familiar, who was clutching something hard and heavy, heading straight for her head.

A white hot pain ripped through her and then Mrs. Sugarman felt nothing at all.

THIRTY-NINE

"WHAT ARE YOU DOING?" Mrs. Johnson asked as soon as Mrs. Hopwood picked up the phone.

"I'm waiting for Monte to come home. I think he's having an affair."

"Why?"

"He seems to be working late much more often."

"Well, he's fairly new at the job and maybe he's just trying to prove himself."

"I don't think so. He says that all I ever do is talk about St. Polycarp and he's sick to death hearing about it."

"We're all sick to death hearing about it," Mrs. Johnson said.

"I discovered a dead body. Do you have any idea how horrible that was? I'm going to see that face forever. Trouble seems to follow me wherever I go!"

Mrs. Hopwood expected some sympathy but instead Mrs. Johnson said, "Listen, I'm not so sure that I should be telling you this, but we've been friends for a long time and I have to confide in someone…"

Mrs. Hopwood felt her heart thump a bit faster at the thought that someone else might be in trouble. "What?"

"I think Mrs. Sugarman is a drug addict."

"Why?"

"A lot of things are starting to make sense. The way she's desperate for money. She told me that her niece needed a dress for the prom and then she asked if I could lend her two hundred and fifty dollars. Well, of course, I couldn't and I didn't, but I offered to give her a dress."

"I remember."

"Well, do you remember when we were talking to her? She said she had no family?"

"That's right!"

"And then there were Addison's missing pills, which were blamed on Jason Briggs."

"Addison was missing pills?"

"And then she gave the dentist a bum check."

"You didn't tell me any of this." For a moment Mrs. Hopwood was miffed and saddened, remembering the days when the two teachers shared everything.

"Because at the time it didn't seem relevant. But I wouldn't be surprised if she was behind those handbag robberies. I think she took my pain pills from my purse today."

"But why would she rob my purses? I don't have any pills."

"Maybe she was looking for more vintage handbags to sell."

"What are you going to do?" Mrs. Hopwood asked, wondering how she could become involved.

"I don't know. I can't just ignore it and allow her to keep teaching. That would be irresponsible. Plus she's got a big mouth. She could go around and tell people that the dead guy could have made a bed out of the clothes you're looking to sell for thousands of dollars. I hate this job. It's as though St. Polycarp School is cursed."

"Oh my God!" A memory flashed for Mrs. Hopwood and she wondered why she hadn't thought of it sooner.

"What's the matter? Did you see a mouse?"

"Worse. Do you remember the girl in my second grade classroom who had bugs in her hair?"

"Your entire second grade classroom always had bugs in their hair. I think *you* even had bugs in your hair."

"Maybe. But this particular girl would not delouse. And Father Felix told her grandmother that the student was not welcome in the school until she did. The grandmother stood in the hall and pointed her bony finger at us, me and Father Felix, and cursed the school. Don't you remember?"

"No. I was probably upstairs preparing for the morning."

"And, right after that, all those people got murdered. Now do you remember?"

"I could hardly forget."

"Do you remember the name of that girl? Sunlight, maybe or Moonbeam? She had dark hair and big brown eyes."

"How am I supposed to remember the names of all those ragamuffins you taught?"

"Some of those ragamuffins are now my fifth graders, although this girl never came back. Father Felix would remember her name. Do you happen to have an address for him?" Mrs. Hopwood asked hopefully.

"No, but..."

"But what?"

"He's my friend on Facebook."

Mrs. Hopwood felt a flash of envy. "Really? Why didn't he ask to be my friend?"

"Do you ever go on Facebook?"

"Not a lot."

"Why do you want to get in touch with him anyway?"

"I have to find that old woman."

"I'm afraid," Mrs. Johnson paused, "to ask why."

"She has to remove the curse."

"You have got to be kidding."

"You believe in God, don't you?" Mrs. Hopwood insisted.

"Of course."

"Then you have to believe in the devil."

"I believe in the devil," Mrs. Johnson said, "but I do think with everything that is going on in the world, the devil has better things to do than think of ways to torment the teachers at St. Polycarp."

"The devil is everywhere. I have to go." And then because she didn't want to appear unsympathetic, Mrs. Hopwood added, "I'm sorry for your troubles."

"You don't get it. My troubles are your troubles."

"They'll be no one's troubles, if I have anything to say about it."

QUARTER PAST SEVEN and still Monte wasn't home. Well, maybe that was for the best.

She opened her Facebook apt, went to the search button, punched in Father Felix's name and immediately sent a friend request.

And then she waited.

The watch told her it was time to breathe. Yeah right.

She waited for Father Felix to get back to her. She waited for Monte to come home and while she waited she clicked on her apple watch, on apps she would never use, checking her Facebook page every fifteen minutes. And then one hour later, she got a response.

Hello, Julia Hopwood. So nice to hear from you. Miss you and Amelia Johnson but loving Rome and the Vatican. Missing St. Polycarp too. Heard about what happened in the fall and hoping things have calmed down. Let's keep in touch and let me know when you'll be visiting Italy.

Visiting Italy? Was he kidding? She wasted no time responding.

Things are not calm at St. Polycarp. Not at all. The school is in total shambles and Mrs. Johnson, who is the interim principal, is clearly overwhelmed. We just found out that one of the teachers is a drug addict and the diocese is threatening to close us. And a homeless man died in our basement. Can you believe it? Do you remember that old woman who cursed the school, when you threw her lice infected granddaughter out? I can't think of her name! I have to find her and beg her to remove the curse.

She was reading what she had written when the front door slammed. She quickly jabbed the post button. Monte looked exhausted and slightly irritated, so she offered to make him some scrambled eggs. He declined, said he had already eaten, and just wanted to watch a little television and go to bed.

She stayed up a bit longer, waiting for a reply, which came just before she turned in.

Curses? I don't know about curses, but I do remember the woman. Can't remember her name, but I believe the student was Starlight Moony. Maybe you should try praying, Julia, and, of course, you're always in my prayers as well. Ciao.

Mrs. Hopwood would find that woman, if it was the last thing she did.

SHE WAS DREAMING of the fun house at Mountain Park— an amusement park which had long ago closed—when she heard the theme from *The Alfred Hitchcock Presents* playing.

Like most people who wake from a sound sleep, at first she thought it was just part of a dream. But when she heard Monte grunt and he nudged her, her eyes flew open.

The look of terror in Monte's face brought her back to reality. She knew exactly what her husband was thinking. Alex. Their son was away at college and, while he didn't have a car, his roommate did and they often went out drinking in town with the locals.

Drinking and driving.

"I can't," she whispered, her chest tightening, her breath coming fast and shallow.

Monte reached over, shoved her aside and grabbed her cell phone off the bedside table.

"Hello." Mrs. Hopwood heard his voice quiver and she watched as the worried expression on his face changed to one of annoyance. "It's your partner." He threw the cell phone at her.

"What's the matter with you?" Mrs. Hopwood looked at the cable box, her fear changing to fury. "It's four thirty in the morning. You scared us half to death."

"What's the matter with me?! I think the question

has to be, what's the matter with you? I got up at four, to say the rosary, but first I check my e-mail..."

"Well, that's very nice, but why should I care?"

"And then I check my Facebook page."

Mrs. Hopwood was a fully awake now and when she heard the word Facebook, she quickly said, "I got in touch with Father Felix and he answered me. I told him..."

"I know exactly what you told him. So do thousands of other people."

"What are you talking about? I only have fifty friends."

"You have no idea how social media works, do you?"

"Well," Mrs. Hopwood mumbled nervously.

"Fifty people share your post with fifty of their friends and then you have two thousand, five hundred people who share the post with fifty of their friends. You criticized my leadership..."

"I did not. I just said you were overwhelmed. Besides, I thought I was answering him privately. How did I know it was going out to all those people?"

"It clearly was. You wrote about a curse in the school. You don't think that someone from the diocese will hear about that? You sound like a deranged woman. And then to make matters worse, if it were possible to make matters worse, you posted that one of the teachers is a drug addict and a dead man was found in our basement. I wouldn't be surprised if Mrs. Sugarman decides to sue the school and you in particular."

"That's ridiculous. I never mentioned her by name."

"Every parent at St. Polycarp will be wondering if it's her child's teacher whos's the drug addict. I knew I never should have shared that information with you. I knew that you couldn't be trusted. You're right, though. I'm not a very good leader. I have very bad judgment. But you, you're the reason that St. Polycarp won't be opening in the fall. That's all on you."

The connection was broken.

Mrs. Hopwood glanced at her husband, who had snatched two pillows and the pink comforter off the bed. "I'm sleeping in Alex's room, that's if I can go back to sleep."

Mrs. Hopwood wasn't even going to try. She glanced down at her phone and saw on the Facebook app that she had seven messages.

She was too frightened to look.

FORTY

TRACY HEARD THE sounds of wailing sirens as she woke on that overcast April morning. That screeching noise had always frightened her. She had a recurring dream that she was terrified might come true. They were coming for her, coming to arrest her, to put her in some tiny cell, for some imaginable crime, just because she happened to be homeless.

She opened her eyes and realized that she and Sugar Daddy who was cuddling next to her heart weren't alone. A frail stick of a man, dressed in ragged clothes, had been sleeping almost on top of her. She could smell his breath, a combination of tobacco and whiskey, and she could smell his body, feces and urine.

At first she thought it was Robert but then she remembered that Robert was dead. The poor guy—who never done anything to anyone—died—probably with a bottle beside him. Well, at least it was painless. Hopefully he closed his eyes and just never reopened them.

Grabbing her purse, she checked her meager belongings. A ripped and ragged wallet, a key to her apartment where she had been evicted twelve years ago, a worn down red lipstick, some sanitizing wipes she had stolen from a ladies' room, some broken and stale cookies, a cracked mirror, two wrinkled dollars and a picture of her and Victor. She got up quickly, shoving the man off of her. He didn't stir.

It had turned cold, a spiteful chilly spring wind under an iron gray sky. She tightened her hoodie around her. She had only walked a few steps when she spotted a small purse thrown carelessly near the gutter.

She picked it up and slowly unsnapped it.

A wallet with ten dollars in it, an unwrapped mint and a single bobby pin. But at the bottom of the purse she found something else, also. Something else that made her everything around her spin. A bulky envelope, with two tiny initials in the corner, TT. Before she even opened it, Tracy guessed that it probably contained cash, and she was right.

A lot of cash.

Her eyes darting in disbelief, she quickly counted it. Two hundred and fifty dollars.

Someone must have dropped it but, even if she wanted to give it back, she would hardly know to whom. The purse contained no identification. If she turned it into the police, they might even keep the money, split it amongst themselves.

Two hundred and fifty dollars would buy a lot, maybe even a room somewhere. She could sneak Sugar Daddy in and they could sleep in a real bed and she could take a shower. Have a piece of steak, a baked potato and green beans.

What she should do was to go into a drugstore and get some stomach medicine. The fast food from the night before—the fish sandwich and the crispy onion rings—had not gone down well. The cash she just found would give her some relief but how long could she go eating all that cheap food with so little nutritional value before she developed some horrible disease?

Well, a disease would put her in the hospital and that wouldn't be such a bad thing.

Except what would become of Sugar Daddy, her faithful friend, who never left her side? Tracy knew that she didn't have long to go, living on the streets. But she wasn't about to die, not until she found a nice home for Sugar Daddy. Sugar Daddy was old though—probably never saw a vet in all of his miserable life. Who would want him?

She had just reached High Street when she saw it.

A bevy of policemen, police cars, fire engines, reporters, all gathered together. One of the policemen had yellow tape in his hand and he was partitioning off the area.

She spotted a blue purse and lying several feet away the body of a woman with a bloody face and an expression frozen in fear. Tracy recognized the lady, the lady who had offered to buy Tracy's flowered handbag.

She couldn't help but scream, the sound instantly drawing the attention of the surrounding police. They gaped at her curiously.

Tracy hadn't survived this long on the street without developing some strong instincts and every instinct was telling her to run. Of course, she couldn't run. That would look suspicious and one thing she didn't want to do was to draw any more attention to herself. But she had to leave fast.

She turned around and scuttled in the opposite direction, as quickly as possible, ignoring the man who called after her.

She couldn't return to the church. They would identify the dead woman soon enough, connecting her to

St. Polycarp. Someone would talk about the homeless lady who hung out in the church.

Was the woman murdered?

Suddenly the money which had been so welcoming and so tempting made her wonder. Could it have been connected to the dead woman? If they found out that Tracy took the purse, they would think that she had killed the lady and then robbed her. The small handbag was swinging wildly from her hand. She threw it in the first a trash bin she saw.

But somehow Tracy could not bring herself to throw away the cash.

Meanwhile, she would hide in the public library.

FORTY-ONE

MRS. JOHNSON FELT as though she was trudging through a nightmare. Just when she thought that things had to turn around, something more horrific happened.

And now this. How on earth was she supposed to do damage control? She had no idea. She was an elementary school teacher, that's all she ever wanted to be. Well, Mrs. Hopwood was right about one thing.

She was clearly overwhelmed.

And about to layer on more trouble.

SHE WAS COMING out of the shower, into the kitchen, to brew her first cup of morning coffee. She glanced down at her cell phone. Missed call.

Probably from some hysterical parent, who managed to get her personal number. No doubt Mrs. Johnson was going to spend the entire morning dodging questions about the drug addict teacher. But when Mrs. Johnson looked again at her phone, her heart gave a hard thud.

Dr. Winters.

Dr. Winters was her primary care doctor, and, no doubt, he was probably calling about the results of her MRI. But what doctor called at six thirty in the morning, unless it was urgent—unless they wanted a patient to come in immediately to see an oncologist, to talk about options.

Suddenly the problems at St. Polycarp seemed insignificant, even silly. Who cared about one lone Catholic school in the middle of nowhere? What did her job really matter? She could do something else, go into real estate, run for office—open a restaurant.

She could do something else, as long as she was healthy. As long as there wasn't a tumor growing inside her spine, a tumor that may have spread to organs. Maybe chemo would help, she would get a wig, if she had too. But the thought of her little boys growing up without her…

She would fight. She would win. She would do whatever it took to stay alive for them.

Should she wake her husband?

No, not until she knew what she was dealing with.

With a shaking finger, she pressed the call back button.

Dr. Winters answered right away.

"Amelia."

"I'm so sorry I missed you," she said in a hushed voice. "I was taking a shower."

"No problem. I apologize for calling so early but I wanted to get back to you as soon as possible." The sentence sounded ominous to Mrs. Johnson. If it were good news, he wouldn't care about getting back to her soon. "Did you listen to my voice mail?"

She hadn't noticed any voice mail. It didn't matter. She needed to talk to the doctor directly. "Is it bad?" She was gasping for breath. "Do I have to come in for a biopsy? Can we schedule it as soon as possible? Maybe today?"

"No, no, no, to all of your questions." The tight, heavy feeling in her chest eased slightly. "There is nothing wrong with you, Julia. Your MRI was clean, no disc problems, no sign of inflammation…"

Mrs. Johnson sank on the kitchen floor. One moment relief flooded over her, the next moment she was skeptical. "But how can that be? I'm in pain."

"Are you under a lot of stress?"

"As a matter of fact, I am."

"Well, that could explain it. If you want, I could prescribe some anti-anxiety meds for you, but long term, I think you might benefit by talking to a good therapist."

"I will get back to you on that. Thank you."

Well, she wasn't dying, that was the good news, even though she experienced some apprehension. She had heard numerous stories of negative tests, of pain that didn't go away, and then a few months down the road, the patient was hospitalized with stage four. The moment she got into work, Mrs. Johnson was going to google what MRIs don't show.

This was the sort of thing she would have shared with Mrs. Hopwood, who could be supportive and comforting in times of crisis.

But not now.

And the way that Mrs. Johnson was feeling, not ever.

SHE WAS GULPING down her coffee and taking big bites of her cream donut, when Miss Turnipseed burst into her office, tightening her lumpy olive green cardigan around her bony shoulders, looking haughty and unruffled. Well, why shouldn't she be unruffled? She didn't have to solve any problems.

"Deborah Harris just sent a note up with a student. She's down in the cafeteria, ready to bring her pupils up and start the day."

"What's the trouble?" Mrs. Johnson couldn't keep the bitterness out of her voice.

"She said that there is no teacher for the seventh grade," Miss Turnipseed said solemnly.

Mrs. Johnson felt a sharp pain run down her back. "What?"

"Mrs. Sugarman is not there."

"Didn't she sign in?"

Miss Turnipseed whipped out the sign-in pad, which she had been keeping behind her back. "No, she did not."

"Did she call in?"

"No, she did not."

All Mrs. Johnson could surmise was that somehow Mrs. Sugarman found out about the Facebook post and she was too mortified to do her job. "That's just great. I'll have to go down. In the mean, call someone on the sub list and have him here as soon as possible."

"Should I tell them not to send the cross eyed man with the crooked bow tie?"

"They can send a rabid dog for all I care. Just get someone in here. Please!"

WHEN MRS. JOHNSON stepped inside the cafeteria, the seventh grade class was clearly out of control.

But not for long.

Just the angry expression on her face quieted them down.

"We're going upstairs," she told them, "and I don't want to hear a sound."

They were mute until they hit the classroom and she started to take attendance. Then they all began speaking at once.

"Sunshine is absent."

"So is Grayson."

"He's faking it because he was up all night playing games on his iPad."

"I didn't ask who was absent, did I?" Her thunderous voice broke through the babble. "I will call your name. If you're here, you will say present. If not, I will assume you are among the missing. In the meantime, please turn to page," she grabbed the religion book off of Mrs. Sugarman's very messy desk and she flipped through the pages, "turn to page ninety-two. There you will find a list of the seven deadly sins. You are to choose one of the sins and explain the sin in detail, writing it in your journal. You are to use not less than one hundred and fifty words."

The assignment caused bedlam.

"We don't have journals."

"We already did page ninety-two. We're up to page one hundred and eleven."

"I can pass out the lined paper."

"There isn't any lined paper. I can pass out the construction paper."

"Can it be a short story?"

"Does it have to be a sin we committed?"

"Quiet!"

The deafening tone of her voice caused the class to be silent except for one skinny boy, Caleb Clarin, who had red streaks in his blond hair—clearly against St. Polycarp's rules. "All we ever do in this class is write," he complained.

Mrs. Johnson slapped the attendance book across the desk and sprang to her feet. She reached for her cell phone and then she made her way down the aisle to the last desk.

"What's your mother's phone number?"

"Oh please, please, don't call her. Please. She'll be so mad. She'll whip me when I get home. I promise you I won't say another word. I won't even breathe."

Mrs. Johnson returned to her desk, grabbed some computer paper and asked Chanel Mason, who had a ring in her nose—again against St. Polycarp's rules—to pass it out. "To answer your questions, it can be a short story. And it doesn't have to be a sin you committed. Get going. You have twenty minutes."

Although what she was going to do with them after that, she had no idea.

She sat down on Mrs. Sugarman's chair, the flowered mat swaying under her weight. One thing she knew was that she couldn't return to teaching. All of this was just too much for her. Mrs. Hopwood was right.

The thought of perhaps going into politics took hold of her again and brought her a wisp of euphoria. She could run for office, maybe city council.

She was a black woman, who had been a Catholic school teacher for years. She would take on the Board of Education, question the common core, the standardized tests. She would endorse charter schools and stand up for inner city kids. She could do it.

She would do it.

But in the meantime, she wasn't about to be known as the woman who closed down St. Polycarp School. No doubt an opponent might use that against her. It wasn't just that. It was a matter of pride, of love for the school. She looked at Mrs. Sugarman's laptop. She would love to open and read what the woman was up to. Probably protected by a password.

She glanced at the door and saw to her irritation that Miss Turnipseed was hovering in the hall. Seconds later she inched her way into the classroom with a grim expression on her wrinkled face.

"What's the problem?" Mrs. Johnson said.

Miss Turnipseed, smelling of peppermint and ginger, leaned down and lowered her voice mysteriously. "You have had several phone calls from distraught parents. Something about face time."

"I think you mean Facebook. But I can hardly return those calls now, can I?" Mrs. Johnson snapped. "Did you reach a substitute?"

"Yes, the woman with the glass eye. She said she'd be here in about a half an hour. There is something else."

Mrs. Johnson hated the way Miss Turnipseed teased her. "Well, what?"

"Two policemen are downstairs. They want to talk to you."

Mrs. Johnson sat up.

"They look very serious. They insisted on speaking to you right away."

Something had happened to one of her twins. Her heart beating fast and furious, she stood up. "Watch this class," she instructed as she made a beeline to the door.

"I don't know anything about teaching," Miss Turnipseed whined. "I'm just a secretary."

"You don't have to do anything. They have an assignment."

"But…"

Mrs. Johnson did not stick around to hear any of the

protests. She could have told the students to stay on task, but she simply didn't care.

She didn't care about the boisterous students, or the future of the school. She didn't care about being a glamorous and productive politician. She didn't even care about dying of a horrid disease. If something happened to one of her boys, she was already as good as dead.

She ran down the stairs, at a breakneck speed, almost falling. Again she had the feeling that she was trudging through a nightmare, unable to wake up.

She didn't recognize the two policemen, who were standing in the hall. But Miss Turnipseed was right. They appeared grim and, when she approached them, Mrs. Johnson thought she saw a spark of pity in their eyes.

"Are you Amelia Johnson?" A paunchy man with a billowy abdomen and a fleshy face asked. He had his hand in his pocket. Mrs. Johnson held on to the wall—decorated with spring flowers by the first graders—to keep herself from fainting. Was he going to take out a photo and ask her to identify one of her twins?

The phone on Miss Turnipseed's desk rang shrill and insistent. Maybe it was her boys' school, trying to get in touch with her, to tell her devastating news.

"Is it one of my sons?" she asked breathlessly, her stomach plummeting. "Have they been hurt?"

"This has nothing to do with your sons," the woman answered. She looked too young to be a cop, almost like a teenager. Her red frizzy hair was tired back and orange freckles dotted her pale skin. "Or your husband, or your mother, or your sister."

Mrs. Johnson breathed a sigh of relief.

"I'm Officer Cook," the male cop said, "and this is

Officer Ross." He eyed a parade of little third grade girls coming back from the bathroom. "Is there somewhere quiet where we could talk?"

"Of course." She led them into her office and closed the door. "Please sit." She pointed to the chairs.

They declined.

"Is this about the dead man who was found in our cellar?" Mrs. Johnson had to sit down. It was barely ten o'clock in the morning and already the day was terrifying. "Honestly, I never saw him before. The poor guy was probably camping out there."

Mrs. Johnson stopped talking when she saw the look of bewilderment on both of the policemen's faces.

Officer Cook finally took his hand out of his pocket. Mrs. Johnson was surprised when she saw a vial of prescription drugs encased in a plastic bag. "Do you recognize these?" He slid the bag across her desk.

They were hers and she told them so.

"Did you give these pills to someone?"

"No."

"Did you sell them to someone?"

"No, of course not."

"Then how," Officer Ross' tone was accusatory, "did they go missing?"

Mrs. Johnson had to be honest. "I think they were stolen."

"By whom?" Officer Ross almost jumped at her.

"I'd rather not say. I have no proof and I don't want to get anyone in trouble."

"Would it surprise you to know that these pills were found on a dead woman?" Officer Ross reached inside her pocket and pulled out a photo. She handed it to Mrs. Johnson.

Slowly Mrs. Johnson lowered her eyes.

Mrs. Sugarman was lying on the concrete. Her short curly gray hair was streaked with blood, her legs sprawled on the pavement.

"Do you know this woman?" Officer Cook asked.

"Yes. She's a teacher here. At least she was a teacher here. Her name is Mrs. Sugarman, Nancy Sugarman. What happened to her?"

"We're not sure," Officer Ross answered. "Not until after an autopsy. There was a blow to her head. Maybe she fell. You said that she was a Mrs. Does that mean she was married? Do you know where we can get in touch with her husband?"

"I believe he died."

"Would you know her next of kin?" Officer Cook asked.

Mrs. Johnson shook her head.

"Well, certainly you must have a personal file on her." Officer Ross was clearly disgruntled. "We would like to see it."

Mrs. Johnson glanced over at the file cabinet, which she had never opened. "I'm just an interim principal and to tell you the truth, I'm not acquainted with the filing system. My secretary knows, of course, but right now, she is covering Mrs. Sugarman's class and I would rather not involve her. I would be happy to dig it out for you, but it might take a few minutes."

"We're not going to wait," Officer Ross said. "But we would like you to bring it down to the precinct. You can come after school."

Mrs. Johnson was about to tell them that she thought Mrs. Sugarman might be a drug addict, but she thought the less said the better. As Officer Ross reached out for the photo, Mrs. Johnson noticed a blue handbag in the corner of the sidewalk. "That purse," she said suddenly.

"Do you recognize it?"

"Maybe. It might be part of a vintage collection. But I thought someone else had it."

"Well, the purse was empty. No wallet, no ID."

"When I come to the precinct, do you mind if I bring another teacher with me?" Mrs. Johnson could see the reluctance on Officer Ross's face.

"Was she a friend of Mrs. Sugarman?" Officer Cook asked.

"No, but," Mrs. Johnson wasn't sure how to begin to explain, "there were some problems with the handbags that Mrs. Hopwood donated to the school. It really is very complicated and it would be best if she were the one to explain. It may have something to do with Mrs. Sugarman's death."

"All right," Officer Cook agreed, "but in the meantime, we would appreciate if you didn't share this information with anyone else. At least until we notify her family. Also we wouldn't want to upset the other teachers or the students."

"I understand."

"We'll be waiting for you," Officer Ross made it sound like a threat.

The moment that they left her office, Mrs. Johnson reached for her phone and sent Mrs. Hopwood a text, brief and to the point.

Find that old woman.

FORTY-TWO

MELISSA WOKE TO the sound of screeching sirens. Her first thought upon opening her eyes was that her father had done something horrible, something which caused him to get arrested again.

She had heard him leave the house in the middle of the night, her mother snoring beside her. The front door opened and then closed softly.

Melissa had not heard him reenter.

The thought that her father had gotten in trouble so soon after his release did not displease her. Last night dinner had been tense, her mother trying too hard to be cheerful, her brother smiling but somehow wary, and she herself, still and silent. Her father was also quiet, concentrating on the rubber chicken, the undercooked French fries, the overcooked broccoli and the chocolate cake, in which she found an egg shell.

Of course, if her father had done something terrible, it would be embarrassing and humiliating in school, but people would no doubt at first feel sorry for her, pity her situation and in time they would forget.

Maybe.

SHE WAS COMING out of the bathroom, when she encountered her father in the hall.

"Getting ready for school?" he asked.

Obviously. She just nodded and her stomach flipped

when he followed her into the bedroom. How was she supposed to get dressed with him staring at her like that?

"I didn't do it," he said suddenly.

"It doesn't matter. You served your time."

"It matters to me. I don't want to go down as a murderer, even one in self-defense. Yeah I realized your mother was running around with Holtz, but I had a few rolls in the hay myself. Nothing like that is worth killing for, you get what I mean? I only confessed because of the plea deal and because the stupid lawyer convinced me if it went to trial, I wouldn't have a chance." He paused and then said, "You know what I was thinking?"

Melissa didn't comment. She really didn't need to hear any of this. Instead she reached for her underwear, hoping he would take the hint and leave.

"That old woman next door, is she still there?"

"Mrs. Sterling?"

"That's the one, the one who was going to testify that she heard me arguing with Victor the night he was murdered. But it wasn't me. It couldn't be me. I'd love to question her but she won't talk to me. She and your mother have never been friendly and I think she's afraid of your brother. Can you talk to her?"

"That was twelve years ago."

"You don't have to tell me how many years ago it was. I counted every single damn day locked up in that hell hole."

Melissa grabbed her uniform. If she didn't get dressed soon, she would be late.

"If you could talk to her, ask her what she thought she heard…"

Rather than argue with him, which would take a

massive effort, Melissa just mumbled, "If I should run into her, I will ask her."

"Thanks." He put his hand on the door. "I got a little money. We're going to be taking that trip, all together. Won't that be good? Like a real family. Going to enjoy the ocean, the warm breezes. It's going to be all right, Melissa. Really."

She managed a weak smile, although she doubted that. She doubted that very much.

MELISSA MADE IT into the classroom, just as the final bell rang. It wasn't only her father who had delayed her. A section of the street had been roped off with orange tape declaring it to be a crime scene.

The thought that her father had something to do with the trouble crossed her mind again but this time only briefly. He wasn't a serial killer—according to him, he wasn't a killer at all. The crime probably had to do with drugs since the area was well known to be infested, and, as far as she knew, her father wasn't a druggie.

Melissa had no sooner arrived in class when Mrs. Hopwood asked to speak to her privately. As much as Melissa welcomed the attention from Mrs. Hopwood, private conversations with her filled Melissa with dread. She was always afraid that she was going to disappoint the teacher somehow.

Today Mrs. Hopwood was wearing a pretty violet dress that ruffled at her slim waist and her shoes were decorated with lilacs on the toe area. Her make-up was carefully done, but black circles lingered under her eyes and her hair was pulled back in a high pony tail with several wisps that had broken loose. She looked tired.

"Melissa," Mrs. Hopwood started, as soon as they

stepped into the hall, "do you know a girl by the name of Starlight? She would be several years older than you, but I believe she lives in your neighborhood."

Whatever Melissa had expected, it was not this. "No. Well, yes. Yes and no. I know of her, but I don't know her personally."

"Do you know her address or whether or not she is still living with her grandmother?"

Melissa shook her head. "She used hang out with my brother, although she is younger than him. But I don't think she's seen him for a while. I'm sorry."

"That's okay."

"But," Melissa hesitated, "I might know where she works, at least where she used to work—in the bowling alley on the corner of Maple and Portland."

"That's great," Mrs. Hopwood immediately perked up. "Thank you so much."

As Melissa went back into the classroom, she couldn't help but wonder why Mrs. Hopwood wanted to find that girl and if it had anything to do with the policemen she saw out the window pulling up to the school a few minutes later.

FORTY-THREE

MRS. HOPWOOD WAS tempted to give the children a written assignment and then thought better of it. It really wasn't fair and there was no question that she wasn't doing justice by them. In spite of everything that was happening, they deserved to be taught. She didn't want them to remember fifth grade as being the worst experience in elementary school.

So instead she posed a moral question—if you knew that your friend was doing something wrong, where would you draw the line—and she put them into groups for discussion. They liked to talk to one another and she floated through the panels.

Until she noticed a text on her phone from Mrs. Johnson.

Her heart fluttered and fluttered even more once she read it. Now Mrs. Johnson wanted her to find Starlight's grandmother. Something must have happened, something horrible. Mrs. Hopwood immediately texted back.

Why?

Can't say. Be in my office not later than three fifteen.

Why?

Can't say.

Mrs. Hopwood was tempted to run down and actually speak to Mrs. Johnson when her students were in art class but she thought better of it. Perhaps she was still angry and Mrs. Hopwood would learn what had precipitated the mysterious text messages soon enough.

But she had a pretty good idea when she saw that there was a substitute in Mrs. Sugarman's classroom.

SHE HURRIED DOWN at three-fifteen, although that meant canceling a meeting with the models for the fashion show. She could read their disappointment but it couldn't be helped, none of this could be helped.

Mrs. Johnson was waiting for her at the front door.

"What's going on?" Mrs. Hopwood couldn't get the fear out of her voice.

"I can't tell you until we're in my car." And then she added with a threatening stare, "I don't trust you."

MRS. HOPWOOD DIDN'T push it. She had seen Mrs. Johnson angry before but never at her. Her fury and her coldness were scary.

When Mrs. Hopwood finally settled in the car, she asked in a meek, little voice. "Where are we going?"

"To the police station."

"The police station? Mrs. Sugarman is having me arrested? How is that possible, when I never mentioned her name?"

"How do you know this is about Mrs. Sugarman?" Mrs. Johnson was managing to keep her eye on the road, without looking at her passenger.

"Because I noticed there was a substitute in her classroom. Is she planning to sue me? Is that what this is about?"

"Mrs. Sugarman won't be suing anyone. She's dead."

"Dead?"

"Dead."

"How?"

"She was found in the street. They are going to do an autopsy. They think she died from a blow to the head."

"That's terrible. But what does it have to do with me?" The seat belt tight around her shoulders, Mrs. Hopwood felt as though she was suffocating. She couldn't break free, trapped.

"It might have something to do with those damn vintage purses. One was found close to her body."

"Oh God! Which one?"

"I think it was blue."

"That's not possible. Mrs. Sugarman sold her blue purse to the Tristen's Treasures and I bought it back. It's under my bed as we speak."

"I'm bringing you with me because you're the only one who can explain it."

"Explain what? I'm just as baffled as you are."

Mrs. Johnson did not respond.

"You're still angry about the Facebook stuff?"

Mrs. Johnson stopped suddenly at a yellow light. As Mrs. Hopwood plunged forward, Mrs. Johnson lashed out. "I'm angry about all of it."

"But it's hardly my fault."

"It's all your fault."

"How?"

"You're the one who brought those vintage bags into the school. You should have thrown them all in the dumpster or sent them to Goodwill. Instead you involved St. Polycarp..."

"I thought I was doing a good deed. Those handbags are valuable."

"So valuable that someone is willing to murder for them."

"How could I know that?"

"Did it ever occur to you that the old woman wasn't cursing the school at all? That maybe she was cursing you personally?"

"I understand that you're distraught and you have every right to be but still you can't be serious."

But Mrs. Johnson was. "And thanks a lot for asking me about the results of my MRI."

"How did it turn out?" Mrs. Hopwood's tone was slight.

"I'm fine." Mrs. Johnson's tone was bitter.

Mrs. Hopwood didn't know what to say. She just stared at Mrs. Johnson who put her foot on the gas and sped down the street.

Neither women spoke until they reached the police station.

WHEN MRS. HOPWOOD saw Detective Paneretto and Detective Hargrove, she realized that she was in trouble. She had met the two detectives in the fall and she knew that their division was homicide. She also knew that, for some reason, Detective Hargrove, did not like her.

Mrs. Hopwood told herself to stay calm, to concentrate on her breathing. She had done nothing wrong, well, nothing really criminal, so there was no need for her to panic. She repeated this to herself, as she and Mrs. Johnson were led into a small cell like room, a room she remembered all too well.

"Okay," Detective Paneretto started, once they were all seated, "what can you tell us about Mrs. Sugarman?"

"I have her file right here." Mrs. Johnson reached into her tote bag and pulled out a rather stained and wrinkled folder. She opened it up and began reading. "She lists her next of kin as a sister in Ohio. She's been with St. Polycarp for eleven years. Up until this fall, she was the librarian but then she had to teach seventh grade because…" Her voice trailed off as though she realized that the detectives already knew why Mrs. Sugarman had been switched to a teaching position.

"Anything else?" Detective Paneretto lifted his eyebrow.

"She was a drug addict," Mrs. Hopwood said suddenly, not missing the scowl on Mrs. Johnson's face.

"We know that," Detective Hargrove spoke for the first time. "We read your Facebook page."

A deeper scowl from Mrs. Johnson.

Officer Paneretto slid a photograph across the table in Mrs. Hopwood's direction. Reluctantly, she picked it up. Grimacing she viewed the dead body of Mrs. Sugarman. Not a graceful way to die with her legs sprayed that way. But it was the expression on her face which confirmed Mrs. Hopwood's worst fear. This was no accident.

"Look at the blue purse," Detective Paneretto instructed. "Does it look familiar?"

"No."

"No?" Mrs. Johnson piped up. "It's one of those awful handbags."

"No, it's not. It resembles the purse I gave to Mrs. Sugarman, but it is definitely not the same handbag. For one thing, it's not the same color. The original handbag is a bright blue, this is more of an Aegean blue. Also the hardware is different. The one in the photo is decorated in cheap metal, the vintage one's has brass. I can tell from the picture that this purse is plastic, not leather." Six eyes listened to her, dumbfounded. "I know my purses," she said proudly.

"Do you have any idea why she would have this imitation?" Detective Hargrove asked.

"No, unless," Mrs. Hopwood paused, "she wanted to sell it, to pass it off as vintage. I gave her one of the originals because she asked me. I found it in a thrift shop window. She had sold it. I bought it back. These handbags," Mrs. Hopwod swallowed hard, "they have been involved in several robberies."

"We know that also." Detective Paneretto's voice was flat. "The robbery you reported on at your aunt's house and the one at your own home. And you're right. Mrs. Sugarman was trying to sell this purse, pass it off as vintage. She had already contacted someone called Stronghold…"

Mrs. Johnson'e eyes bulged. "How do you know that?"

"You gave us permission to look in her computer."

"He contacted me first, wanted to buy the handbags," Mrs. Hopwood said. "I refused. Do you know who Stronghold is?"

"We're still investigating." Detective Hargrove took the photo from the table. "But it looks as if he used a public computer in the library. We'll follow up, of course. We're going to have to take possession of all those vintage bags."

"No problem." Mrs. Hopwood was happy to be rid

of them. "They were five in total. I have two, hidden under my bed."

"She gave me one," Mrs. Johnson volunteered. "It's in my car."

"I gave one to Tracy Holtz, the homeless woman." Mrs. Hopwood wanted to be completely up front. "I don't know if you're aware of it, but that homeless woman is the wife of a man who was murdered twelve years ago, Victor Holtz." They didn't react, making Mrs. Hopwood suspect that they already knew this information.

"And the fifth one?" Detective Hargrove asked.

"I gave it to a student of mine, Melissa Ortiz, to use in the fashion show. To be honest with you, I was going to let her keep it after the show."

"Ortiz," Detective Paneretto said thoughtfully, "any relation to George Ortiz?"

"He's her father." Mrs. Hopwood watched as the two detectives exchanged uneasy glances. "But I can't see how this has anything at all to do with the purses."

"And these vintage purses, they came from where?" Detective Hargrove asked.

"They were my Aunt Eunice's. She owned a high end thrift shop years ago and they were all stored in her attic. When she died, she willed all of her belongings to myself and my four siblings. My sister told me that I could keep whatever I found in the attic."

"Is there any more of this vintage stuff?" Detective Hargrove interrupted.

"Yes, there are some clothes."

"We're going to need those also."

"No. I mean, you can't have them. We need them for the fashion show." Mrs. Hopwood looked at Mrs.

Johnson, hoping for support but Mrs. Johnson's eyes were downcast. "We have been planning this fashion show for months…"

"Where are the clothes now?" Detective Paneretto asked.

"Well, we stored them in the school basement and then I gave them to the girls, the ones who are modeling in the fashion show. They took them home."

For a few agonizing moments Detective Paneretto stopped and stared at her. "The basement?" he repeated. "The same basement where that homeless man was found?"

The most that Mrs. Hopwood could manage was a nod.

Detective Hargrove stared at both teachers for several long seconds. "A little bit of coincidence, isn't it?"

Mrs. Hopwood thought it best if she didn't answer at all.

"I mean, you got one homeless person who you gave a purse to, and then you got another homeless person killed in your basement. And now you have a teacher who died from a blow on the head." Detective Hargrove turned towards Detective Paneretto. "Was there an autopsy scheduled for that homeless man?"

She shrugged. "I don't think they thought it was necessary."

"Well, maybe," Detective Hargrove said. "Maybe now it is. After the fashion show, what happens to those clothes?"

"People are free to purchase them. It's a fund-raiser."

"All right," Detective Paneretto agreed. "After the show, we're going to have to examine them more before anyone gets to take them home."

Mrs. Hopwood was at a loss for words because she knew now that the show was bound to be a complete fiasco. Who would want to buy clothing that had been implicated in a murder?

As though Detective Paneretto could read her mind, he said, "We're not sure that Mrs. Sugarman was murdered. She could have just easily have fallen and hit her head, especially if she was on some sort of drugs. And the homeless man could have just drunk himself to death. Until the results of the autopsies, we won't be sure of anything."

"Do you know where we could find this Tracy person?" Detective Hargrove asked.

"She used to spend a lot of time at St. Polycarp Church," Mrs. Hopwood said.

"That's it for now." Detective Paneretto stood. "Mrs. Johnson, if you could remove the purse from your car and bring it in, we'd appreciate it. Mrs. Hopwood, we'll send someone to pick up the two purses in your possession. And then we will be in touch. In the meantime, if you can think of anything else, let us know."

THE MOMENT THAT Mrs. Hopwood got into the car, she could hardly resist. "None of this makes any sense."

Mrs. Johnson did not react at all. It was as if Mrs. Hopwood was speaking to herself.

"The question still remains if the robber wanted something in a vintage handbag, but he wasn't sure what the handbag looked like, then what made him think that the article was in one of Aunt Eunice's bags? Unless he had prior knowledge that Aunt Eunice had the bag, but if that were the case, why did he wait until she was dead to claim whatever it was he was looking for? And really, what could possibly be the connection between the homeless man and the purses?"

"I'm sorry," Mrs. Johnson said, as she started the car. "I shouldn't have said all those horrible things to you. You're right. I'm so overwhelmed." Mrs. Johnson rested her head against the steering wheel. Mrs. Hopwood could never remember seeing her friend look so discouraged and downtrodden. "I don't know how much more of this I can take."

"You're not thinking of quitting, are you?" Mrs. Hopwood had a sick, burning feeling in the pit of her stomach. "You only have two months to go."

Mrs. Johnson started the car.

"I found out the name of the girl, whose grandmother cursed us. Starlight works at the bowling alley on the corner of Maple and Portland." She thought that Mrs. Johnson would ask how she came upon this information but she was silent. "Do you think you could run me over now so I can talk to her?"

Mrs. Johnson released an exasperated sigh.

"I know you're not a taxi service, but we have to try, Amelia. We really do."

"It's going on five o'clock. My nanny has a fit if I'm late." She hesitated. "I'll do it but just make it quick."

Mrs. Hopwood was hoping that Starlight was there but she didn't dare voice that concern aloud.

MRS. JOHNSON STOPPED the car, cursing under her breath. Mrs. Hopwood didn't necessarily want to know what was wrong but she was going to be told anyway. "See that boy hanging out in the corner?"

Mrs. Hopwood spotted a tall teen leaning against the building, playing with his phone.

"He goes to St. Polycarp. He's in the seventh grade. His name is Shawn Caffety. And you know what's worse? He saw us and probably is wondering what the hell we're doing here. Something I'd like to know. So please, make it fast."

Mrs. Hopwood got out of the car, aware that the student in the corner was staring at her.

The bowling alley was dark and almost looked deserted. Mrs. Hopwood could hear the sound of balls being tossed down the lanes and just when she thought that this might be a dead end, she noticed a young girl, leaning against the vending machine, talking to an older boy.

Mrs. Hopwood approached her cautiously. "Starlight?"

Starlight looked up. She had always been a pretty little girl, but with a little bit of make-up, she had turned into a real beauty. Her lashes were long and curled, her skin, glistened like cocoa butter. Her lips were moist and pink.

"Do you know who I am?"

"Yeah, I know who you are. You were my second grade teacher." She studied Mrs. Hopwood with an expression of shock and suspicion. "Before you threw me out of the school."

"You were thrown out of school?" The boy wasn't as good looking as Starlight was pretty. Acne covered his face and his flat, broad nose but his biceps were bulging with tattoos.

"I didn't throw you out of the school. Father Felix asked you to leave. But all he wanted you to do was..." Mrs. Hopwood looked at the boy, whose small, beady eyes were squinting. "I need to speak to your grand-mother. Do you still live with her?"

Starlight gave an odd, twisted smile. "It's more like she lives with me. What's this about?"

'I'd rather talk directly to her."

"You want her to take a curse off?"

Mrs. Hopwood tried not to act surprised. "You remember that?"

"No, but my grandmother is always cursing people left and right. Everyone laughs at her, then they're back a few months later, crying their eyes out, begging her to remove the curse."

Mrs. Hopwood wasn't about to admit that she was one of those people. "Please, Starlight, I just need an address."

"What do I get out of it?"

The boy forced a laugh, exposing uneven, yellow teeth.

Mrs. Hopwood thought for a moment. "Do you want to come back to St. Polycarp?"

"Yeah, like I would ever want to go back to that ghetto school."

"Then what?" Mrs. Hopwood thought she might want money, but unfortunately, Mrs. Hopwood only had a ten dollar bill in her wallet.

"I heard," Starlight continued, "that you're having some sort of big fashion show. I want to be one of the models."

"I'm afraid that's not possible. The models have already been assigned to dresses and the show is just a couple of weeks away."

"Forget it then. Besides, my grandmother won't talk to you."

"Starlight, this is so important. Please!"

Starlight seemed to be mulling it over. She turned towards the boy who shrugged his skinny shoulders.

"When I said that my grandmother wouldn't talk to you, what I should have said was that my grandmother can't talk to you. She lives with me, all right. She rests right by my 46 inch television in a tin can. My grandmother died six months ago."

IT WAS ALL OVER, nothing else to be done. When she conveyed this to Mrs. Johnson, the only response was a shrug.

WHEN MRS. HOPWOOD entered her house, she heard footsteps coming down the front staircase.

"The police were here," Monte said, "tearing apart our bedroom, looking under our bed."

"I don't know why they should be tearing our bedroom apart. I told them exactly where those purses were."

"They found them and they took them."

"They can have them, all of them." Mrs. Hopwood headed for the living room. She wished that drinking wine didn't make her stomach queasy. She could use a drink.

She saw Monte whirl around and grab something from the landing. That something was suitcase.

She felt dizzy and sick as she tottered back to the hall.

"What's going on?" She held her breath and grabbed the banister.

"I think we need some time apart. This marriage isn't really working for me. For the last couple of years, you've been involved in one murder case after another. This isn't what I signed up for."

"But none of this is my fault! Really! An old woman cursed the school when Father Felix asked her to have the lice removed from her granddaughter's hair. Amelia and I went looking for her today, but she's dead. Her ashes are in a tin can—the grandmother, not the girl."

Monte had his hand on the front door. "I'll be in touch."

"Twenty-five years of marriage and that's the best you can do? I'll be in touch?"

He didn't bother to say anything else. Just opened the front door and closed it gently.

Mrs. Hopwood sank on the bottom stair and stayed there for a long time.

FORTY-FOUR

TRACY DIDN'T FEEL at home in the library, not like she did in the church, even though there was more to do in the library. And even though they allowed her to bring in Sugar Daddy, when she said it was a service dog. One of the librarians even gave Sugar Daddy a treat. Tracy had found a book of short ghost stories, which she was attempting to read, although people watching often interrupted her. The thought that there was an afterlife was a comforting one.

It wasn't only that she was people watching, but people were watching her as well. The reading room seemed to attract old folks, who probably had not much else to do and just wanted to get out of their one room studios which Tracy would never leave if she was fortunate enough to have one. They eyed her apprehensively and one elderly woman with steel gray hair and poppy eyes actually got up and moved to the other side of the room. Tracy knew that she smelled. She hadn't had a shower in two months. She reeked and her stomach growled from hunger. Yes, she had money but she thought it best if she waited until dark to venture outside. Then she could get something to eat and maybe walk to the motel on Riverdale Road.

She was watching the door, which turned out to be a mistake because at that precise moment two policemen marched into the library.

How could they have found her so soon?

No, it didn't appear as though they were headed her way. They went over to the front desk and pointed to the computer room. She saw them follow the librarian and disappear from sight—nothing to do with her. She was safe.

Now and then she looked up, but she didn't see them again. And then she did.

She stared straight at one of the policemen and what was worse was that he stared straight back at her. She knew then that it was all over.

Because the next moment he was looking at his phone.

She should get up and leave but that would mean walking by them and would certainly look suspicious. So instead she put her head down and pretended to be reading about the ghost of Ivan the Terrible, who haunted Russian castles.

She heard the footsteps coming towards her but she was too scared to look.

Until she heard a male voice ask her if she was Tracy Holtz?

She nodded.

"We would like you to come down to the precinct. We have a few questions to ask you."

She lifted her head and faced a cop, with a glistening bald head, who seemed to mean business. Nobody was reading anymore. They were all staring at her in amazement, as though she were dangerous.

"I didn't do anything," she said in a hoarse whisper.

"No one said that you did." The young African American cop seemed sympathetic and kind. He even managed to smile. "We just want to ask you a couple of questions." He glanced down at her purse.

"I didn't steal this!"

"No one said you did," the cop repeated.

They led her outside and into a police car. A pretty girl, who was texting on her phone, and looked as if she didn't have a care in the world, took a picture of Tracy, probably hoping that Tracy was a killer and she would have a scoop.

They pushed her head down roughly and shoved her into the back of a police car, behind those bars, with locked doors. Did they think she had stolen the purse? Or, and this thought, filled her with terror, did they think she had something to do with that teacher's death? This was her worst nightmare. And it was coming true.

Sugar Daddy jumped in the car beside her and then the black cop spoke. "We're going to have to drop him off at the shelter. Dogs are not allowed at the precinct."

"Please!" Tracy felt panic rising. "If you take him away from me, I'll never see him again. Can't I keep him with me when you ask questions? He's no trouble. And he's a service dog."

The bald headed guy, who was driving, turned around. "Just for a little while. But I'm not making any promises."

SHE DIDN'T UTTER another word as she followed both policemen through a maze in the precinct, finally stopping in a tiny room, where they left her alone, sitting at a table.

She knew that they were watching her on the other side of the mirror. She once read that innocent people act nervous, shaking with fear, while guilty people are more relaxed because they need a breather, after being jazzed up from the crime.

She wasn't sure how she should be acting. She bent down to pet Sugar Daddy, to reassure him. He was shaking. He knew this was serious. It was as if he had an inkling that they might be separated. But she also knew that he was hungry and thirsty.

Would they offer her something to eat? Should she take the food and leave her DNA on the utensils? She didn't care as long as Sugar Daddy had food.

The door burst open but it wasn't the two policemen who had brought her here.

Instead it was a heavyset man, who introduced himself as Detective Paneretto and a grumpy looking woman, who said her name was Detective Hargrove.

Detectives—not good.

Paneretto slumped down but Hargrove stood, setting up a small camera. "Do you mind if we record this conversation?" she asked.

Tracy could hardly say no, but perhaps this was the time to ask for food. "We're really hungry. Do you think you could get us something to eat? And water for my dog?"

"Sure. A tuna sandwich, okay?" Paneretto asked.

Tracy hated tuna and Sugar Daddy didn't much like it either. But this wasn't the time to be fussy. Paneretto opened the door, said something in a soft voice and waited there. Meanwhile Hargrove was staring at her with big round brown eyes. She stared back until she finally lost the contest and lowered her eyes.

Paneretto returned with a skimpy sandwich on stale white bread wrapped in plastic. The tuna was fishy, the sprite was flat and the water was warm. She gave half

the sandwich to Sugar Daddy and asked for a small bowl.
Hargrove grumbled but came back with a plastic bowl
and she watched as Sugar Daddy lapped up the water.

"We'd like to know about your purse," Paneretto started.

"It was a gift," Tracy answered, her mouth thick with
tuna, "from a friend."

"From Mrs. Hopwood?" Hargrove's tone was accusatory and aggressive.

"That's right. You can ask her if you don't believe
me."

"I'm afraid we're going to have to take it from you,"
Detective Paneretto said.

"No." Tracy grabbed the purse and hugged it to her
chest. "You can't! This is one of the nicest things I've
ever had. I don't have any other pocket books."

"We can give you a plastic bag for your belongings,"
Hargrove said, as she stood her arms folded.

"The reason we want it," Paneretto said, "is because
there's a possibility that it might have been involved in
a crime."

"What are you talking about?" Tracy asked, truly
bewildered.

Hargrove left the room and Paneretto was silent, until
she returned with two plastic grocery bags.

"This isn't fair," Tracy protested.

"Would you mind emptying your purse?" Hargrove
asked.

Tracy minded. She minded very much. Her eyes
filled with tears. She opened her purse, aware that she
was being watched as she removed all of her earthly
possessions.

And then that envelope.

She could hardly miss the knowing glance that the two detectives exchanged.

"Do you mind if we count that?" The woman detective leaned in so closely that Tracy could smell her powdered deodorant.

"It's mine," Tracy said quickly. "Money I've been collecting from generous people for months."

"You know what else I think?" Detective Hargrove said as she handed the envelope to Detective Paneretto "I think if you had this money for as long as you said you did, you wouldn't be so hungry now."

Tracy didn't answer. Instead she watched the money being counted and heard her heart thump when Detective Paneretto stopped suddenly to examine the envelope. He studied it for a moment and then handed it to Detective Hargrove who looked down and then up at Tracy.

"Do you know what this is?" she asked Tracy.

"No."

"Of course, you don't. Because this is not your money. So let me tell you what this is. It's an envelope from Tristen's Treasures. Did you sell something there?"

Tracy could have lied. But they could have checked.

"You know what else I think?" Detective Hargrove was leaning over her again. "I think you killed Nancy Sugarman, after you robbed her. We saw you at the scene. Would it surprise you to know that there was a witness who saw you arguing with Mrs. Sugarman the afternoon she was murdered?"

"No!" Tracy jumped up and then glided down again. No way were they going to railroad her for murder. "If you're talking about that woman, that mother in the street, you should know that she was the person who was angry with Mrs. Sugarman. Mrs. Sugarman asked me if I wanted to sell my handbag and I said no."

"And she just gave you the money?" Detective Hargrove asked sarcastically,

"I found it. I saw the dead body and I rushed away. The money was on the ground in a handbag a few feet away. I didn't connect it to the murder. I just took it and left."

"Well, we're just going to take it now," Detective Hargrove said, "as evidence in what may be a crime scene."

"May be a crime scene," Tracy repeated. "So you don't even know if the woman was murdered."

"How well did you know Robert Ryan?" Detective Paneretto asked suddenly.

"He was my friend," she blurted out, jolted by the question.

"Do you know anything about his death?"

"I know that he died in the basement of St. Polycarp School." No one responded and the way that they were eying her made her add, "I saw him carried out on a stretcher."

"Do you know anyone who might want to harm him?"

She shook her head. "He was a nice man who had a hard life. He drank too much and I thought that's what killed him." She hesitated. "Isn't that what killed him?"

No one answered.

"Can I go?" she grabbed the plastic bag and scooped her belongings into it.

"I'm afraid not," Detective Panerotta spoke.

"You can't keep me on suspicion of murder, if you're not even sure there's been a murder committed."

"No," Detective Hargrove said, "but we can hold you on possession of stolen goods."

"I didn't steal anything!"

"Wait here," Detective Hargrove said, "someone will come along to take you to lock up."

"But my dog!" Tracy shouted.

They didn't bother answering her. They just left and Tracy felt like crying. Maybe she should cry. Maybe people on the other end of the mirror would see her, would take pity on her. Maybe they would see themselves in her and realize something like this could happen to them as well, that in a moment, without any warning at all, your entire life could change.

Minutes later, the door opened violently and an overweight policewoman swept into the room, holding a set of handcuffs.

"What about my dog?"

"I guess we'll have to put him in a shelter."

"No, please don't put him there! They kill animals there!"

Sugar Daddy, no doubt reacting to her hysteria, started to whine.

"I'm entitled to a phone call," Tracy insisted.

"You are."

"Please, please, don't take my dog anywhere, until I make the phone call. And please, I'm not sure of her number. Could you look it up for me?"

"Okay," the officer said. "But you better be speedy. I don't have all day."

FORTY-FIVE

"I DON'T KNOW how much longer I can do this," Mrs. Johnson confided to her husband after she settled the twins in bed and she was drinking her nightly glass of red wine.

"So quit," Mr. Johnson said. "We'd have to cut back for a little while, but you could do something else. Why should you be miserable?"

Mrs. Johnson knew that her husband didn't like it when she was miserable. When she was miserable, the twins were miserable and when the twins were miserable, everyone was miserable. "I'm thinking of going into politics."

He reached for the remote control. "Sounds like a plan."

"How would you feel about that?" she probed.

"Whatever you want to do is fine with me." He turned the television on and started to click through the channels.

"I just can't quit. If I quit, it will go on my record and my opponent will use it against me."

The phone rang and Mrs. Hopwood's name flashed across the television screen.

"I'm going to let the machine pick it up," Mrs. Johnson decided. But then after a second glass of wine and five handfuls of potato chips, curiosity got the better of her and she listened to the voicemail.

Mrs. Hopwood seemed to be sobbing. "Please call me back," she begged. "Something horrible has happened."

Mrs. Johnson's first thought was that something horrible had to do with Alex. The boy had been nothing but trouble ever since he started high school. Well, teenagers could be trying and maybe Mrs. Johnson should not be so judgmental.

She phoned right back without hesitation. She and Mrs. Hopwood might have their differences but when catastrophe struck, they were family.

Mrs. Hopwood picked up right away.

"What happened?" Mrs. Johnson thought it best to take the phone call in the kitchen.

"Monte is gone."

"You mean he's dead?"

"No, He left me."

Mrs. Johnson breathed a sigh of relief and then asked if Mrs. Hopwood was sure.

"What do you mean am I sure? Do you think that this is something I'm uncertain of? The police came looking for those darn purses and he freaked out. He said he was tired of being involved in murder and mayhem."

"Join the club."

"Like all of this is somehow my fault!" Mrs. Hopwood sniffled.

"He's overreacting. Give him a few days. He'll calm down."

"I doubt it. He sounded very serious and very disgusted."

"Get a good night's sleep. Things will look brighter in the morning."

"I doubt it," Mrs. Hopwood repeated. "But you were right about one thing. It's not the school that's cursed. It's me."

AT TEN O'CLOCK when Mrs. Johnson had just settled into bed after giving Justin Joseph his third glass of water, the phone rang again. And again the name of Mrs. Hopwood appeared on the screen right on top of the pundits who were talking about North Korea.

"I suppose I should take this," Mrs. Johnson said. "I'm sure it will be short."

But knowing Mrs. Hopwood she knew that probably would not be true.

"Go ahead," Peter said but with a dash of irritation in his tone.

Reluctantly she picked it up. "Monte's come back?"

"No. But I got a call and you'll never guess who from."

"It's been a long day, so just tell me."

"Tracy, the homeless woman. She's in jail."

"Why?"

"They holding her because she picked up some money which they believed belonged to Mrs. Sugarman. And they suspect that she had something to do with Mrs. Sugarman's death."

"But why is she calling you? And how on earth did she even get your phone number?"

"I have no idea."

"I hope you said no. We don't know one thing about her. Except that her husband was murdered. Why she could be a serial killer herself."

"I thought the same thing. Like I really have the money. And I told her that. Then she asked me to go and get her dog out of the pound. I think his name is Sugar Daddy."

"That's just what you need is a dog." Mrs. Johnson said drowsily.

MARIANNA HEUSLER   225

"They're going to kill it."

After lapsing into a thoughtful silence, Mrs. Johnson asked Mrs. Hopwood what she was going to do.

"I guess I have to go and get it. I mean it's all the poor woman has. At least Monte won't be complaining. He hates dogs. Come to think of it, he hates people too. I'll go first thing in the morning and hope he's still alive. The dog, not Monte."

"What?"

"I might be a few minutes late because I have to drop him off at my house."

"Really, this is…"

"I'm trying to do a good dead," Mrs. Hopwood argued.

"Your good deeds are always an inconvenience to me."

"Then they're good deeds for you too," Mrs. Hopwood said brightly, as she hung up the phone.

MRS. JOHNSON HAD no sooner left her car on the following morning, when she was approached by a student, whom she recognized as Shawn Caffety.

"Hey, can I talk to you about something?"

"I'm not a horse," she said as she walked rapidly. She could tell by the puzzled expression on his face that her comment had eluded him.

"I saw you in the project yesterday."

"So? Was I trespassing?" she asked sharply.

"Starlight told me that Mrs. Hopwood trying to find her grandma."

"So?"

"To have the curse removed."

"Is this conversation going anywhere?" Mrs. Johnson flung open the door to the school, missing Shawn's face by mere inches.

"I know a way you can talk to her."

"And how is that? When she's dead?"

"You see, there is this guy who lives in the same building as my friend, Adam Ortiz. I think he's the super or something." Shawn entered the building. "Anyway he does these séances, where he can call people back from the hereafter. No kidding. He told us where my Aunt Marina put her silverware. You gotta give him a try."

"Thanks, but no thanks. I'll pass. And you're not supposed to be inside the school until the first bell rings. So please wait outside."

She didn't miss Shawn crestfallen face, but really enough is enough.

Except it wasn't.

Because when she reached her office, Miss Turnipseed announced with some glee—and some lively interest—that Sister Mary Grace wanted to speak to her immediately.

"Hi, Sister, this is Amelia Johnson." Mrs. Johnson was trying to keep her voice upbeat, even though she was flooded with anxiety, and her stomach was dropping inch by inch.

"I understand that there have been a couple of deaths in your school. You lost one of your teachers…"

"Well actually, Mrs. Sugarman was the librarian but we were using her in seventh grade because…"

"I know about that. She died in the street?"

"Yes."

"Of unnatural causes?"

"Well," Mrs. Johnson hesitated as she was gripped with a stabbing pain in her lower back, "They'll be an autopsy, of course."

"I heard rumors that the woman was a drug addict."

"Well…"

"Were you not aware of this?"

"Well…"

"And what about that homeless man who died in your basement and was hiding there for who knows how long?"

"Well, actually…"

"Don't you lock the windows and the doors?"

"Well yes, but…"

"Do you have any idea how much trouble, how much shame St. Polycarp has brought upon the diocese?"

"None of this is my fault!" Mrs. Johnson was aware of just how much she sounded like Mrs. Hopwood. "I didn't hire Nancy Sugarman."

"No, but she worked under you for six months. And if she was having a problem, you should have seen it. And now you need a teacher for the seventh grade."

"We have a sub and he's very competent."

"He won't be staying. I am not paying for a sub."

"Do you want to combine the sixth and seventh grades?" Mrs. Johnson was thinking that Mrs. Thain would not be happy.

"Certainly not. Why should the children suffer because of your lack of judgment? You will return to seventh grade. It was a mistake to appoint you interim principal in the first place. On Monday Sister Maria Anna will be taking over the reins at St. Polycarp. Until then, please do your best not to get anyone murdered."

The connection was broken.

Mrs. Johnson sat holding the phone, wondering how everything had gone so horribly wrong.

FORTY-SIX

MELISSA WALKED SLOWLY to school. She was early because she had to get out of the small, cramped apartment. Her mother still sound asleep in Melissa's bedroom, her father sprawled out on the living room couch watching sitcoms from the 90s.

She was afraid that her father would talk about what happened last night and she had nothing to say.

IT HAD BEEN early evening when the doorbell rang with some insistence. Her father screamed out, "Wait a damn minute," before he flung open the door.

It was the police.

Melissa peeked out of her bedroom as her father growled, "What do you want?"

"Can we come in?"

"You got a warrant?"

"Do we need one?"

"Listen, I've done nothing wrong. I'm keeping a low profile. I barely leave the house. My parole officer with tell you…"

"This isn't about you."

Silence.

"We need to speak to your daughter, Melissa."

This was about her? What on earth could the police want? She tiptoed out of her bedroom, feeling sick to her stomach, her head throbbing.

"What do you want with her? She's a good girl, never done nothing wrong."

"Are you Melissa Ortiz?" A policewoman with red hair and freckles smiled briefly.

"Don't say nothing," her father warned, his voice dripping with bitterness.

"You're not in any trouble," the policewoman reassured her. "We just want to ask you a few questions."

Her friendliness put Melissa at ease.

"We are collecting the handbags that Mrs. Hopwood gave out." The policeman, a heavyset man with wheezing breath, stepped into the apartment.

"Oh, okay. I hid it in my closet."

The moment she uttered the sentence, she knew that she had made a mistake. And the policeman's suspicious expression confirmed her fear. "Why did you feel it was necessary to hide the purse?"

"It's not mine. It belongs to Mrs. Hopwood. She is only letting me use it for the fashion show. I was afraid," Melissa swallowed hard, "I was afraid that if my mother saw it, she would want to use it and she would ruin it."

"Do you know if your mother used it?" the policeman questioned as he followed Melissa into the bedroom, the policewoman and Melissa's father trailing behind.

"No, I'm sure she didn't."

Melissa opened her closet door and lifted up a pair of too small jeans, a stained crop top, her olive green sweatshirt and an old moth eaten army blanket from the floor.

The purse was not there.

Immediately Melissa felt dizzy as panic set in. She knew exactly where she had placed the handbag but nevertheless she found herself looking in other places, on the shelf above, where with worn shoes and stained party dresses came raining down, between bent and broken hangers and, finally in her own bureau where the drawer, with the broken hinges, came tumbling out and crashed on the floor with a muffled sort of thump.

"You can't find it?" Coming from the policeman, it sounded like an accusation, as he advanced towards her menacingly.

"I know where I hid it," she insisted.

"Is it possible your mother did borrow it?" The policewoman's eyes traveled to the floor, where she stared at the debris. Melissa saw a flicker of pity cross her face.

"I don't think she did."

"Where is your mother now?"

"At work," Melissa volunteered. "She's a waitress at Barry's Bar and Grill." Again the wrong thing to say because her father's eye became slits of fury. He glowered even more when both officers turned their gazes to him.

"What the hell would I want with a pocketbook?" he snarled.

"Is there anyone else who might have access to your apartment?" The policeman headed for the living room.

Melissa thought for a moment and then said, "Mr. Penroy, he's the super, he lives downstairs and he's very creepy. My mom told me that a few days ago he came by, saying he had to examine the pipes under the sink. But there wasn't any leak."

"Would you mind if we look around?" Which the policeman was already doing...

"She may not mind, but I sure as hell do." Her father held the door open. "Not without a warrant."

"We'll be back."

As soon as they left her father made an awkward attempt to comfort Melissa by putting his beefy hand on her shoulder. It took all of her self-control not to push her away.

"Don't worry. They're just trying to scare us."

BUT MELISSA WAS SCARED, plenty scared but not by the police. Something sinister was happening. When her mother came home, she woke Melissa up from a restless sleep and began to scream at her for giving information out to the police.

"Do you know that they came to my work, my restaurant? How do you think that looked to Barry? Accusing me of stealing some kind of old handbag…"

"I told them about Mr. Penroy," Melissa said.

"They probably didn't even question him. Do you think I have an easy life? Waiting tables, smiling for a few dollar tips…"

Melissa put the pillow over her ears to drown out her mother's ranting.

BUT SHE COULDN'T drown out the gossip when she entered the classroom the following morning and heard the news that Mrs. Sugarman was dead.

And might have been murdered.

By a purse thief?

Even Mrs. Hopwood did not look like herself. For one thing she was wearing the same outfit she had already worn a few weeks before, a gray sheath with gray and yellow shoes. Everyone knew that Mrs. Hopwood would go the entire year—all 180 days—without repeating her clothes. She had forgotten the pretty gold and silver necklace and the dangling earrings. Her bright red lipstick had been replaced by a sheer lip gloss and her carefully blown dried hair was carelessly placed in a knot on top of her head.

She looked tired and scared.

As Melissa dropped down in her seat, she realized that whatever was happening, Mrs. Hopwood was clearly at the center. And why was she looking for the girl in the project? Did that girl have a handbag too?

The worst part about it was that Melissa only felt it right to tell Mrs. Hopwood that the police had been at her apartment last night.

And the handbag she had given Melissa was missing.

FORTY-SEVEN

Mrs. Hopwood was indeed tired.

Since Monte left, she had barely slept. She realized that he wasn't coming home so fast—maybe not at all. They had been married for twenty-five years and she never saw this coming.

She realized, of course, that they had grown apart. But she thought that once things were settled at St. Polycarp, she could start to pay more attention to her husband, perhaps they could even take a second honeymoon somewhere.

The problem was that things were never settled at St. Polycarp.

And she had run out of tomorrows.

Still, as far as she knew, he hadn't hired a lawyer yet, so maybe, just maybe, he was just thinking it over, or trying to put a scare in her. Maybe he needed a little time apart.

She could hope, or she could start making plans as a single woman.

But right now all she could think of was Sugar Daddy, who had clearly invaded her life. He was obviously an outdoor dog and did not appreciate being inside. She walked him before her bedtime—9:30—again at midnight—then at five in the morning—and finally, just before she left for school at seven.

These frequent walks did not prevent him from crying, wandering from room to room, probably looking for Tracy. And he peed and defecated wherever he went.

No way was this mutt going to have the run of the house. So before she left, Mrs. Hopwood put him in Alex's room—Alex would hardly notice if he peed in there—with a bowl of water and a quarter pound of ham.

Then she left for work, happy to be away from his loud barking.

AND MRS. HOPWOOD was indeed worried. She had received a text from Mrs. Johnson, which was mysterious and concerning.

You have a prep at 10:15. Please come to my office.

Was she about to be fired? Would Mrs. Johnson do such a thing? All right, so Mrs. Hopwood was a little distracted. Who wouldn't be with handbags being stolen and teachers being killed, and her husband of a quarter of a century walking out on her, but surely she deserved some leeway.

Now more than ever, Mrs. Hopwood was going to need money. How long would Monte continue to pay the bills, the mortgage—the cable? She might even have to hire a lawyer. Her life had turned upside down. And the only thing of certainty was that she couldn't lose her job.

So she floated through the morning, beginning, as always, with religion class. She broke the students up in groups where they had a spirited discussion on whether annulments should be allowed in the Catholic Church.

At exactly 10:15 Mrs. Hopwood trudged down to the principal's office, telling herself that she was being silly.

Mrs. Johnson had been her best friend for years, her advocate—her mentor. No way would Mrs. Johnson ever betray her, especially now when she was so vulnerable.

Would she?

"Come in and shut the door." Mrs. Johnson's tone was gloomy, as she slumped behind her desk. "I received a call from Sister Mary Grace."

"And she wants to fire me," Mrs. Hopwood guessed.

"Why do you immediately think everything is about you?"

Mrs. Hopwood relaxed, sitting down.

"Actually she's firing me."

"What?" she asked in a stunned voice.

"Of course, she knows about all about Mrs. Sugarman's death, or maybe her murder. Either way it involves drugs. Sister Mary Grace was furious and demanded that I return to seventh grade. They're going to replace me with a nun."

"What about the fashion show? It's next week."

"She didn't mention that."

"Well," Mrs. Hopwood took a deep breath, "I guess that's not so bad. I mean, you hate this job."

"That is not the point," Mrs. Johnson snapped. "In essence I was fired. How on earth am I going to get another job?"

"Well," Mrs. Hopwood hesitated. "You weren't fired as a teacher."

"That's not going to be my next job."

"What do you mean?"

"I'm going to run for city council."

A wave of excitement rushed through Mrs. Hopwood. She'd welcome something new, different for both of them. "I could be your campaign manager. We should start planning, branding you..."

"I think we're getting ahead of ourselves."

Mrs. Hopwood voice quivered as she felt the euphoria escape her like a leaking balloon. "You don't want me to be your campaign manager?"

"Right now, I just want to get through the year. I've got to answer a few e-mails, although God only knows what I'm going to say. Not a word to the teachers. Understand?"

"Yeah, like I'm really friendly with the teachers."

"And don't even think about putting it on Facebook." Her voice dropped. "How are you doing? With Monte gone I mean?"

"I don't know. I'm still shell-shocked."

"He'll probably come back. Have you heard from him?"

"Not a peep."

Mrs. Johnson shook her head, rose and opened her office door. Mrs. Hopwood had no recourse but to follow her.

"Damn," Mrs. Johnson suddenly cursed.

"What's the matter?"

"Mr. Caffety," Mrs. Johnson said. "Please return to your classroom."

"But I wanted to give you this." The student held out a scrap of paper. "It's the man I was telling you about, the one who can get in touch with the dead. His name is Mr. Penroy. I got the address from my friend, Adam."

"I have no interest in psychics." She grabbed the paper, crumpled it and threw it into Miss Turnipseed's wastepaper basket.

'What was that all about?" Mrs. Hopwood said in a

whisper that didn't contain her curiosity. Miss Turnipseed was coming down the hall, holding a cup of tea
in one hand, and a prune in the other—and a piece of
paper in her mouth.

"I told you. He saw us outside the bowling alley and
found out you were trying to get in touch with the dead
grandmother. I guess he's trying to be helpful."

Mrs. Hopwood felt a flicker of hope and that flicker
must have shown in her eyes.

"Don't even think about it," Mrs. Johnson warned.

MRS. HOPWOOD DIDN'T have time to grab a cup of coffee from outside so she had to made do with the pot
from the teacher's room. She had never felt comfortable there, not after Mrs. Pinkerton had been poisoned
in that exact spot.

She had reached her classroom just in time as the
fifth graders came barreling in. They were singing some
sort of rap song and Mrs. Hopwood was betting that
they'd hadn't learned it in music, at least not by Father
Manuel.

"Can I talk to you for a moment?" Melissa approached
her. Mrs. Hopwood tried not to show her annoyance. No
doubt it would involve some sort of problem and Mrs.
Hopwood had so many, many problems of her own.

After Mrs. Hopwood had threatened the class with
no recess—which they knew was an empty threat because she herself needed them to be outdoors so she
could stay indoors alone—and after she escorted Melissa into the hall and shut the door, Melissa began.

"You know that green purse you lent to me? Well,
the police came last night and asked for it."

"Well, I hope you gave it to them. Those handbags

have been nothing but trouble. I wish I had never set eyes on them. Why couldn't my Aunt Eunice have left me something else?"

"I didn't give it to them."

"Why?"

"I couldn't. It was gone. Missing…"

This fact gave Mrs. Hopwood a most unsettled feeling.

"We think it was the super," Melissa said. "He was in our apartment when we weren't there a while ago. Something about a leak, but really, there was no water damage. He's very weird. Probably was hoping he'd find something inside. Well, he'll be disappointed."

A loud crash erupted from the classroom. Mrs. Hopwood rushed in to find that a chair had overturned on someone's toes. Tears were flooding down Claire Waterson's round face, so Mrs. Hopwood asked Melissa to accompany her to the nurse's office.

"He did it on purpose!" Clarice sobbed.

"Did not!"

"Yes, you did."

"You tripped because you're a fat girl!"

"That's enough!" Mrs. Hopwood thundered. It had been enough in September. "Especially since you're not so skinny yourself. Clarice, go to the nurse. Everyone else we're having a spelling test. Avery, pass out the lined papers. Number one to fifty."

"Fifty?"

"This is unfair! You didn't tell us!"

"Should we skip lines?"

"Do I have to write my last name?"

"Or the date?"

"What is the date?"

"Complete heading." Mrs. Hopwood figured that would take about five minutes.

Something Melissa said was whirling around in her brain. "He was looking for something inside."

And just like that the pieces fell into place.

MRS. JOHNSON APPEARED in her classroom as soon as the dismissal bell rang. She had on her light spring coat and she was carrying her briefcase.

"I got your text but I can't stay long. I'm sick of tired of staying late, trying to make things better. I don't even know why I'm taking this darn briefcase home. No one appreciates what I've done"

"I figured it out."

"Figured what out?"

"Remember we kept asking if the murderer was looking for a handbag, how did he know it was among the purses from Aunt Eunice's attic?"

"No, I never wondered that—just you." She collapsed on one of the student's chair, which created a loud creak.

Mrs. Hopwood remained standing to make her point. "He would know if he recognized something that had been in one of the purses."

"What are you talking about?" Mrs. Johnson asked irritably. "We didn't take anything from the purses. They were empty."

"No, they weren't. One of them, and I have to tell you I have racked my brains trying to remember which one it was, had the compact in it. Remember? The compact had the name Dagny engraved on it. And I used that compact as a logo. It appeared all over the flyers. So what if the murderer, if he was a murderer, recognized the compact Dagny always carried with her, and then

he knew that I had one of her purses? And don't you remember the piece of paper I found in the cellar? It had
Dagny's name on it. That had to have been inside one
of the purses. All right, that was just a dry cleaner receipt. But what if someone was looking for something
else—something that belonged to this Dagny—that she
had hidden in her purse. Maybe, just maybe that's why
that poor homeless man was killed because someone
thought he had it, whatever it was."

"We don't know that was why the homeless man was
killed," Mrs. Johnson corrected her. "And anyway, what
does all this prove?"

"It answers the question of how the murderer—if
there was a murderer—knew I had the purse!"

"It might tell us how, but still doesn't answer the
question of why."

"I did some research."

"When?"

"When the students were doing DEAR."

"What?" Mrs. Johnson perked up.

"You know, drop everything and read. You liked
that idea."

"And how long were they reading? Oh listen to me,
I'm sounding like a principal, or someone who cares.
Let them read until June for all I care."

"Anyway," Mrs. Hopwood thought it best to continue with her theory, "Dagny is not a common name
especially in this town. At first the only thing that came
up in Google was Dagny Taggart, you know the char-
acter from *Atlas Shrugged*. But then I put in the name
of this town."

Mrs. Johnson had her eyes closed as though she was
napping.

"A woman by the name of Dagny Danvers popped up. She slipped and fell on the ice, causing a brain bleed. And you will never guess what she did! She was a photographer. There was even a picture of her, a kind of buxom blonde with frosted hair."

"And now you think *she* was murdered?" Mrs. Johnson asked wearily.

"No, I don't think she was murdered. Because the murderer, if there was a murderer…"

"Stop saying that!"

"All right, the thief then, he would have just grabbed her purse at that time. You know what's really puzzling?"

Mrs. Johnson clearly did not want to know.

"Dagny's death occurred just one week after the murder of Victor Holtz. Now, there aren't many murders in this town…"

"And most of them have happened at St. Polycarp."

"So maybe, just maybe, there's a connection. Maybe Dagny was on her way to meet the murderer—maybe she had something which proved he committed the murder of Holtz."

"I thought George Ortiz murdered Victor Holtz."

"He swears he didn't. But the murderer never got the proof and all he knows was it was in one of Dagny's purses and he terrified that someone else will find this proof. And what if—what if the murderer is this Mr. Stronghold?"

You know what I think?" Mrs. Johnson rose wearily.

"What?" Mrs. Hopwood was happy that she was taking an interest.

"I think if you don't have a teaching job next year, you should seriously consider becoming a detective."

"I can't be a detective. You have to be a policewoman first and no way would I wear that drab uniform."

"And that's the only thing holding you back?"

"That and the fact that I'm easily frightened."

"Well, maybe," Mrs. Johnson was heading to the door, "you could be a police consultant. You know, like Monk."

"I don't think the police like me too much."

"I gotta go." She ambled out, closing the door behind her.

Mrs. Hopwood sank in her chair with a wave of sadness. She had not only lost her husband, but her best friend as well.

FORTY-EIGHT

"YOU HAVE A VISITOR."

Tracy opened her eyes. Had someone spoken to her? Was this just a dream? Had the entire arrest been just that reoccurring nightmare? Was it winter and was she holed up against some building trying to keep warm in the snow?

Was she dead?

"Holtz, get your butt up. Someone wants to talk to you."

"My lawyer?"

"The lady don't look like no lawyer."

Tracy walked stiffly from her cell, following the guard through a series of cells, lined up against either wall. It was the odor that got to her. On the street at least there was fresh air. If not, you could always move to a different location. Here she was stuck in a place that reeked of urine, feces, blood, sweat, musky perfume and something else, which she had come to identify as fear and shock. She could put toilet paper in her ears to block out the noise at night, and she could close her eyes to forget where she was, but she couldn't stop smelling.

At least she had her own cell. But even that had a downside because she was lonely. Of course, she had been lonely on the street, but here the loneliness seemed worse, deeper. It wasn't only that she missed Sugar Daddy desperately but this was just a holding place.

One of the guards had told her that she would soon be transferred to a state prison. Who knew what awaited her there?

The noise was deafening as she passed. Some of the inmates were cursing at her, some of them were cooing with soft romantic language and some of them were shouting out questions.

Tracy looked straight ahead.

Another set of bars, a dark and deserted corridor and then Tracy was led to a small room and, when she saw Mrs. Hopwood sitting there, she breathed a sigh of relief.

She rushed forward, collapsed in the chair opposite her, a table in between them and said, "You've come to bail me out!"

Mrs. Hopwood shook her head. "I'm sorry. I can't. I just don't have the money."

Tracy looked at the guard, who had closed the door and was now leaning against the wall, a blank look on her flat face. "Don't I get any privacy?"

"Not unless this lady is your lawyer."

Tracy turned to Mrs. Hopwood. "You got a house you could put up. And I swear to you, I won't skip out. My dog, did you get him out of the shelter?"

Mrs. Hopwood nodded.

"How is he?"

"A pain in the neck. He's not happy living indoors and being away from you."

"Then get me out of here!"

"Do you know anyone by the name of Dagny?"

Tracy was startled by the odd question. "What kind of a name is that?"

"Do you?" Mrs. Hopwood pressed on.

"No."

"Are you sure? She was a photographer."

"I guess I would remember someone who had a name like that."

"What about your husband? Had he ever met a Dagny?"

"I'm not sure. I thought I knew Victor. I thought we had a decent marriage, not perfect, but not any better or worse than anyone else's. Then I find out that he had this whole different life. Maybe it was because I wasn't able to give him children. He really wanted a big family. He would get teary eyed every time he saw a baby carriage. Of course, at first he thought it was his fault, because he had some blood disease. But then I took tests…" Tracy leaned over and began to whisper—why should the guard overhear every word. "The day he died he told me that he had a big surprise for me. I thought at first he was going to tell me that he was leaving me. But no, he said I would be very happy with the news. And that he loved me. And then, and then he was murdered."

"I'm sorry," Mrs. Hopwood muttered.

"After he died, I rummaged the apartment, looking for a clue to what he was going to tell me. Maybe he won the lottery, or got an inheritance from a distant relative. For days I waited for a phone call, but it never came. Whatever Victor was going to tell me, he took it to the grave with him." Tracy paused and took a deep breath. "Isn't there something you can do for me? Anything? You don't know what it's like here. Sure, I was homeless, but I was free. I could move around. Here they tell you when to eat, what to eat, when to go to bed, when to get up. You don't know how lucky you are. You're pretty, got yourself a husband, a nice house, friends. You don't know how quickly it can all change."

"I'll talk to the detectives."

"I didn't steal that money or hurt that woman."

"I believe you."

"Please, please, take care of my dog! Don't let anything happen to him! I love him more than life itself."

"Time's up," the guard shouted.

"I'm afraid my time was up a long time ago," Tracy said sadly.

FORTY-NINE

MRS. JOHNSON WAS sitting at her desk, when Miss Turnipseed wrenched open her closed door, hurried inside and whispered in her ear. "A nun has just arrived. Her name is Sister Maria Anna and she says she's the new principal. I told her we already have a principal, but she was pretty insistent. I tell you," Miss Turnipseed's leaned in even closer, "she keeps on grinning and it's making her look cuckoo."

So that was it. So soon. "Send her in."

"Are you sure? I could call Mr. Salisbury." Mr. Salisbury, seventy-eight year old, sometimes doubled as security.

"I'll be fine."

The woman, who reluctantly entered the office, was not at all what Mrs. Johnson expected. She was slightly overweight with a round, smiling face, warm brown eyes, a sharp nose like the end of a sharpened pencil and a few gray springy curls sticking out from her black veil. She was dressed in the usual nun habit, navy blue mid length skirt, white button down blouse, a huge silver cross around her neck, ending on her full breasts and sturdy, brown, laced shoes. "How do you do?" she extended a warm hand to Mrs. Johnson. "Do you mind if I sit down?"

"Of course. After all, this is your office now."

Sister plopped down on the chair. "I have to confess

I really don't know how this came about." She turned around and eyed Miss Turnipseed, who was casting curious looks, as she pretended to file papers very close to the office. "Do you mind if we talk alone?"

Mrs. Johnson nodded and watched as a gleeful smile spread across Sister's full face and then she gently closed the door. "Anyway," she sank down again, "I've been teaching first grade for thirty-five years. Can you believe it? I thought it was time for me to get out of the classroom and try my hand at administration. I got my masters but I never expected to get a job so soon. I certainly didn't anticipate being yanked out of my classroom, when there are only a few months left of school. But when Sister Mary Grace called—Well, I don't have to tell you. You can hardly say no to her."

Mrs. Johnson was silent as she tried to think of how to respond.

"I'm afraid I'm going to need a lot of help."

"I'll do whatever I can to make the transition smoother for you."

"Another thing, if anyone should ask me, I'm going to tell a little white lie and pray that God will forgive me. But, you know, the seventh graders have been through so much. Having you as a teacher at the beginning of the year, and then having Mrs. Sugarman die suddenly, you felt that was just too hard on them. So you decided that, for their sakes, returning to the classroom where you started would give them some stability."

Mrs. Johnson still didn't know what to say but she was grateful.

"Now, if you want to go around and introduce me to the staff, I will say I am here at your request."

"That would be fine," Mrs. Johnson said. "Just fine."

MRS. JOHNSON SPENT the rest of the day taking Sister Maria Anna on a tour of the school and the church, introducing her to all of the staff—including Father Bartholomew who continued to be baffled as to who she was and why she was at the school and Pearl who offered her a lukewarm cup of tea and a stale cupcake. Mrs. Hopwood spent her entire prep describing the fashion show and explaining why it would be the highlight of the year, if not the decade.

"Tomorrow is the dress rehearsal in the auditorium we're renting from Saint Fabius. Would you like to come and watch?"

"I certainly would! It is all so exciting and wonderful that you were able to put together such a worthwhile project. Mrs. Johnson, you probably should open the show—then introduce Mrs. Hopwood. There will be no need to refer to me at all but I'll be in the audience cheering you on."

Mrs. Hopwood exchanged a smile with Mrs. Johnson. For the first time in a very long time, Mrs. Johnson thought everything was going to turn out just fine.

Until she went to the dress rehearsal the following morning.

MRS. JOHNSON ARRIVED early and, because she knew that her friend was going through a tumultuous time, she brought with her a chocolate croissant and a cup of hazelnut coffee. Mrs. Hopwood was appreciative but Mrs. Johnson had not thought of bringing anything for Sister Maria Anna so it was a bit awkward. Especially since Sister Maria Anna looked like a woman, who liked to eat.

And unfortunately, the rehearsal was not getting off to a good start.

For one thing quite a few people were late, which created a real problem since the auditorium was booked by the local Sons of Jacob for their annual talent show.

The girls and their volunteer parents came strolling in a half an hour after the appointed time, carrying coffee—which Mrs. Hopwood could hardly object to since she had her own cup, and then they insisted on talking amongst themselves.

It took Mrs. Hopwood several minutes to get their attention.

"We're not actually going to try on the clothes. It's just important that you know, and the volunteer assigned to help you knows, when your change of clothing occurs. Yesterday I gave you all the information."

"I lost the paper."

"My mother couldn't come. She had to go to court."

"My aunt is coming but first she has to bring my brother to the ER. He got bit by a snake."

"I need another paper too. My father used it to line the parakeet's cage."

"Mrs. Hopwood, could I speak to you for a moment?"

Mrs. Hopwood nodded and directed the woman to a corner—where much to Mrs. Johnson's dismay—she was sitting with Sister Maria Anna.

"I'm Melissa Ortiz's mother."

"Yes, we've met." Mrs. Hopwood looked helplessly at Mrs. Johnson, as though Mrs. Johnson was in a position to help.

"I don't know if Melissa told you but the police came

looking for that green bag, you know the one with the leaf on it. But Melissa couldn't find it."

"Yes, I spoke to your daughter."

"I know who took it. It was that creepy super, who lives above us, Mr. Penroy. I never trusted him."

Mrs. Johnson could tell by the flicker of recognition on Mrs. Hopwood's face, and the indistinct noise which came from her throat that she had made the connection.

"Mr. Penroy?"

"When I got home from work the police were still searching, rifling through the garbage in the alley. I don't think they found it though. He's not stupid enough to throw it in his own trash bin."

"This Mr. Penroy," Mrs. Hopwood forged ahead, "does he by any chance communicate with the dead?"

"I think that's against our religion," Sister Maria Anna said quietly.

"That what he claims. I can't say whether he's successful or not. What I can say is that all those séances have brought roaches into our building. You know, the dead don't like to be disturbed."

"They shouldn't be disturbed. That's against our religion," Sister Maria Anna repeated.

"Thank you for telling me all this. If you could go behind stage and stand with your daughter, I'd appreciate it. We'll be ready in a few minutes." Mrs. Hopwood nudged Mrs. Johnson and stepped aside and—much to Mrs. Johnson's irritation—they were followed by Sister Maria Anna.

"Don't say it," was all Mrs. Johnson could utter.

"You don't see this? You're going to deny that there's a connection?"

"I am not going to a roach infested apartment to get in touch with a dead woman."

"Against our religion," Sister Maria Anna said firmly.

"We don't have to go for that purpose. We could go there and just ask a few questions, find out whether or not he actually took the green bag."

The confusion on Sister Maria Anna's face told Mrs. Johnson that she needed to nip this in the bud.

"It doesn't matter whether or not he took the purse. The police have the other four handbags and they were empty. So whatever was hidden had to have been in the green bag. If Penroy is the culprit and he stole the bag, then he got exactly what he wanted and that is the end of the entire matter."

"No, it's not."

Mrs. Johnson was afraid to ask what she meant.

"Melissa told me that Penroy came into the apartment several days ago. If had stolen the purse, it was before Mrs. Sugarman was murdered."

"Murdered?" Sister Maria Anna piped in.

"If he had found what he was looking for, then he would have no reason to meet Mrs. Sugarman in order to get a hold of what he thought was another handbag. And he wouldn't have killed her."

"We don't know that she was murdered," Mrs. Johnson argued.

"Yes, she was. It was on the news this morning. She was hit over the head with a heavy object."

Mrs. Johnson was resisting the urge to hit Mrs. Hopwood over the head with a heavy object, especially when she caught the expression on Sister's face. "We don't know that her death had anything to do with the handbags. It could have just been a drug deal gone wrong."

"A drug deal?" Sister Maria Anna sank down on one of the rickety chairs as a rumbling of angry voices broke out.

"Mrs. Hopwood said that I could wear the red dress."

"Well, the blue dress doesn't fit me!"

"I don't think we have enough chairs."

"This red carpet is not long enough to go down the aisle."

"That's because you cut it crooked."

"I did not!"

"Can we get started here? I have to take my husband for a colonoscopy."

"I had no idea." Sister Maria Anna paled. "I gave up watching the news for Lent and never went back. Sister Mary Grace told me that the school had some problems, but I never expected..." She stopped in mid-sentence, and made the sign of the cross.

"Why don't we go back to your office?" Mrs. Johnson suggested. "I'll give you the keys and wish you luck. Oh, and I'll be praying for you."

FIFTY

MELISSA WAS HALF ASLEEP, dreaming of school, and Mrs. Hopwood, and the strange smiling nun, when she heard a furious rapping on the front door. Her eyes flew open and she saw her mother spring up.

"What the..." She stopped suddenly. "At eight o'clock on a Sunday morning. Give me a break!"

"Who is it?" her father's voice bellowed from the other room.

"Police. Open up."

She watched as her mother's face turned ashen. "Oh God!" She hopped out of bed and Melissa reluctantly followed her into the living room,

"You got a warrant?"

"We just want to talk. Here or down the precinct. You choose."

In the hallway a door opened—the nosy neighbor, Mrs. Sterling.

They stood there the three of them, eying each other, her father in his boxer shorts, with a paunchy stomach, a stained undershirt, her mother, in a ribbed tank top, her breasts spilling out, her shorts, exposing white, flabby legs, streaked with cellulite. Melissa was in a jogging suit.

Her father threw her mother a sweatshirt and ordered her to cover herself and then he opened the door wider.

It was the same two cops who came bursting through the door.

"What do you want now?" her father demanded. "More questions about the pocketbooks?"

"No," the policeman answered as his eyes scanned the room.

"Well, I got nothing to say." He looked at Melissa. "She ain't talking either."

"We don't want to talk to either one of you," the policewoman said, not looking quite as friendly this time.

Both Melissa, tingling with fear, and her father looked over at her mother, who was nervously using her fingers to sift through her greasy hair.

"We're here to speak to your son, Adam," the policewoman said.

"What for?" her mother questioned. "My son is a good boy."

Melissa didn't miss the smirk that the cops exchanged.

"He's a minor," her father said. "You're not allowed to speak to him without my permission."

"That's entirely true." The policeman said in a self-satisfied tone. "Technically we cannot question a minor without a parent present. So you're free to stay, or again, if you'd rather, come down the precinct with us."

"Does he need a lawyer?" Her mother's wide eyes traveled to the closed door.

"That might depend."

"On what?" Her father was worried also, but his anxiety came out as anger.

"Would you mind waking him?" The policewoman asked politely.

BUT THERE WAS no need to wake him. Adam's door opened. He stood there, in a deep stupor, rubbing his eyes, looking at his parents and then to the police—clueless to the thread of the conversation.

"What's going on?" he asked in a feeble and exhausted way.

"Are you Adam Ortiz?" the policeman asked.

"Yeah."

"What do you know about the murder of Nancy Sugerman?"

"Who?"

"Murder!" Melissa's mother gasped. "You're accusing my son of murder?"

"He doesn't know Mrs. Sugarman." Melissa thought it was about time she intervened. "He never even went to St. Polycarp. Why would he murder someone he doesn't know?"

"Get out of my house. Right now." Her father stood in front of his son.

"We can go," the policewoman said in an agreeable voice. "But I'm afraid that we're going to have to take your son with us."

"You haven't read him his rights." Melissa knew that she sounded rather foolish.

"That's because he's not officially a suspect. But since you brought it up," the policeman began, "You have the right to remain silent. If you give up that right…"

"Please!" Adam bellowed, finally jerked out of his trance. "I know my rights. But I don't understand what's going on." He managed to sound confused but Melissa knew when her brother was lying. And he was lying now. He had a tell-tale sign, rubbing his chin with his left hand. Obvious to the police as well. "What are you talking about?" He swallowed hard.

"Your cell phone puts you in the exact location at the exact time Nancy Sugarman was murdered."

"I lost my cell phone."

Except at that exact moment, as though God Himself was signaling, a cell phone rang from the open door where Adam was standing.

"Your cell phone and your buddy's, Logan Briggs."

Adam's face had turned a funny shade of gray and his eyes veered left and right.

"Tell them, tell them that you had nothing to do with that," her mother begged.

"We didn't kill her," Adam blurted out. "She was already dead when we got there!"

"Oh my God!" Melissa's mother staggered sideways and then sank to the floor.

"Don't say another word," her father cautioned. "We're getting you a lawyer."

"You will feel better if you come clean," the policewoman said soothingly.

"That's a crock." Her father stood eye to eye with the policewoman who stared right back at him. "They tell you that just to make their job easier. They need to convict you, guilty or not."

"Were you there, Adam, to sell drugs?" the policewoman asked.

"No, not me. Logan's the one who is the dealer. I just went along to keep him company. She was supposed to give us two hundred and fifty dollars for some Percocet. But the deal never went down. We found her lying on the ground like that. We just took off."

"And that's all you know?" the policewoman urged.

"Yeah, that's it. But think about it. Why would we murder the woman? She's our ideal customer, a lady from the right side of town, a teacher with money. She might even bring some of her friends…"

Melissa closed her eyes, confirming what she already knew. Her brother was a complete idiot, unaware of what he had just said. But her father had caught on. He released a sigh of disgust.

"Did you hear yourself?" the policeman asked, with a judicious air. "You said, she's our ideal customer."

Adam's face crunched in confusion.

"*Our* ideal customer?" the policeman repeated, "That means you were dealing too."

Adam hung his head.

"As to why you would murder her?" the policeman continued. "Maybe you thought she was a snitch and was going to turn you in."

"Nah. She was a drug addict."

"How could you be sure of that?" the policewoman asked.

"Read it on Facebook."

"We're going to have to take you in." The policeman reached in his pocket for handcuffs. "Your parents can come with you."

"You're dealing!" his father roared. "What the hell were you thinking?"

"Maybe," her mother said in a terrified whisper, "just maybe he was thinking he was trying to be like you."

"So this is my fault? What the hell were you doing when I was locked up? At least I'm healthy. Nothing wrong with my genes. I didn't pass nothing on to my children."

"Can I get dressed?" Adam asked sheepishly.

Melissa retreated into the bedroom, crawled under her covers, and stayed there for the remainder of the day.

FIFTY-ONE

THE WEEKENDS WERE the hardest. It wasn't that she and Monte ever had a lot to say, but he was there, and there was something comforting having someone else in the house, watching television, drinking coffee, commenting on the news.

She hadn't lived alone for years and years and she didn't like the way that the house felt so empty.

Maybe it wasn't so much that she missed Monte but she missed the companionship.

It had gotten so bad that she was even grateful for Sugar Daddy's company. He had become better adjusted and had taken to sleeping on her bed. Maybe it was a good thing that Monte left. He would never allow her to take a homeless animal.

Still she didn't want Sugar Daddy to get used to a warm bed and two meals a day. Because when Tracy got out of jail, she would, no doubt, want her dog back.

Mrs. Hopwood hadn't told Alex about Monte leaving yet. If she hadn't heard from Alex, she always assumed that he was doing fine. She didn't want to give him any reason to fall off of the narrow path.

Except on Sunday night he phoned.

"What is going on there?"

"What do you mean?" She decided it was better to act bewildered.

"Dad called. He said that the two of you have separated, that the marriage just wasn't working out."

"Well, that's not quite true. It was working just fine for me. He walked out."

"Why?"

"He was tired of my working at St. Polycarp. He said that there was too much drama." Alex didn't answer, so she launched into an explanation. "But it's important that you know, Alex, that you understand, that none of this is my fault. My Aunt Eunice died, she's your great aunt, and your Aunt Roseanne said I could have whatever I wanted. So I took some vintage clothes, and some vintage handbags, shoes too—but no one wants those—for the express purpose of having a fashion show at St. Polycarp—because the school needs money. But someone thought that there was something hidden in one of the purses. He could have even been a murderer. So he started stealing the purses. Meanwhile, this teacher, well, she's really a school librarian, she was a drug addict, so she stole one of the purses to buy drugs, I guess..."

"Have you considered counseling?" Alex interrupted her.

"Yes, I have. But I doubt your father would go. You know how he doesn't like to talk in front of strangers."

"I mean, for you, Mom. You should go by yourself."

"That's ridiculous. Why would I do that? You're not understanding, Alexander. You see this old woman put a curse on the school, some years ago, and we want the curse removed, Mrs. Johnson and I. But she's dead, the old woman, not Mrs. Johnson. Anyway, there is this creepy super, who may have stolen one of the handbags, but he communicates with the dead, and if we can hire him…"

"Do you want me to come home, Mom? Because if you want me to come home, I will."

"No, absolutely not. How would that be helpful? I want you to stay where you are, finish your last semester and graduate."

"Yeah about that…"

Mrs. Hopwood didn't think she could take any more bad news. "What do you mean?" she asked slowly.

"I'm short a few credits."

"How many?"

"Twenty-two."

"Twenty-two?"

"I have been under a lot of pressure, you know, family problems."

"What are you talking about? I am your family and your father and I have just started to have trouble. Until recently, we were perfectly normal."

"You think?"

At that precise moment Sugar Daddy started to bark. The scary thing was that Mrs. Hopwood never knew what he was responding to.

"Is that the television?" Alex asked.

"No."

"You bought a dog?"

"Not really. I'm holding it for a homeless woman, who is in jail. I gave her one of the purses but somehow she's also involved in this horrible murder…"

"Mom…"

"Just stay where you are, Alex, and I'll find a way to fix this."

"Yeah, well, I hope you can, Mom, I really do."

"I can."

Mrs. Hopwood hung up the phone, but the truth was that she couldn't shake off the lurking feeling that the worst was yet to come.

THE HOUSE WAS so lonely and so quiet that Mrs. Hopwood was actually looking forward to going to school on Monday morning. After all, Sister Maria Anna seemed like a mild mannered person, who was unlikely to cause trouble and who, hopefully, wouldn't bother her too much. And now that Mrs. Johnson was back in seventh grade, she'd have to stop bossing Mrs. Hopwood around.

Mrs. Hopwood had no sooner entered her classroom, when she saw Melissa waiting for her at her desk.

"You're not supposed to be in school until the first bell." The moment she said it, Mrs. Hopwood felt a pang of regret. Melissa's face puckered as though she was about to cry.

"I'm sorry, but I had to talk to you. Yesterday the police came and arrested my brother, Adam."

"For what?"

"For killing Mrs. Sugarman. It's so crazy. Adam admitted that they went there to sell her drugs, but Adam says that it never happened because when they got there, she was already dead, so they just ran away. The police don't believe him. My parents tried to talk to the police, but they hate my father because he's been in prison and my mother gets verbally abusive—I was wondering if maybe you could call them."

Mrs. Hopwood heard footsteps in the hall. She was hoping that it was Mrs. Johnson but when she turned around, it was Addison.

"Do you know where Mrs. Johnson is? The copy machine is broken and someone has to call the repair man."

"Mrs. Johnson is no longer principal." She saw the look of surprise on both Addison's and Melissa's face. "I suggest you talk to Sister Maria Anna." She turned to Melissa. "I'll see what I can do," she promised, knowing that she could probably do very little.

And since the three people she seemed to love most thought she had lost her senses, her husband, her son, and her best friend, all she could hope to do was to prove them all wrong.

"DETECTIVE HARGROVE, PLEASE."

"Who's calling?"

"Julia Hopwood."

"Hey, Hargrove, Nancy Drew is on line two."

It took several minutes for Detective Hargrove to come to the phone. "What can I do for you, Mrs. Hopwood?" From the tone of her voice, it was obvious that she didn't want to do anything.

"I'm actually calling on behalf of the Ortiz family. I understand you're holding Adam for the murder of Mrs. Sugarman. He told you that the drug deal never happened and you have to know that's true, because you found that money on Tracy Holtz. I know because Tracy called me, asking me to bail her out. So I don't really understand…"

"Well, quite frankly, you don't need to understand. But I'll tell you anyway. We're not holding him on murder. We're holding him on possession with the intent to sell."

Mrs. Hopwood didn't know what to say, so she asked about bail.

"It hasn't been set yet. Any more questions?"

Mrs. Hopwood had already called twice, once to tell them how she believed the murderer knew that she had the handbag and once to discuss her theory about how the murderer could not have found what he was looking for, even if he had the green bag. Evidently from her cold and clipped tone, Detective Hargrove was getting tired of Mrs. Hopwood's interference.

So Mrs. Hopwood just hung up.

MRS. HOPWOOD MADE the decision before her prep was over. She would walk home with Melissa and talk to her parents, tell them what she had learned from the police. What she really wanted to do was contact Mr. Penroy and she doubted very much if Mrs. Johnson would take her.

When she told Melissa of her plans, Mrs. Hopwood was surprised by her reaction. She seemed skeptical, but, because she could hardly refuse after she had asked for help, Melissa agreed.

So at the end of the day, they walked to the tenements, making small talk about the upcoming fashion show, which was less than a week away. Mrs. Hopwood wished with her heart and soul that she had never agreed to any of this.

Too late.

WHEN THEY ARRIVED at the building with the broken entrance door, the wobbly stairs, and the graffiti spray painted on the walls, Mrs. Hopwood noticed that Mr. Maurice Penroy lived in 2A.

And Melissa lived on the fifth floor. When they finally reached her door, with Mrs. Hopwood, huffing and puffing, trailing behind, Melissa asked her to wait in the hall. "I have to tell my mother that you're here."

Mrs. Hopwood had no choice but to wait, fiddling with her phone, wondering how safe she was, if someone should suddenly burst out of their apartment and rob her, and feeling guilty for even thinking such thoughts.

"Mrs. Hopwood." Melissa's mother, dressed in a skin tight black uniform with a tag that read, *Welcome, my name is Winifred*, threw open the door. "Melissa said you wanted to speak to me. Is something wrong?"

"No, not at all. Melissa asked me to call the police and find out what was going on with your son. I spoke to Detective Hargrove."

"That witch."

"Anyway, she told me that they're holding your son on drug charges, not on murder, and no bail has been set yet."

"I already know that."

"Oh."

"Look, I realize you're just trying to be helpful, but the truth is that I wish I had never heard of St. Polycarp. Besides the police breaking in and demanding we give them the green purse, which has strangely disappeared, and the murder of that seventh grade teacher, it's just been too much. We are going to transfer Melissa for the fall semester. I'm sure you understand."

"Of course. Well, I guess I'll see you Saturday night."

Mrs. Ortiz didn't even answer. Instead she just slammed the door. Considering the chilly reception she had received, Mrs. Hopwood was thinking maybe it wasn't such a good idea to visit Mr. Penroy. But then again she was here, and she might not have the opportunity again.

She hobbled down the stairs and wasn't surprised when she saw the sign on his door which read, *No solicitors*. The bell was broken, so she knocked once, almost hoping he didn't answer.

Her heart quickened when she heard footsteps and the door flew open. A little man wearing baggy pants and a crisp white shirt, with a red bow tie, glared at her with small, gray, beady eyes covered with round glasses. He was missing several front teeth.

"Are you Maurice Penroy?" Mrs. Hopwood detected the odor of a cat.

"Who are you?"

"My name is Julia Hopwood. I'm trying to get in touch with someone who is dead."

Mr. Penroy didn't even blink.

"She was an elderly lady, who put a curse on our school. I don't really know her name but she was Starlight Moony's grandmother. Maybe you knew her." The way he was staring at Mrs. Hopwood gave her the willies. "I heard you do that kind of work."

"What about her?"

"Pardon?"

"Your friend?"

"If you're referring to Mrs. Johnson, well, I don't know if she really believes…"

"I'm referring to your dead friend, your murdered friend."

A wave of fear enveloped Mrs. Hopwood and it occurred to her that he knew all about Mrs. Sugarman because he had caused her death. She backed away just slightly, as to not arouse suspicion. "Well, yes, I wouldn't mind talking to her also. Maybe at the same time?" She tried to sound hopeful. He was studying her red patent leather Mary Janes. "Well, maybe not at the same time. Maybe one after another. And then there is that homeless man, who died in our cellar. Maybe he knows something, you can never tell."

"Five hundred dollars."

"Pardon?"

"That's what it will cost you."

"Well, yes, but what if no one comes?"

"Then it's your hard luck. The truth is there's no guarantees. Some dead like to stay dead—others—they like the company of the living."

After an awkward pause, Mrs. Hopwood blurted out, "Can you find something for me?" And then she added hastily, "A green purse?"

"What do I look like? Lost and found?" His expression remained blank.

Mrs. Hopwood stepped back even further. "I'd also like to get in touch with Victor Holtz."

His blank face changed from annoyance to confusion to anger in a matter of minutes. "Who are you again?"

"I told you. My name is Julia Hopwood."

"You from the police?"

"No, I'm a teacher."

Mr. Penroy started to close the door so Mrs. Hopwood talked quickly. "No, really, I want to hire you. I'm not sure when. Can you do it in the afternoon, like at this time?"

He nodded.

"Do you take credit cards?"

"Cash only."

"Do you have a card with your number on it?"

Mr. Penroy reached inside his clearly pressed pants and pulled out a crisp, white business card, his name written neatly in olive ink, on a pink background, Maurice Penroy, Communication with People Who Passed.

"I'll be in touch. My name is…"

"Julia Hopwood. And the woman you want to get in touch with. Her name is Mrs. Mooney." Then Mr. Penroy did slam the door.

Now all Mrs. Hopwood had to do was find a way to get Mrs. Johnson to 13 Lyman Street.

FIFTY-TWO

SHE WAS OUT.

Tracy didn't know why but the guard had come for her and told her that she was free to go. Free to go after days of being locked up in a cell, alone. But the guard did caution that she shouldn't leave the area.

"Right," was Tracy's response. "That means I have to cancel my flight to Paris."

When she walked out of the prison, clutching her plastic bag, with her ripped wallet and her two dollars, with her shredded tissues and her broken red lipstick, after she got caught in the pouring rain, she made a decision.

Her life was simply not worth living.

Twelve years—twelve years for destroying two lives.

And it wasn't just George, who should have been serving time. What about his wife, who started all the trouble, who lured Victor, a man who had been faithful and loving until he met her.

There was no way Tracy was going to let them get away with this.

Then there was poor Robert. The police suspected that he might have been killed. If that were the case, if she didn't avenge his death, who would?

If she had to spend the rest of her life in jail, so what? Sugar Daddy was in a good home. Mrs. Hopwood would no doubt take care of him, feed him well, and give him a better life than Tracy ever could. Because Tracy loved him so much, the best thing she could do was to let him go—and as for her? Was being in jail so much worse than living in the streets? Maybe they would give her some training, so when she left she could find a decent job. Maybe the jury would take pity on her.

A plan was beginning to form in her mind, a plan to even the score.

All she needed was a weapon.

FIFTY-THREE

"WILL YOU BRING me to a séance?"

"What?"

"I met the super in Melissa Ortiz's building, Mr. Penroy. I have to admit he's very strange, could even be a killer."

"They why would we want to…"

"He says that he can get in touch with Starlight's grandmother and even Mrs. Sugarman."

"That's probably because he killed Mrs. Sugarman. Then she's going to come back from the dead and point the finger at someone else. Why do you care anyway?"

"Because I have nothing left. I come home every night to an empty house except for Sugar Daddy. Alex called me. It's obvious that Monte got to him first."

"Have you heard from Monte?"

"Nothing. He's convinced Alex that I'm insane. And if I lose my job, how will I support myself?"

The last thing that Mrs. Johnson felt like was going to a séance in some creepy man's apartment, who might just be a murderer. But she felt terrible for Mrs. Hopwood, who was obviously in the deepest state of gloom. Maybe, just maybe, a curse could be lifted and things could return to normal.

But shouldn't she believe that only God could lift a curse?

"I'm not even going to ask you to pay for it." Mrs. Hopwood, if nothing else, was relentless.

"And just how much are you going to pay?"

"Five hundred dollars."

"That is beyond crazy."

"I know. But I'm a desperate woman."

"All right. I'll go, but," and then Mrs. Johnson repeated the phrase, which she had said so often to Mrs. Hopwood, "I don't like this. I don't like this at all."

MRS. JOHNSON RECEIVED a text right in the middle of when she was trying to explain the causes of World War II to her bored and sullen seventh graders.

Séance is set for Thursday at four o'clock.

Thursday at four o'clock was a bad time for Mrs. Johnson. It was the day when she had to take her twins to tennis, wait for them, and then drive them home. She'd have to ask her nanny to do it, pay her nanny overtime, which she should really charge Mrs. Hopwood for. After all if Mrs. Hopwood had money to throw around at a charlatan…

The three little dots which lingered on the page told Mrs. Johnson that Mrs. Hopwood had not finished.

Why don't you come over to the auditorium if you're not busy now? We're setting up for the fashion show.

I am teaching. Which is something you should do.

You're not the principal anymore and Sister Maria Anna said it was fine.

Mrs. Johnson had a feeling that everything was just fine for Sister Maria Anna, which was probably a good thing.

Thanks for wishing me a happy birthday.

Oh, is it your birthday. I am so sorry. But at least you have a family to spend it with.

Mrs. Johnson turned off her phone.

MRS. HOPWOOD MIGHT have forgotten her birthday, but her students had not.

Sister Maria Anna came bustling down the hall, just as Literacy was about to begin and asked Mrs. Johnson to step out of the classroom for a minute. She was guided down the hall quite a distance and then Sister asked her a nonsense question about a folder which had been misfiled.

Mrs. Johnson kept her eye on the door because she heard a ruckus developing inside her classroom and she was eager to return before she heard chairs overturning. So she quickly made her way back and was pleasantly surprised when the buzz of chatter ceased and a group of girls began to sing, a bit off key, *Happy Birthday*, and then presented her with a sloppily iced cake. Then the students took out the other treats, potato chips, cheese doodles, pretzels, Oreo cookies, donuts, gummy bars, and a bag of sour apples.

Sister Maria Anna insisted that Mrs. Johnson cut the cake, except that a knife was lacking, so Sister sent Chestnut Postel down to the cafeteria to fetch one, and he returned with a meat cleaver. The cleaver made jagged edges into the cake, but the excitable crowd hardly seemed to mind as they ate heartily on copy paper. Even Sister joined in on the festivities.

Luckily, the festivities only lasted forty long minutes, because it was the last period of the day.

After the students flew from the room—no doubt

feeling high after ingesting so much sugar and salt—
Mrs. Johnson looked at her classroom in horror. Chips
were scattered on the floor, spilled soda on the desk,
half eaten cookies on the book shelves and dirty nap-
kins strewed everywhere.

"I hate to leave this for the janitor." Mrs. Johnson
grabbed the trash can.

"No worries," Sister Maria Anna said cheerfully.
"I'll put a little something extra in his paycheck this
week. After all, you only have one birthday a year!"

"What happened here?" Mrs. Hopwood approached
the threshold.

"My students remembered my birthday."

"They're dear children," Sister Maria Anna said. "If
you ladies will excuse me, I have to meet with some
parents."

"She is about to learn that the dear children aren't always the products of dear parents," Mrs. Johnson said,
as soon as Sister was out of reach. "Do you want a piece
of cake?" Mrs. Johnson shoved the plate of crumbs in
front of Mrs. Hopwood's face.

"Absolutely not. Remember last time I ate a piece of
a student's cake? I found the lucky little doll buried in
the middle and I broke a tooth."

"Yes, but two days later you won one hundred dollars from the lottery."

"Which didn't begin to pay for the broken tooth."

Mrs. Johnson looked up and was startled to see Tracy
entering the classroom.

Mrs. Hopwood was the first to speak. "They let you
go."

"They did. I'm not sure why." Tracy entered the classroom and Mrs. Johnson gave her a fleeting, frightened

look, edging away as though Tracy was dangerous. She seemed different somehow, which Mrs. Johnson was guessing a stint in jail, even a short one, could change a body. "Would you like a piece of cake?" She held the paper platter out again and the meat cleaver fell to the floor.

"No, thank you."

Mrs. Johnson reached for an unopened bag of chips. "How about this? They haven't been open yet."

Tracy nodded.

Mrs. Johnson gave Tracy not only the chips, but a package of half eaten Oreos, some fruit rollups, two blueberry muffins, and a half a bottle of grape soda.

Then she threw the cake into the trash bin. And minutes late, Mrs. Johnson was dipping her hand into the garbage to retrieve the meat cleaver.

"I suppose now you're going to want Sugar Daddy back?" Mrs. Hopwood asked hoarsely.

"No, not now. Not until I get settled."

Mrs. Johnson noticed the relief on Mrs. Hopwood's face.

"WHAT HAPPENED HERE?" Mr. Salisbury, the janitor, asked the same question Mrs. Hopwood had asked, a look of disgust on his wrinkled face as he walked in.

"I can help you clean it." Tracy rested her plastic bags on one of the cleaner desks.

"You don't have to do that," Mrs. Johnson reassured her.

"It's okay. I don't have anything better to do or any place better to go."

Well, Mrs. Johnson did. And she was going home to her birthday celebration.

FIFTY-FOUR

"YOU SENT THAT woman to our home." Her mother hurled the accusation at Melissa.

"I thought she could help. She has a relationship with the police…"

"You don't get it, do you, Melissa? She's a rich teacher, playing the part of Mother Teresa. You're going to a new school next year and she's never going to give you a second thought. You're just going to be one of a hundred students whose name she can't even remember."

The lump in Melissa's throat prevented her from speaking.

"I've got to go to work. Your father is down the police station, trying to get some legal aid for Adam. Don't go anywhere, just stay put. I got enough trouble without you adding to it."

AFTER SHE LEFT Melissa went into her room and sat on the small twin bed. Her mother's cot was littered with clothing, dirty underwear, wet towels, and a pair of orange high heels.

A few moments alone. She'd raid the cabinets and pray that her father didn't come home for a long, long time.

But the cabinets were bare, a few broken crackers, a box of stale ginger snaps, a few lingering popcorn kernels and two scurry roaches.

Melissa was advancing towards the refrigerator—
where she didn't anticipate having any better luck—
when she heard a loud banging on her door.

Her first thought was that her father had forgotten
his keys—after all, he had lived twelve years in a cell
where no one entrusted him with a set of keys. Her second thought, coming soon after, was that maybe the
police were outside.

Or worse.

She waited a few minutes before tiptoeing towards
the door. She peered into the peep hole but all she saw
was a sea of black.

"Who is it?" she asked as she secured the chain on
the door. "What do you want?"

"I have to talk to Winifred Ortiz." The voice was
deep and indistinguishable.

"My mother is not here."

"What about your father?"

"He's not home either. He's down at the police station." The minute that Melissa uttered those words, she
knew that she had made a mistake. She had just admitted that she was alone in the house to a complete
stranger. "He should be back any minute," she added
quickly.

"Then I'll wait. Can I come inside?"

"No. I'm not supposed to let strangers into my apartment."

"I'm not a stranger."

"You are to me."

"Okay, I'll wait right here in the hall."

The threat scared Melissa, but if the person wanted
to wait outside, there wasn't much Melissa could do
about it. Except watch the door and pray.

"What are you doing here?" Mr. Penroy's voice rang out. "Who are you?"

"I'm waiting to speak to the Ortizs."

"Well, you can't wait in the hall. You're blocking traffic."

"I don't see any traffic."

"We don't let strangers in the building."

"Like I told the girl, I'm no stranger."

There was a moment of silence.

"I'm Tracy Holtz, Victor Holtz's wife."

Another moment of silence.

"You still can't wait here."

Melissa heard footsteps and then another threat. 'I'll be back."

She stood away from the door, trying to decide whether or not to phone her mother. Her mother didn't like to be disturbed at work. A ringing cell phone was a problem when she was taking an order, carrying a tray, and the boss didn't like it either. Except in cases of emergency.

Was this a case of emergency?

A loud knock interrupted her train of thought.

"Melissa?" She recognized Mr. Penroy's voice. "Are you okay?"

"I'm fine. Why wouldn't I be?"

"I just thought," he hesitated. "Anyway, maybe you'd like to know your teacher is coming to me on Thursday night. Wants me to lift a curse. Would you like to join us?"

"I don't think I can."

"I'd like you to come, Melissa. I have a feeling you'd find it beneficial."

"I'll see." She wouldn't even consider it without first

talking to Mrs. Hopwood. Although maybe it wouldn't be safe.

But Mrs. Hopwood would protect her. At least Melissa hoped that she could.

FIFTY-FIVE

"I CAN'T TELL you how much I don't want to do this," Mrs. Johnson whined as she turned on to Lyman Street.

Mrs. Hopwood thought it best not to comment.

"This entire thing is utterly ridiculous, agreeing to meet a man for a séance. He could murder us while we're sitting there in the dark and he could blame it on the dead."

"He invited Melissa Ortiz and she asked me if she could come. I could hardly refuse but I doubt if he would murder us in front of a child."

Mrs. Johnson stopped the car abruptly, pulling Mrs. Hopwood forward. She didn't complain.

"I think you should have refused," Mrs. Johnson said. "You are endangering a child. Who knows what he might do?"

Mrs. Hopwood had enough of remaining mute. "Why on earth would he steal handbags and murder drug addict teachers? What could possibly be his motive?"

"How on earth am I supposed to figure out what his motive could be? For all I know he could be mentally ill. Most serial killers are." Mrs. Johnson looked at the little knot of teenagers congregating on the corner, "I am not comfortable parking my car in such a seedy area."

"It's the neighborhood where most of our students live."

"Which is precisely why we are trying to educate them."

Mrs. Hopwood could have argued further. She could have reminded Mrs. Johnson that removing the curse would benefit St. Polycarp. But there was no advantage to arguing. It might just inflame Mrs. Johnson further.

She didn't utter a word when Mrs. Johnson cursed about the broken outer door, or the rickety stairs, that thankfully they didn't have to climb.

Mrs. Hopwood was just about to knock when the door flew open. Mr. Penroy was dressed all in black, right down to his bow tie. "Salutations!" he greeted them while chewing gum vigorously.

"Yeah, whatever." Mrs. Johnson pushed her way into the apartment.

Descending footsteps caused Mrs. Hopwood to look up. Melissa was running down the stairs in her pajamas and fluffy slippers. She flashed a quick smile but the corner of her mouth twitched ever so slightly, and there was a fearful look in her eyes.

As they followed Mr. Penroy from a living room, heavy with antiques, into a darkened room with lit candles, Mrs. Hopwood wondered who would be smiling after the séance.

They took their seats around a small wooden table, a Ouija board set up in the middle. Mrs. Hopwood sat in between Mr. Penroy and Mrs. Johnson and Melissa sat between Mrs. Johnson and Mr. Penroy, although she leaned towards Mrs. Johnson.

"Before we start, do you have my five hundred dollars?"

Mrs. Hopwood picked up her handbag from the floor, unzipped it, extracted her wallet and handed Mr. Penroy ten fifty dollar bills. He examined them carefully and then said that they didn't look real.

"I got them from the ATM machine," Mrs. Hopwood protested.

He shrugged, folded the money and stuffed it into his pocket. "I've given this a great deal of thought on how to proceed. I decided the best thing to do was to call Mrs. Mooney back. She's been on the other side for a long time, so she might be able to answer all of your questions."

He reached for the pointer and instructed Mrs. Hopwood to put her hands on it lightly. "Do not push. Let it glide on its own."

"I've done this before."

"Never with me. Let me ask the questions." He cleared his throat, continued to chew his gum and then said in a loud voice, "Ethel Mooney, are you here with us?"

Mrs. Hopwood felt the pointer travel to YES.

"Do you remember putting a curse on the school?" He turned towards Mrs. Hopwood. "What's the name of your school? St. Hedwig?" He spat through a missing tooth.

"St. Polycarp!"

"Shouldn't he have known that?" Mrs. Johnson questioned doubtfully.

Mr. Penroy glared at her. She glared right back.

The pointer jumped to YES.

"So ask her to remove the curse, please," Mrs. Hopwood said.

The pointer navigated to NO.

"This is a waste of time," Mrs. Johnson mumbled.

"Why won't she?" Mrs. Hopwood demanded. "It happened a long time ago. Her granddaughter doesn't have head lice anymore. She doesn't even go to our school…" Mrs. Hopwood was barely touching the pointer when it gave a sudden frightening lurch and began to jump all over the board.

MELISSA IN DANGER

All eyes turned toward Melissa. "I'm in danger?" she asked, in a somewhat chocked voice.

"From whom?" Mrs. Hopwood demanded.

Again the pointer moved with an alarming rapidity, spelling out…

MRS. SUGARMAN'S KILLER

Melissa scrambled up and so did Mrs. Johnson.

"How dare you!" Mrs. Johnson bellowed. "This is unforgivable, involving a child!"

"Madam, I can assure you, it's not I who is involving the child."

'Oh, and we're supposed to believe that this Ethel Mooney has returned from the grave to issue warnings to poor Melissa."

"I don't feel so good," poor Melissa said. "Like maybe I've already been poisoned."

"No one said that you're going to get killed." Mrs. Hopwood tried to be soothing.

"What else am I to think?" Melissa argued, "If I'm in danger from a murderer? I'm going back upstairs."

"I'll walk you." Mrs. Johnson offered.

As soon as they left, Mrs. Hopwood turned towards Mr. Penroy. "Can you ask her what happened to the green purse?" Of course, she was upset about Melissa but still she wanted and needed answers. And she had paid for them. So maybe she could figure out who the culprit was and prevent whatever was destined to happen.

The pointer began to move and stopped at the P.

PURSE NOT IMPORTANT

"It is to me!" Mrs. Hopwood rose. She stepped back when Mr. Penroy spit on her again. She thought she should go soon or Mrs. Johnson might leave without her. "I haven't got my five hundred dollars-worth of information. You have told me absolutely nothing."

Mr. Penroy pushed the Ouija board in the middle of the table. "They're the ones who told you nothing. It's not my fault, if the dead have better things to do."

"Well," Mrs. Hopwood hesitated. "Can you tell me if my husband is coming home?"

"Is he dead?"

"I don't think so."

Mr. Penroy balked. "I'm not a fortune teller."

"You're not much of anything," she mumbled, and then she made a beeline for the front door because she was a little frightened. Frightened but still annoyed. She had been conned by this strange man and now she was five hundred dollars poorer and Melissa was rightfully upset.

She remembered the quote by Pascal—"All of man's misfortune comes from one thing, which is not knowing how to sit quietly in a room."

She should have sat quietly in a room.

SHE FOUND MRS. JOHNSON waiting in the hall with a grumbled look on her face. Mrs. Hopwood was feeling grumpy herself. "Melissa was the only one who got information," she complained. "Maybe if she wasn't there, it would have been more productive for me."

"Don't tell me you believe this nonsense." Mrs. Johnson hurled the front door open.

"I don't know."

"Sister Maria Anna was right. All this hocus-pocus is against our religion. If I were you, I'd go to confession and start praying the rosary every night."

WHEN THE PHONE rang at eleven at night, Mrs. Hopwood snapped on the light. She hadn't been sleeping but still the jarring noise scared her. She didn't recognize the local number—it could be anyone. Maybe Monte with a new cell. Or a friend of Alex's.

"Hello."

"Is this Mrs. Hopwood?"

"Yes."

"This is Winifred Ortiz, Melissa's mother. I'm sorry for calling so late."

"Is Melissa all right?"

"No, she is not. And I take that back. I am not sorry for calling so late. Not sorry at all. Melissa is scared out of her wits. What sort of teacher are you? What kind of person are you? Inviting my daughter to a séance, where the dead are supposed to visit…"

"Actually I didn't invite her. Mr. Penroy did."

"She asked your permission and you should have said no. Did you have any idea why Mr. Penroy wanted her there? Well, I'll tell you why. Because he had plans to make the séance all about my daughter. He wanted to threaten her, frighten her, which he did. He is a dangerous person, whom Melissa's been told to avoid. I don't know if you know this, but my daughter, she's not well. She has a disease Haemochromatosis, which she inherited from me. She doesn't have any symptoms right now, but it could start at any time, trouble with her liver, her joints. She doesn't need to be stressed out. I won't be volunteering for the fashion show and Melissa won't be participating either. Thank God, this year is almost over. It's been a nightmare from start to finish."

Before Mrs. Hopwood could utter a word, Mrs. Ortiz had hung up.

Well, it was just as well.

Mrs. Hopwood had no defense.

SHE GOOGLED HAEMOCHROMATOSIS out of curiosity and read about the cause and the symptoms—tough luck for Melissa. For a girl, who already had a lot of tough luck.

And all Mrs. Hopwood could hope—there wasn't more trouble forthcoming.

FIFTY-SIX

AT FIRST TRACY was convinced that everything was going to work out in her favor.

She had planned on sneaking into the cafeteria and stealing a weapon. But the minute she walked in the door, she was greeted by a prissy, old maid of a woman, who, with a pained look, demanded to know what she wanted.

Tracy said the only thing she could think of—she had an appointment with Mrs. Hopwood.

"Her classroom is upstairs." The woman eyed Tracy with suspicion.

Tracy took her time climbing the stairs and then she followed the voices. She had interrupted some sort of birthday celebration. She couldn't remember the last time her birthday had been celebrated—the truth was sometimes she lost track of the days and her birthday went unnoticed, even by her. The African American teacher offered her a piece of crumbling cake and then kept throwing junk food at her.

When the janitor saw the classroom, he didn't look happy, so Tracy offered to help him, her eye on the meat cleaver, which had been used to cut the cake. She even offered to bring it down to the cafeteria, but he grabbed it first.

It didn't take a genius to know that the janitor— an elderly guy with a dripping nose—didn't trust her.

Maybe he didn't like homeless people and resented the fact that Robert had died in his basement. He told her not to bother. But Tracy said that sometimes Pearl left a sandwich for her on the counter and she wanted to go down and check.

The janitor grunted an agreement.

She followed the janitor down two flights of stairs.

No sandwich rested on the counter, of course. All the food was locked up for the night—but not the silverware. And while the janitor was busy emptying the trash can, Tracy was able to slip a sharp knife into her plastic bag.

Then she proceeded to Lyman Street.

Where she learned that the Ortizs weren't home and she was thrown out by peculiar looking man with a bow tie. She was planning to return until she saw the sign announcing St. Polycarp Fashion Show on Saturday night.

The perfect place to end it all.

FIFTY-SEVEN

MRS. JOHNSON WAS in the process of using the copy machine, when Sister Maria Anna glided by. "Good news!" she said, her eyes shining.

Mrs. Johnson couldn't imagine what sort of news could change the doomed course of events.

"I persuaded Sister Mary Grace to come to the fashion show!"

Mrs. Johnson did not consider this to be good news, but she managed to flash a weak smile. "I hope everything goes well."

"I just spoke to Mrs. Hopwood. She did say that the bidding has been a bit sluggish."

Mrs. Johnson hadn't asked Mrs. Hopwood about the bidding. She did not want sluggish news.

"So far it's up to one hundred and thirty-three dollars and thirteen cents."

Mrs. Johnson wasn't sure why anyone would bid thirteen cents and she wasn't about to ask.

"But I think that a lot of people will be bidding the night of the show, don't you?" Sister Maria Anna asked hopefully.

Another paper jam—and Mrs. Johnson needed these Math quizzes in fifteen minutes. "I hope so," she mumbled as she bent down and opened the copier door and began fumbling with the roller.

"I hate to bring this up," Sister said rather sheepishly, "but I have a complaint from Mr. Salisbury."

"I know my room was a mess after the party and I should have stayed to clean it up..." Right now Mrs. Johnson was hoping that she wouldn't be cleaning up her hands from the black toner.

"No, not that." A pained expression crossed Sister Maria Anna's usual beaming face. "He says there is a bag of shoes in Mrs. Hopwood's room and he's trying to tidy up. A group of people will be coming by to look at the building." Sister lowered her voice. "In case the school doesn't open in the fall. I think they might turn the space into some sort of clinic."

Then as far as Mrs. Johnson was concerned, the school should stay as messy as could be. But she didn't say any of this. Instead she just muttered. "He should talk to Mrs. Hopwood."

"Talk to me about what?" Mrs. Hopwood breezed down the hall, carrying a honey dip donut and a cup of coffee.

"The janitor says you have to get rid of the old shoes in classroom." Mrs. Johnson pulled on the stuck paper and it ripped. "Sister, I'm afraid you're going to have to ask Miss Turnipseed to call the repair man." And Mrs. Johnson would have to think of something else to do with her class during Math.

"What am I supposed to do with the shoes?" Mrs. Hopwood took a large bite from her donut.

"Just throw them out." Mrs. Johnson slammed down the lid of the copy machine in anger, almost catching her fingers in the process.

"I can't throw them out," Mrs. Hopwood followed

Mrs. Johnson down the hall as Sister bustled away, promising to call the repair man. "They're vintage."

"They're old."

"By the way Mrs. Ortiz called me late last night, screaming at me for involving Melissa in the séance."

"You can hardly blame her."

"She said Melissa wouldn't be participating in the fashion show, but I guess Melissa cried enough, because she told me this morning, her mother said all right." Mrs. Hopwood trotted alongside Mrs. Johnson. "I have a bad feeling about Saturday night. Everything is set to go, but what if no one comes?"

"Well, at least you tried. No one can say you didn't."

"What if no one buys the clothes?"

"You can throw them away with the shoes. Look, I have to figure out something to do in Math. Don't worry, it will be fine," she lied.

But Mrs. Hopwood had known her too long. "Yeah, sure it will," she mumbled.

Mrs. Johnson took the easy way out. She told the students to make up the problems and then solve them. The students would trade papers and anything that they didn't complete in class would be done at home.

The students fell silent, eager to get the work done.

In the meantime, she would correct the history essays and maybe give out some stickers. Even teenagers liked stickers. She had stashed some in the bottom drawer but, she had a feeling, Mrs. Sugarman had gotten to them first, too cheap to buy her own—too poor because she was spending all of her money on drugs.

She shouldn't think ill of the dead.

The stickers were gone, of course, only a blank sticky

page remained. But she found something else, on the bottom of the drawer. It was a small pill box with the initials DD engraved on the top. Dagny Danvers, and it matched the compact.

She reached for her phone and immediately sent a text to Mrs. Hopwood.

The first chance you get, come to my classroom.

Can't do it now. Teaching the objective case.

Never mind the objective case. This is important.

Twenty minutes to dismissal. See you then.

"OH MY GOD!" Mrs. Hopwood exclaimed the moment Mrs. Johnson handed the pill box—which she dropped immediately as though she had received an electric shock. "You know what this means. This means that it was in the purse I gave to Mrs. Sugarman, which is where the compact must have been. That was Dagny's purse. But I bought that purse back. And it was empty by the time I got it. But maybe there was something else in it. And maybe Mrs. Sugarman, not realizing the significance, tossed it somewhere. Or maybe she didn't toss it at all and that's what got her killed."

"We should call the police," Mrs. Johnson decided.

But Mrs. Hopwood had other plans. "Not until we search this classroom top to bottom."

MRS. JOHNSON WANTED nothing more than to put the entire matter into the hands of the capable law officers, to go home, and to cook lasagna while she enjoyed a glass of red wine.

But she thought her days of humoring Mrs. Hopwood were numbered so she went along with the suggestion.

While she emptied out the desk, Mrs. Hopwood, in a frenzy of excitement, searched through the closets. Mrs. Johnson discovered a crossword puzzle book—many started, none completed—a pair of heavy socks with small holes in the heel, three bottles of sanitizers, a box of Ritz crackers and a ripped copy of Donald Trump's, *Art of the Deal*.

Mrs. Hopwood found nothing more significant and she jammed the contents back into the closet, the contents consisting of wrinkled and torn bulletin board paper, paper stencils, broken and uncapped markers, paper clips and a copy of the Bible.

Mrs. Johnson gathered her belongings. "You call the police. I have to go home."

"What if they want me to bring the pill box to them?"

"They'll send a car."

"Can't you wait a few more minutes? Really?"

"I have a family!" The moment she uttered those four words and saw the sad expression which flashed on Mrs. Hopwood's face, she uttered, "All right. But hurry."

She sat down at her desk, held her head with her hand and waited, only slightly relieved when Mrs. Hopwood put the phone on speaker.

It took several minutes to reach Detective Hargrove and, as usual, she didn't sound happy.

"Mrs. Johnson found something in her desk drawer," she announced in a loud, jaunty voice.

"All right."

"If you remember, Mrs. Sugarman was teaching in that classroom."

A sigh. "Yes, I remember."

"Anyway, Mrs. Johnson found a pill box with the initials DD on it, Dagny Danvers."

A pause. Mrs. Hopwood shot Mrs. Johnson a hopeful look.

"And that is significant—why?"

Now it was Mrs. Hopwood who released the exasperated sigh. "Because that means that Mrs. Sugarman had the purse which the compact had originally come from, and that was the purse that the killer as after. Now I bought that purse and handed it over, it was the blue one, by the way, but at the time I got a hold of it, it was empty. Mrs. Johnson and I did a thorough search of this classroom, looking for something else that might have been hidden in the purse."

A longer pause, while Mrs. Johnson was wishing that Mrs. Hopwood's explanations didn't always sound so convoluted.

"Detective Hargrove, have you heard anything I told you?"

"I heard you. Now it's your turn to hear me. We don't know that Mrs. Sugarman's death has anything to do with these handbags that you and your friend have been chasing. The poor woman was a drug addict."

"I know. But I thought you cleared Adam Ortiz of that charge, because of the money Tracy found."

"No one has been cleared—just not charged. And by the way, drug addicts usually have more than one supplier. We searched Mrs. Sugarman's apartment thoroughly. We found nothing incriminating, certainly not something that would result in her murder."

"Oh." Mrs. Hopwood took a deep breath, after being jerked from the thought that she had discovered something of significance. "And what about the homeless man's autopsy?"

"He died from a blow on the head."

"He was murdered?" she shrieked.

"I didn't say that. He could have just as easily have fallen and hit his head. There was quite a bit of alcohol in his system. By the way, what time is your fashion show tomorrow night?"

"Why?"

"I may drop by."

"Seven o'clock."

"See you there."

Mrs. Hopwood put down her cell phone.

"You better hope it goes off without a hitch," Mrs. Johnson rose.

"Tell me something I don't know."

FIFTY-EIGHT

MRS. HOPWOOD WAS about to leave the building wher she spotted Mr. Salisbury, dragging a trash bag through the upstairs hall.

"Can't store these no more," he said.

"What are you throwing away?" she asked, her hear hammering.

"Bunch of shoes at the back of your classroom. got to clean before those people coming next week. told Sister all about it. She said I could toss whateve wasn't useful."

"The shoes are useful! And they're vintage!"

"So take them home."

"I can't. At least can you carry them to Mrs. Johnson's car?" Mrs. Johnson would have a fit but what else coulc Mrs. Hopwood do? She knew what she wanted to do, go home to her empty house and finish the half a pound o fudge she had bought for dinner. She wanted to crawl intc her bed, with Sugar Daddy at her feet, and turn her televi sion to a TCM black and white movie and never move. She didn't want to be stuck in the school for one moment longer

She followed Mr. Salisbury, listening as he grumblec something under his breath. She limped beside him ir her too tight cerise shoes, the white plastic bag behinc them. Suddenly Mr. Salisbury stopped.

"This bag is broken," he announced as he took a slug of his crème soda.

The shoes were all over the floor, the robin egg blue stack heels, the olive green round toed Mary Janes, the beige T straps, the brown and white oxfords, the brown loafers, the kitten white heels…

"So now what?" Mr. Salisbury stood with his hand on his skinny hip and burped noisily.

"Throw them away," she said with regret.

"You mean I got to pick up all this junk?"

Frantic footsteps were running up the stairs, which was just the diversion Mrs. Hopwood needed. She was too tired and too discouraged to be gathering old shoes.

Melissa stopped, stared at the shoes, at the janitor and finally at Mrs. Hopwood. "I need to speak to you. It's really important."

"I'm really sorry," Mrs. Hopwood told the janitor, as she guided Melissa away from the scattered shoes and down the stairs. "I'm in a hurry, so we can talk as I leave."

"We're going to the Dominican Republic," Melissa said breathlessly.

"Does that mean you're not going to be in the fashion show?" Mrs. Hopwood was feeling dizzy and nauseous.

"No, it's not that. I told you. My mom didn't want me to be in the fashion show. But when I threatened suicide, she finally agreed."

"I wished you hadn't done that, Melissa. Suicide is a pretty serious thing and making threats like that, not a good idea." She hesitated. "Your mother told me about your illness."

"Yeah, it's a bummer. Something I inherited from my mother."

"And your father?"

"My mother."

For a moment Mrs. Hopwood was stunned. "Are you sure?"

"Oh yeah, my father loves to throw it in her face. How he has perfect genes, never passed anything on to me. I'm very nervous about the fashion show."

"Don't be, Melissa, you're going to be fine. We are all going to be fine."

Even as she said it, Mrs. Hopwood suspected that it was a lie.

IT WAS A MISTAKE. Mrs. Hopwood knew that as she lay in her bed, watching television as the clock ticked towards midnight.

She should have kept the shoes, or at the very least, looked them over more carefully. Some of them were darn pretty, especially the blue ones. And it was nearly impossible to find a pair of white shoes with kitten heels, she could have at least tried them on.

Maybe they wouldn't be her size, but if something was spectacular then she knew how to make do. She wore a size 8 shoe, but in a pinch, she could fit into anything from size 7 to size 9.

And was she ever going to get those handbags back? After all they were hers and she could really use them. Nothing incriminating had been found in them. Even the police weren't interested in them anymore.

She'd like the green one with the copper leaf and the robin egg blue one she gave to Mrs. Sugarman. And her own violet purse as well.

But right now those handbags were the least of her problems.

Because tomorrow evening was the night of the fashion show.

MRS. HOPWOOD WASN'T sure what she was going to wear. She had to be on stage to introduce the fashion show, so everyone would expect her to look, well, fashionable. She should have bought something new, but with all the chaos around her, she simply hadn't the time. After rummaging anxiously through her closet, she finally settled on a spring like dress, with morning glories climbing on a white background.

She grabbed her blue shoes, which she seldom wore because they were much too high and the fabric was a little stained. But she wasn't really walking anywhere, just on stage and who could see that far? Hopefully, she wouldn't fall and break her neck in full few of the audience.

Which would probably consist of ten people.

SHE HAD SITUATED a group of eighth grader boys at the front of the auditorium to take care of the tickets. So far all they were doing was eating Kit Kats and chatting with one another.

Backstage was bedlam. A few girls were crying from nerves, one mother was sewing a ripped hem—another mother—who was doing make-up, poked a model in the eye and the girl was claiming she couldn't see. Melissa's mother paced, looking irritated. Mrs. Hopwood hobbled over to one of the models who was whining that the skirt was too big and unflattering, when another model threw up, right on Mrs. Hopwood's blue shoes.

Mrs. Johnson came rushing over. "You know who just came in? Tracy."

"Someone just threw up on my shoes."

The model had disappeared, wearing the last dress of the show, a gold lame sheath.

"Well, just wipe it off."

"They're powder blue. It's stained. I can't go out like this."

"Do you want my shoes?"

Mrs. Hopwood looked down at Mrs. Johnson's brown clogs. "There was a pair of vintage shoes, this exact color."

"We can't go back to the school for a pair of vintage shoes."

"It wouldn't matter. They weren't my size anyway and they got trashed." She limped over and grabbed a make-up wipe, which didn't work very well, leaving a curious white spot on the toe of the shoe. Then the insole came loose and went flying across the room.

"This is going to be a disaster," Mrs. Johnson said. "I can't bear to watch. Can't I go out in front?"

"Mrs. Hopwood," Pearl, who was supplying vitamin drinks for all the working models, approached, "I think you should start. The crowd is getting antsy."

"There's a crowd out there?" Mrs. Hopwood picked up the insole and stuffed it back in the shoes. And just like that something clicked in her brain.

She pushed Mrs. Johnson aside. "What if…"

"You're kidding right?"

"We know that the blue purse belonged to Dagny, correct?"

"Right now I don't know anything."

"What if whatever the killer was looking for wasn't in the purse at all, but in a pair of matching shoes? You can hide something under the padding? Something like a photo."

Mrs. Johnson didn't answer. Instead she whirled

around. "Excuse me, you can't come back here. Girls are dressing."

"I just want to wish my daughter good luck. I'm Melissa's father."

"You want to try to throw him out," she asked Mrs. Johnson. "Good luck." Mrs. Hopwood eyed George Ortiz bulging biceps and colorful tattoos. He smiled with three gold teeth.

"Are you going to go out now?" Pearl asked.

Mrs. Hopwood drew a deep breath, looked down at her shoes and tried to find the opening in the curtain, her insides somersaulting.

At the same time she saw Tracy Holtz, standing at the exit door with a knife in her hand.

FIFTY-NINE

THEY WERE ALL staring at her, wide eyed, but not particularly frightened. And then Tracy knew that this plan would be a complete fiasco. How could she have possibly thought she could get away with hurting George Ortiz or even Winifred, when there were so many others around?

Pearl, who was one of the few people who hadn't glanced at her, pushed Mrs. Hopwood through the curtains, causing Mrs. Hopwood to lose her balance and almost fall over.

"I want to take this opportunity to welcome all of you to our annual fashion show." If Mrs. Hopwood was nervous, it didn't show. Her voice was strong and loud.

Tracy heard a storm of applause.

"Everyone here line up and be prepared to walk," A heavyset woman with honey colored hair ordered, as she corralled the girls away from Tracy.

"We have some wonderful vintage clothing," Mrs. Hopwood spoke on, "which is being modeled by our own beautiful students. They will be parading down the runway with grace and glamour."

"Put the knife down, Tracy," Mrs. Johnson ordered flatly. "This is silly."

But Tracy had come this far and she wasn't about to give in so easily. Although she knew now all she would be able to do was scare the Ortizs. She had forgotten how large George was, how formable.

"You have your booklets," Mrs. Hopwood's spoke with confidence, "so if you see an outfit that you like, put a check beside it, noting what the starting bid is. Then you can write down your bid. At the end of the show, which will run about a half an hour, our eighth grade boys will collect the booklets. It may take a couple of days for us to determine who gets what, just make sure you contact information is at the front of your booklet, so if you do win the bid, we can get in touch with you."

"Will we get our booklets back?" A woman shouted from the audience, "I want it as a souvenir."

Mrs. Hopwood hesitated and then said a quick yes.

"Can we put in a lower bid than what's in the book?" someone else bellowed.

"Yes, you can. But please understand that you probably won't win the outfit."

"You murdered my husband," Tracy roared. "You killed him and you ruined my life, the life we might have had."

"My husband paid his debt to society," Winifred shouted shrilly. "So leave him alone!"

"I didn't do it," George insisted. "I swear to you! It was someone else!"

"Be quiet!" Pearl demanded. "They can hear you in the audience!"

"I will be describing each of the outfits as the models come down the runway, for those of you who are in the back seats. But before we start I have to say that most of you know that, like a lot of Catholic Schools, St. Polycarp is experiencing some financial problems.

It's our hope that this fashion show will keep our school open another year. I can't tell you how much I value my Catholic education and how important I think it is that your children are educated in the faith. You cannot separate God from the process of learning. Without God there are no standards, there are no absolutes, there is no hope. As Catholic teachers, we do our best to ensure that your children learn how to be strong communicators, orally and in the written word, that they understand math and use it in their daily lives, that they learn another language, which will broaden their horizons globally. But we go far beyond that. We teach your children a whole new way of thinking. We give them a strong moral code and a value system. Without that, we will become a nation of lost souls."

The clapping was deafening so Tracy had to scream. "I can't let you get away with this." She stepped towards George, and held the knife above her head as the first model paraded on stage.

"Gabriella is wearing a red shirtwaist dress with a flowered belt. This dress is a size ten, but could easily fit a woman who wears a twelve."

Tracy felt a firm arm behind her. She whirled around and saw Mrs. Johnson, trying to wrestle the knife. She was torn between the horror of what she was about to do and the disappointment that she might not accomplish what she had planned so long. And then suddenly that awful woman, the woman Mrs. Ortiz, who had started it all, jumped in.

If it hadn't been for her!

Tracy kicked Mrs. Johnson in the knee. She released a long, piercing scream, as the next model, about to go on stage, stared in shock. Pearl pushed her and she stumbled forward onto to the stage.

Tracy slashed Winifred Ortiz in the arm, sank to the floor and dissolved into tears.

"I've had enough of this nonsense," Pearl said, while George Ortiz went immediately to his wife. Pearl yanked the knife away from Tracy.

And the music from Rocky played on.

SIXTY

I⊤ WAS ALL happening so fast that Mrs. Johnson felt as though she were walking in a dream, that none of this could be real.

Her bruised knee, Tracy with the knife, Mrs. Ortiz bleeding from her right arm, but insisting on going to the hospital alone, so George could watch Melissa, the policemen which included Detectives Paneretto and Detective Hargrove, who happened to be in the audience suddenly surrounding the models back stage, Mrs. Hopwood's voice in the background talking about an ivory lace blouse with twenty-one tiny pearl buttons in the back. "They don't make blouses like this anymore. No one has the time or the energy."

And when Mrs. Johnson took a peek from the curtains, she saw everyone writing frantically in their booklets.

The show ended with a huge applause. Mrs. Hopwood was presented with a dozen red roses and box of Godiva chocolates—and a standing ovation.

For one brief moment a flash of envy rang through Mrs. Johnson. How wonderful to get all that attention! But then again Mrs. Hopwood deserved it. She really worked hard to make the fashion show a success and that was going to be good for everyone.

A reception had been planned in another room, with

cakes and cookies and brownies and assorted beverages. Mrs. Johnson would grab a cup of coffee, a chocolate brownie and then slip out with her husband and her sons to the peace and quiet of her own home.

Mrs. Hopwood beamed as parents and teachers scrambled to congratulate her. She flopped the flowers up and down and held on to the Godiva chocolates tightly.

"The music was too loud," Father Bartholomew complained, "And you talked too much. All that earsplitting racket gave me a headache."

"I had to describe the clothing," Mrs. Hopwood shouted.

"What for? No one in the audience is blind or deaf."

Mrs. Hopwood caught the eye of Mrs. Johnson and then pushed through the people, no doubt to railroad Mrs. Johnson and to gloat.

When she finally made her way through the hordes of buzzing congratulations, she pushed Mrs. Johnson aside.

"I have to talk to Tracy. Where is she?"

"The police are taking her away now."

"Come on." She shoved Mrs. Johnson towards the back door and caught up with the policemen, who were exiting.

"Tracy," she screamed.

Tracy looked back.

"Can I ask her a question?" Mrs. Hopwood looked at Detective Hargrove, who just shook her head.

"You said that Victor wasn't well. That he had a disease. Do you know the name of that disease?"

Tracy looked at both the detectives. "I don't know it was an odd name. Something that began with H. I could never pronounce it. It meant there was too much iron in his blood."

"Was it Haemochromatosis?"

"Yeah, that sounds right. Why? Will that help me?"

"I don't think anything is going to help you now." Detective Hargrove pushed Tracy forward.

"WE HAVE TO go back to St. Polycarp," Mrs. Hopwood said as soon as they were out of sight.

"Why?" She voiced the question in a hesitant tone.

'We have to go into the alley and find those blue shoes."

Mrs. Johnson looked down at Mrs. Hopwood's own blue shoes, which were badly soiled. "No one is looking at your shoes, especially now. It's over."

"No," Mrs. Hopwood said. "It has nothing to do with me. I told you. I think something was hidden in those shoes."

Mrs. Johnson shook her head and wondered how soon she could plan her escape. "First the purses and now the shoes?"

"Excuse me, Mrs. Hopwood." A woman Mrs. Johnson had never seen before, and probably wasn't a parent at St. Polycarp, since she was dripping in diamonds, shoved Mrs. Johnson aside. 'What a wonderful show! I've spent time in New York and go to fashion week every year and this rivals their event!"

"How kind of you," Mrs. Hopwood spluttered.

"Now I made a bid on that floral skirt, you know the one, silver and peach. If someone outbids me, I am willing to go higher." She shoved her booklet into Mrs. Hopwood's startled face.

"I don't think that's right," Mrs. Johnson said.

The woman stared at Mrs. Johnson, as though she was a cockroach that had suddenly appeared on the kitchen counter.

"I'll take that into consideration," Mrs. Hopwood said.

Mrs. Johnson led Mrs. Hopwood towards the exit. "Let's get out of here. And I don't care where we're going."

SHE THOUGHT THAT Mrs. Hopwood would be smug, chattering in the car about the success of the fashion show, but instead she was quiet and pensive. She was afraid to ask what was wrong because she knew that Mrs. Hopwood would tell her soon enough.

"I have to congratulate you." Mrs. Johnson stopped the car in front of the school. "I saw Sister Mary Grace approached by some of the parents. Maybe they can talk her into keeping the school open."

"I hope so. I'm about to do something I don't want to do."

Mrs. Johnson didn't want to reply that with Mrs. Hopwood that was not a rare occurrence.

"Remember that handbag I gave Melissa? It was green and it had a copper leaf, which opened and closed."

"Vaguely. Why?"

"It was never found. And I think Melissa's mother was the person who took it. She was able to describe it once to me and, by her own admission, she never saw it."

"That's crazy. Why would she steal a handbag that was already in her house? She could have just looked inside of it."

"What if she wanted to cut out the lining?"

"I don't see it." Mrs. Johnson hesitated. "For one thing what's her motive?"

"I was hoping you would ask that. Melissa mother told me that Melissa wasn't well, that she had a disease which puts too much iron in your blood, a disease she inherited from her mother. I did some research and in order to inherit the disease both parents have to be carriers. George Ortiz was not."

"What are you saying?"

"You heard Tracy. Victor was."

"So," Mrs. Johnson hesitated while she thought it through, "you're thinking that Victor was Melissa's father."

"I think he was."

"So what? That only gives George Ortiz a better motive. He found out that his wife was pregnant by another man, so he killed the other man."

'I don't think George knew about that. But what I do think is that Victor might have fought for custody or at least joint custody of Melissa. Tracy said that he always wanted children—that he had a surprise for her the night he was murdered. If George didn't know, and Victor was about to tell him…"

"And what about Dagny? How does she fit in? And your Aunt Eunice?"

"Dagny was a photographer. She could have seen the crime being committed and taken a picture. Somehow my aunt got a hold of the handbag and the shoes that Dagny was wearing the day she died. Maybe a relative sold them to her. You know what I'm thinking?"

"I never know what you're thinking." Mrs. Johnson hated to get out of the car.

One of the streetlights was broken and she thought she saw someone hiding in the shadow behind the school building. St. Polycarp looked spooky at night, eerie and deserted.

"I'm thinking," Mrs. Hopwood continued, obviously not in the least discouraged by Mrs. Johnson's lack of interest, "that Dagny never hid the photo in the purse but in her shoes."

"And how are we supposed to know what shoes she wore?"

"Well, we know that she was carrying the blue purse, and I'm betting that her shoes matched the handbag."

"I don't like this at all." Mrs. Johnson threw the car door open, fumbled with her keys, and approached the front door. Mrs. Hopwood stood close by on her dirty blue heels.

Mrs. Johnson flung the door to the school open and turned on the hall lights. "Where are these elusive blue shoes?"

"We have to go through the trash in the alley."

"Oh no!" Mrs. Johnson stood firmly in the hall. "No way. I'm dressed!" Granted it wasn't quite the same way as Mrs. Hopwood, who looked like a morning glory that had suddenly sprung to life, but Mrs. Johnson was wearing her favorite faux black leather dress and her good black kitten heels. "Besides, I have a bad back. I can't be bending down."

"All right, I'll go through the trash. You just stand behind me."

"Why don't we just call the police, like normal people? I mean, they were right there in the audience."

"Because those detectives don't like me. They think I'm deranged."

"Well…"

Mrs. Johnson trailed behind, somewhat reluctantly until she reached the basement She forced one of the keys into the lock. It didn't fit. "Sorry."

"What do you mean sorry? How can it not fit? It always fit before!"

"I don't know if it fit before or not. I never once opened the door to the alley. That's Mr. Salisbury's territory. Here, you try."

She shoved the keys into Mrs. Hopwood's hand.

"Maybe it's not the right key."

"It's the only key. The key to the front door and the back door and the alley are all the same."

"That doesn't seem smart to me."

Mrs. Johnson was prepared to leave. "Well, that was Father Felix's idea. And this is from someone who lost all of her school keys."

"They were stolen. And you know that. Isn't there another entrance to the alley on the other side of the school?"

Of course there was, and Mrs. Johnson knew it. But she was hoping that Mrs. Hopwood had forgotten.

"It's important," Mrs. Hopwood insisted.

"Let's go," Mrs. Johnson agreed, her heart dropping like a stone.

They walked through the deserted front hall together until Mrs. Hopwood halted suddenly. "Did you hear that?"

"No."

"Footsteps."

"I didn't hear anything."

A few more steps and Mrs. Hopwood stopped again, "It sounds squishy."

"That's us!"

Mrs. Hopwood looked down at her own shoes. "Oh my God!"

"More stains?" Mrs. Johnson glanced down and saw that the shoes were dotted with reddish pink.

"It's blood," Mrs. Hopwood whispered shakily.

"Well, maybe it's old—a kindergartener with a nose bleed. Mr. Salisbury doesn't clean so well."

"It's wet."

"That's it!" Mrs. Johnson reached for her shoulder bag. "We're calling the police."

"No, you're not." The voice came first, an easily recognizable voice, but before Mrs. Johnson could say a word, a figure emerged from the shadows, carrying a gun. Mrs. Winifred Ortiz.

"You don't want to do this," Mrs. Hopwood said in a rather breezy tone, the same way she might converse with a fifth grade student.

"What difference does it make now? I overheard you talking. You think that horrid blackmailer hid the photograph in her shoe."

"A photograph of you killing Victor?" Mrs. Hopwood asked and Mrs. Johnson wanted to slap her. Why didn't she plead for their lives or buy time by offering to look for the shoes? Or at the very least keep her mouth snapped shut?

"When I found out I was pregnant I knew the baby was Victor's. But I was going to persuade George that it came early and she was really his. But then for some reason Victor got into his head that he was going to sue for joint custody. He was going to tell George every-thing and I couldn't have that. George would have never forgiven me. I would have lost everything, my husband, my child. And by that time, Victor had already decided to make it work with Tracy. So you see, I really didn't have a choice."

"How could you let your husband serve twelve years in jail for a crime you committed?" Mrs. Hopwood asked.

"I'm sure she had her reasons." Mrs. Johnson's own voice sounded weak and unsure.

"I was not going to leave my baby! Besides, I didn't arrest him, the police did. They're the ones who rail-roaded him."

"After they found the gun that you hid," Mrs. Hop-wood said. "And what about that poor homeless man? Did you kill him too?"

"I told the secretary I was looking for Mrs. John-son. I knew you weren't there because I saw you get-ting out of your car. I went into the basement, hoping to look through the clothes. Then I saw that disgusting man. He had something in his hand, something he had gotten out of one of the purses. I thought it might have been the photo. He wouldn't give it up. I went to take it from him and I pushed him. Then he started to say how he was going to tell everyone who I was and what I had done. I couldn't have someone like him bring me down. Enough of this." She pointed the gun straight at Mrs. Johnson. "I need the keys to the alley."

"What are you going to do with us?" With trembling hands, Mrs. Johnson handed over the keys.

"I feel bad about you, I do. Her," she shot a look of disdain at Mrs. Hopwood, "she's a vain, selfish woman."

And also a crazy person.

"That is so unfair," Mrs. Hopwood said.

They were about to get killed and all Mrs. Hopwood could say was that the killer was being unfair.

"Why did you kill Mrs. Sugrarman?"

"I thought she might have had the purse. I followed her. Would you believe she tried to sell me a handbag she had gotten a few years ago probably in Macys? Like I wouldn't know the difference. I was afraid she was going to tell everyone that I was Mr. Stronghold, someone desperate to get a hold of the purses unless I gave her money. Like I have money. I couldn't let her do that. She was a druggie. I hit her with a rock and then dropped it into the river. I had no idea," her voice softened, "that my son was on his way to meet her."

"And if you had?" Mrs. Hopwood challenged her.

Before Mrs. Ortiz had a chance to answer, sirens blared in the background.

"What's going on?" Winifred said, confused. "How did the police…"

"Open up," a voice thundered, as pounding erupted at the front door.

Winifred started to shoot in the air as Mrs. Johnson attempted to duck and felt a pinch in her lower back. Mrs. Hopwood crawled to the front door.

But someone had already kicked it in. One policeman went after Winifred and another got Mrs. Johnson slowly off the floor.

"I think I broke my meniscus." Mrs. Hopwood patted her knee and attempted to grab her blue shoe, which had gone flying in the corner.

"How did the police get here?" Mrs. Johnson wondered.

"I called 911 on my watch. You really should get one."

"Maybe I will," Mrs. Johnson said, "maybe I will."

SIXTY-ONE

ONE MOMENT WINIFRED ORTIZ was holding a gun in her hand, the next moment she was shooting and the following moment they were all surrounded by a bevy of policemen, including Detective Paneretto and Detective Hargrove.

"She came to look for a photo," Mrs. Hopwood said breathlessly. "I think it might be hidden in a blue shoe, which is in the trash, in the alley."

Detective Hargrove's only response was a puzzled look.

Mrs. Hopwood gave the shivering Mrs. Johnson a gentle push and then led the way outside. Detective Paneretto had no trouble opening the door and turning on the overhead lights in the alley. One woman, wearing pajamas with pink rollers in her hair and a brown hair net, holding a dirty white poodle, gaped at them from outside the fence.

"We're looking for a blue shoe," Detective Paneretto shouted.

Much to Mrs. Hopwood's disappointment, she was not allowed to help in the search. Detective Hargrove found one shoe and then the other. Mrs. Hopwood watched as the detective lifted up the insole and pulled out a photograph and a negative. Mrs. Hopwood thought she deserved to take a peek, so she didn't hesitate to limp over. The faded and wrinkled photo showed a young, pretty Winifred Ortiz holding a gun on a tall, thin, frightened man.

Mrs. Hopwood bent down and picked up the other blue shoe. Size 9. She glanced down at her own stained shoes. "After it's all over, do you think I could have these shoes back?" she asked to no one in particular.

Everyone stared at her, openmouthed.

"Well, maybe not," she muttered.

BY THE TIME Mrs. Hopwood and Mrs. Johnson returned to the auditorium, Pearl, judging by her scowl, distinctly disgruntled, was standing outside, holding a shopping bag.

"I was just about to go home," she said in a grumpy voice. "Where have you two been? They locked up and kicked me out. The clothes are still inside. But I didn't want to leave these booklets there also, in case they got lost."

"We are so sorry," Mrs. Johnson said.

"It's very complicated," Mrs. Hopwood added.

Pearl just shook her head. "With you two it always is."

Mrs. Hopwood didn't bother to deny the statement.

MRS. HOPWOOD WAS up until three in the morning, calculating the highest bids for each item and counting the ticket sales.

$13,333.66

And then she fell into the deepest sleep she had had for months.

THE PHONE RANG at nine on the following morning.

Because Mrs. Hopwood did not recognize the number, she didn't answer. Maybe it was just another telemarketer offering her storm windows—except this caller left a voice mail.

"This is Sister Mary Grace. I've already called Mrs. Johnson."

On a Sunday morning.

"I would like to see you both in my office tomorrow morning at ten o'clock."

What about their classes?

"I've arranged for substitutes to cover your grades. I can be found at 47 Sycamore Street on the fifth floor. Please be prompt."

Mrs. Hopwood wasted no times calling Mrs. Johnson.

"I can't talk. I'm on my way to church, where you should be."

"I got a call…"

"Yeah, me too. We're probably both going to get fired."

"Why?"

"Who knows? Maybe because the bullet made a hole in the wall at St. Polycarp."

"But we raised $13,000," Mrs. Hopwood argued. "I counted it last night."

"They don't know that. Listen we did what we could. We raised money, we caught a killer, who just happened to one of the parents. Not our fault. Now we have to leave it up to God."

Mrs. Hopwood was not comfortable leaving things up to God. She figured He was busy with far important things. But Mrs. Johnson was right. All she could do now was wait.

"Mom?"

"Alex, is everything all right?" Eleven thirty on a Sunday morning, it would be unusual for Alex to call.

"Yeah. I just wanted to say congratulations."

"Congratulations?"

"For last night."

"How do you know about last night?"

"It's all over Facebook."

"You're friends with Mrs. Johnson?"

"No. But a lot of parents posted it and then it got shared. You know no one was going to miss an opportunity to take photos of their beautiful daughters strutting on the stage like models."

"Oh. That. After it was over, we caught a murderer."

"What?"

"It's a long story," but Mrs. Hopwood couldn't resist adding, "Everything I thought, all of my outlandish theories, I was right."

"Oh."

"I'm not sorry I did what I did, or what I thought, even though," she drew a deep breath, "it might have cost me your father."

"Well, about that…"

"Has he been in touch?" Mrs. Hopwood asked, in a hesitant tone.

Alex paused. "He called me once or twice. I don't think he knows what you've been up to. I'm pretty sure he's not on Facebook. But once he finds out…"

Mrs. Hopwood didn't want to articulate what she was thinking. No matter how crazy or zany some of her theories were, she needed to be with someone who believed her, who supported her, not someone she clearly exasperated.

"Maybe if you want me to," Alex said, "I could come home next weekend, you know. Maybe catch a movie, go out to dinner."

"I'd love that."

"Okay. Be there sometime Friday night."

"Love you."

Mrs. Hopwood hung up the phone thoughtfully. Maybe she would try to make the noon Mass. Because heavens knew, she had a lot to be grateful for.

SIXTY-TWO

As it turned out, Tracy only had to spend one night in jail and then they were going to transfer her to a half-way house. Winifred was hardly in a position to press charges, but they did tell Tracy she was guilty of assault, which would result in probation.

When the guards came to get her, Tracy assumed that it was time to leave. But no, she was told that she had a visitor. And even before she left her cell, Tracy could guess who the visitor was.

Mrs. Hopwood was waiting for her, looking pretty, actually glowing in a peach dress with silver accessories. Obviously, in spite of Tracy's antics, the fashion show had been a huge success.

Mrs. Hopwood took a tentative step forward before she sat down.

"I understand you're going to a half-way house."

Tracy nodded.

"You know, Tracy, Harrison Ford said that we all have big changes in our lives, which are really second chances. This is your second chance. You seem like an intelligent woman. You can do something with your life."

"I know that," Tracy said. "I thought about it all night. Maybe I could get a job and save money, go back to school. I'd love to be a social worker, to help the homeless, to make a difference."

"I think you'd be great at that." Mrs. Hopwood paused. "You haven't asked about Sugar Daddy. I've grown very attached to him, but if you want him back..."

"No, I know you're taking good care of him. I love that dog but he'll have a better life with you. At least I did that." Tracy felt a surge of relief flash through her. "I made life better for someone."

Mrs. Hopwood rose. "If you ever need a reference, if I can help in any way, please don't hesitate to call me."

Tracy drew a deep breath. Maybe it was finally going to be all right. And the next thing that Mrs. Hopwood said clenched that feeling.

"Just so you know," Mrs. Hopwood smiled broadly, "meeting you made my life better too."

SIXTY-THREE

ON MONDAY MORNING Mrs. Johnson and Mrs. Hopwood sat outside the superintendent office, trying to guess what the meeting was about.

They were going to be fired.

They were going to get a raise.

They were going to be separated and sent to other schools.

They were going to get jobs in administration.

When the receptionist—a dour looking woman dressed in gray with gray hair and gray earrings and a gray complexion—announced that they could enter, Mrs. Hopwood pushed Mrs. Johnson in first.

To Mrs. Hopwood's surprise and delight, Sister Maria Anna was seated on one of the chairs. The teachers sat on either side of her in front of Sister Mary Grace, who leaned forward on her desk.

"First of all, I'd like to congratulate both of you on the success of the fashion show. It was nicely done," Sister Mary Grace said, her expression, stony.

"Well, it was more Mrs. Hopwood than me," Mrs. Johnson admitted.

"Be that as it may." Sister Mary Grace waved the comment aside. "I also want to congratulate you on solving the murder. That was in the morning paper. I have to remind you though, that is not your job."

"We raised over $13,000 with the fashion show." Mrs. Hopwood thought it best to change the subject.

"That is so impressive!" Sister Maria Anna gushed.

"You know," Sister Mary Grace said, "we were thinking of closing St. Polycarp."

"We're hoping that you'll consider keeping it open," Mrs. Johnson said.

"We did talk about it." Mrs. Hopwood found herself holding her breath. "And we decided it wouldn't hurt to give it another year, especially since the teachers are working so hard for the school. After all," Sister Mary Grace turned towards Sister Maria Anna, "we really didn't give Sister Maria Anna a chance to be principal."

"Thank you," Mrs. Hopwood said.

"There is something else. For a while the diocese has been considering opening up a thrift shop with all proceeds to go towards our schools. We would like you, Mrs. Hopwood, to be in charge."

"But what about her teaching career?" Mrs. Johnson asked. Mrs. Hopwood glared at her.

"Well, of course, you will finish the year as a fifth grade teacher. The shop won't be up and running until the fall. Do you think you could work on it during the summer?"

"Yes, of course. My summer is wide open." The thought of breaking all ties with St. Polycarp and with Mrs. Johnson made her stomach feel hollow. "I have an idea," she said suddenly. "Maybe I could work part time at St. Polycarp as the librarian, since Mrs. Sugarman obviously won't be back."

Mrs. Johnson opened her mouth to say something and then quickly closed it.

"That might work," Sister Maria Anna agreed quickly.

"Well, we'll be in touch." Sister Mary Grace stood, "And again, congratulations."

MRS. JOHNSON AND Mrs. Hopwood didn't speak until they were out of the office.

"What do you know about being a librarian?" Mrs. Johnson asked.

"Nothing," Mrs. Hopwood confessed.

"I think that this summer I'm going to volunteer for the city council just to see if it's something I might want to do. And I read in the morning paper that they're going to get Tracy help. What about her mangy dog?"

"He is not mangy. His name is Sugar Daddy and I'm bringing him to the vets this afternoon for his shots."

"You're keeping him?"

"I am. I went to see Tracy yesterday, just to boost her spirits. I think she's going to be okay."

"Did you say anything about Victor being Melissa's father?"

"I though it over and decided not to. What good would it do?"

"Are you going to tell Melissa?" Mrs. Johnson asked.

"Absolutely not. She'll probably find out eventually but it's not going to be from me."

"Justice isn't perfect," Mrs. Johnson said. "All we can do is pray for her. And in the meantime, let's go and get the vintage clothes, drop them off at your house..."

"My house?"

"And then go for a nice, long lunch and talk about nothing at all."

MRS. HOPWOOD SANK on the bed and pushed the piles of clothing aside. She could talk to Melissa the following day, but she decided to text her instead, thankful that Melissa had shared her number.

Thinking about you, Melissa. I can imagine what a difficult time this must be for you. Please don't be too hard on your Mom. Anything she did, she did for you. You will get through this. And anytime you want to talk, please know that I'm there for you.

She wasn't expecting a response but Melissa texted her right back. Thanks. Had a long talk with my father. I've been writing in my journal. That helps.

Someone once wrote that all sorrows can be borne if put into a book. Remember this, Melissa, you are a strong person, a warrior. And you have a bright shiny future ahead of you.

And so do I, thought Mrs. Hopwood as she pushed the send button. *"And so do I."*

* * * * *

ABOUT THE AUTHOR

Marianna Heusler is the author of eight novels including three prior St. Polycarp mysteries, *Murder at St. Polycarp*, *Cappuccino at the Crypt* and *No End to Trouble*. She is also the author of hundreds of published short stories and her mini mysteries have frequently been featured in *Woman's World*.

A retired teacher, she has taught at all grade levels in Catholic Schools and also taught third grade in a private all girls' school on the upper eastside of Manhattan.

Marianna lives in New York City with her husband, Joel, her son, Maximilian, and her little dog, Dolce. She spends her free time, writing, working out, and volunteering for the Red Cross.

You can learn more about Marianna by clicking onto www.mariannamystery.com
Or by following her fashion blog at mariannaheusler.typepad.com.